THE Rule
MAKER
RULE BREAKERS SERIES

JENNIFER BLACKWOOD

Entangled Publishing, LLC
2614 South Timberline Road
Suite 109
Fort Collins, CO 80525
Visit our website at www.entangledpublishing.com.

Embrace is an imprint of Entangled Publishing, LLC.

Edited by Candace Havens
Cover design by L.J. Anderson
Cover art from Shutterstock

Manufactured in the United States of America

First Edition January 2017

embrace

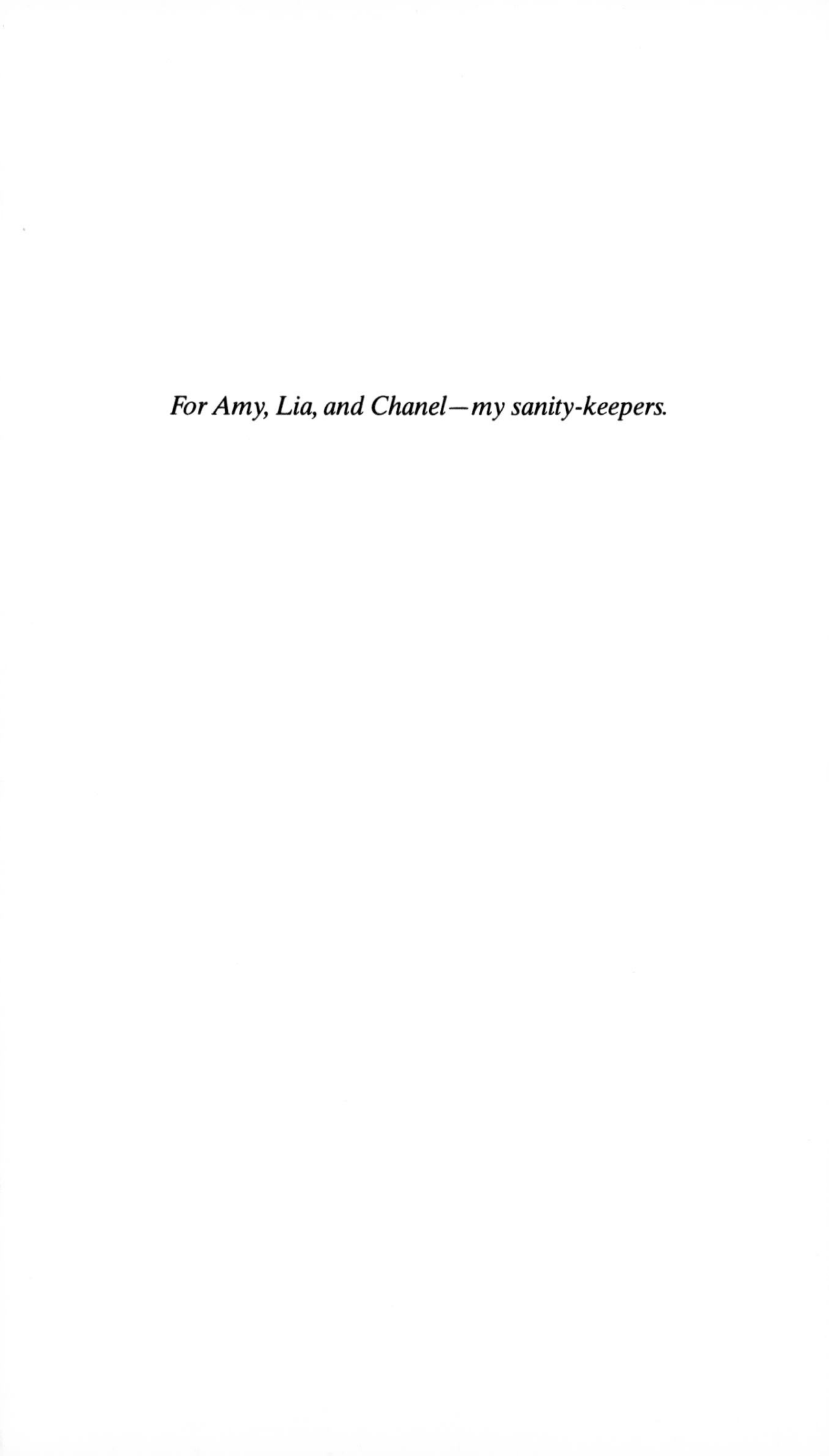

For Amy, Lia, and Chanel—my sanity-keepers.

Chapter One

Rule #1: Never eat while driving.

There was nothing quite like indulging in pity I'm-single-on-Valentine's-Day chocolate. No man candy? No problem. Reese's Peanut Butter Cups would surely fill the chasm that was my love life.

"Siri, read my emails." I unwrapped the candy I'd stashed on my dash, plopped it in my mouth, and put my car into drive.

"You have one new email," Siri replied. I loved my car for the sole reason that it had become my command station, my badass Batmobile that could answer emails, texts, and memos at a voice command. Okay, it was a Prius, but still. "Sender—Jason Covington."

I jerked back in my seat and sucked in a breath, the chocolate hitting the back of my throat. *No.* For the love of all that was holy, why was this man emailing me? Anyone but him. I went to clear my throat, and the candy didn't budge.

Crap.

"Ms. Reynolds, it was a pleasure doing business with

you on the Culver Cove Inn late last year. I have recently purchased a new resort on Mount Rainier and would like to hire your services again," she said in her monotone voice.

Goose bumps flecked my arms as I attempted to cough, to get some air into my burning lungs. I mean, if I had to choose a way to pass on to an afterlife filled with never-ending reruns of my favorite shows, self-filling coffee cup, and unlimited free wifi, death by chocolate was decidedly the best way to go. Chocolate fountain, satin pie, éclair…hell, I'd even settle for a Snickers. And, as fate would have it, I'd be taking a visit to the white pearly gates with a Reese's Peanut Butter Cup lodged in the back of my throat. But I still had seven episodes until I was caught up on *Supernatural,* and I hadn't made it to the highest level in Candy Crush. I didn't have time for dying yet.

My eyes filled with tears as I fought to extricate the candy from my mouth, attempting to give myself the Heimlich maneuver. And, if my burning lungs were any indication, failing miserably. I looked out at the sidewalk, and of course, at this time of day, there was no one in sight.

"I'll need you to take measurements today so we can discuss the design on Monday. Keys will be sent to you within the hour. Best, Jason Covington." There was a pause and then Siri asked, "Do you wish to respond to the email?"

No! I wanted to scream. Instead, salt and pepper particles invaded my vision. This was it, I'd die sitting in the spot outside my apartment, listening to an email from a stupid Covington. Even if this particular one wasn't the target of my wrath, blood relation was enough to taint my opinion.

"I'm sorry, I didn't catch that. Would you like to respond to the email?" Siri repeated.

All I could do was keep pounding my stomach, cursing him seven ways to Sunday. I somehow managed a garbled noise that could possibly pass as a *no*.

"I'm sorry, I didn't catch that."

Screw you, Siri. For what I paid my phone carrier, she should be able to give me a damn Heimlich herself.

My vision continued to fade and the clock was ticking as I choked my way into unconsciousness. This was it. My last meal had been screw-this-Hallmark-holiday candy and a friggin' ex-fling was going to be seared into my final fleeting thoughts. What a way to go.

In a last ditch effort, I took hold of the steering wheel with shaking hands and rammed my stomach into it. The piece of chocolate shot out of my mouth and hit the windshield with a *splat*. It slid down the glass and left a brown slug trail behind it. Sweet, delicious air rushed through my now-clear windpipe and the particles swarming my vision dissipated.

I held my head in my hands, taking deep, shuddering breaths, and cursed the day I decided to take my client's brother, Ryder Covington, to bed.

• • •

Three hours—and much-needed gulping of air—later, I parked my car, facing the snow-capped mountaintop that lay as a backdrop to one of the many ski resorts on Mt. Rainier. This one just happened to be closed for renovations. My renovations. And nothing made me happier than having my mind busy with plans for a new project. It even overshadowed the whole choking incident earlier.

I pulled my windblown hair into a messy bun, smoothed my black eyelet lace skirt, and glanced down at my list of specs I needed to acquire. Room layouts, size, supporting structures, the basics. Then, I had the simple task of creating mock-ups that blew the mind of Jason Covington, the most uptight, eccentric billionaire on the West Coast. He earned that title during our last job together. If I hurried, I could make it back to my apartment in time to implement my original plan for tonight: catch up on *Supernatural* while gorging on microwave popcorn. Maybe if I was feeling really wild, I'd go for the good stuff. The kind where the bag disintegrated into a sopping mess within twenty minutes due to grease concentration. This was obviously the makings of the best Valentine's Day ever. Or most pathetic. I hadn't decided yet.

Air gusted through my open window, ruffling my hair and the pages of my planner in the passenger seat. I took another few seconds to revel in the warmth and give myself a mini pep talk.

Time to get my butt into gear and turn on my designer mode.

Deep breaths. No need to panic just because of the little fact I was working on my ex-fling's brother's resort. Try saying that ten times fast.

I grabbed my camera bag from the floor of the passenger seat, plus my notebook and measuring tape, and kicked the door shut behind me.

Gravel crunched under my heels as I made my way to the main lodge. Normally I liked to go through the space with the client to get a feel for what they had in mind for the remodel. On my first project with Jason, he'd also asked me to scout the place without him. Weird, yes, but it didn't surprise me that I was here solo for this project.

Bring it on, Jason Covington. I can take whatever you throw at me.

I'd managed to hold my own at the most prestigious firm in the city. I was totally ready for this project.

That was until I pulled open the door to the main lodge.

My breath caught in my throat. I'd like to say it was because the entryway was just that beautiful, but what lay in front of me was a chaotic array of chairs, paintings, and wood paneling that screamed *seventies love children were conceived here.* The seventies had a lot going for itself. I mean, there was Clint Eastwood, ABBA, Cher. This did not have any of that charm—it was just plain outdated, ugly-as-sin, burn-this-place-to-the-ground disgusting. I gulped, forcing stagnant, musty air down my throat.

My fingers ran over the burnt orange window casing as I eyed the suit of armor—missing an arm and foot, propped up in the middle of the room—along with the remains of a broken disco ball, shattered into thousands of pieces.

Design situation: nightmare

Designer emotion: tonight's greasy popcorn would better serve as lighter fluid to torch this disaster to the ground.

Jason's email failed to mention that I'd be getting asbestos poisoning and possible death by disco ball with one wrong move. No wonder he sent me to do this alone.

I coughed as I inhaled another breath of noxious air, and beelined for the first available window. After unlocking it, I tugged at the pane and tried to pull it open. It gave a protesting whine as I inched it up the track, and slammed shut when I let go.

I decided not to take that as an ominous clue that I'd entered some kind of resort of tortures, and instead scanned the room for something to prop the window open. After passing over a rusted brass candlestick and a fireplace poker, I settled on an old piece of firewood stacked in the corner. I slid it between the sill and the cracked wood and breathed in the fresh air.

Now that air circulated in the room, making it slightly more tolerable, I took my phone out of my pocket to snap pics for reference when I went back to the office to design the mock-ups…and okay, *maybe* text a few to my best friend Lainey, because she really needed to witness this hellhole. Just as I was about to click into camera mode, a call came through, Jason's number flashing across the screen.

"Hello?"

"Ms. Reynolds. Are you at Divinity?"

"Yes." I sat down on the windowsill, tucked my phone between my ear and my shoulder, and grabbed my pen and notebook in my purse. "It's quite…something." That was the only non-offensive adjective I had readily available at the moment.

"It is." He paused and I heard the sound of papers shuffling in the background. "I expect you'll have ample ideas for renovations."

Burn it all! I ached to say, but I *really* liked my job and Jason wasn't the sort to joke around, even in his best mood. "Of course. I'll have designs ready for you by Monday." I picked at a thread on my skirt and crossed my legs.

"I wanted to give you advance notice—"

His words were lost on me, because at that moment, something black and furry with eight legs skittered across the top of my skirt. A scream that could be heard from the other side of the mountain range ripped out of me, and at once I was on my feet, swiping at my skirt, hopping, cussing, regretting my choice of incredibly high heels.

I stared at the ground, frantically trying to find the culprit. He could have been anywhere. I shuddered.

My ankles buckled as I jerked in an uncoordinated, spastic version of an Irish jig. If I had a most-hated list, spiders took the number two spot, second only to clowns. And maybe this resort.

My pulse pounded as I twisted my skirt around. And a second time, just to make sure. No sign of my eight-legged nemesis. I looked around the floor. Nothing. He was here somewhere, hiding. I could feel his beady gaze on me, plotting my untimely death.

And then my ringtone began to blast.

Crap.

I'd totally just had a freak-out while on the phone

with Jason. So much for acting like a twenty-four-year-old professional. I made a quick search of the ground and the windowsill for my phone and came up empty. I listened for the ringtone, tracking the sound…which came from a distance. I swallowed hard and peeked my head outside and looked down. Nestled between foliage of a bush four feet below, my phone continued to ring. And then cut to voicemail. Followed by another call.

I swallowed hard. The longer I took to answer Jason's call, the angrier he'd get, and I wasn't exactly winning any points at the moment. The phone was well within reach. It would have to be because if I were to go around the building, that would take at least a few minutes, and I already needed to do some major butt-kissing after screaming in Jason's ear. I scanned the sill for any sign of the creepy crawly, and once I was satisfied that he wasn't anywhere near me, I leaned out the window.

In a totally unladylike fashion that would have my aunt raising her brow at me, I reached over the sill, legs seesawing to steady myself so I didn't face-plant into a flower bed. My skirt rode up way past acceptable as my fingers grazed my phone.

I wiggled on the sill, and just as my hand grabbed my cell, I bumped the piece of firewood and the window hit the small of my back with a *thud* hard enough to leave me fighting for air. I struggled to backtrack into the room, and the sill dug into my stomach, the weight of the window pressing into the top of my butt.

This was it. The resort had a death wish for me.

My phone continued to ring, and I had no choice but to answer it. "Mr. Covington. I am so sorry. I don't know what came over me."

"Are you okay?" His tone dripped with more irritation than concern. I'd expect nothing less from him.

I looked behind me at the windowsill. My body was effectively pinned down, the pane too heavy to lift from this angle. He'd be less than sympathetic for my situation. In fact, I'd witnessed him fire vendors for less stupidity than this. "Yes."

Absolutely no need to panic. None at all. Not with a Chewbacca-level-hairy spider on the loose. I bet it made Wookie noises before sinking its fangs into its victims.

"I was going to tell you that I'm sending someone up there today—"

"Great." I knew I was being rude, interrupting him, but I needed to figure out how to get out of this situation before I turned into a human popsicle. "Sounds wonderful." A note of hysteria laced my words.

"Are you sure everything is okay?"

"Of course. I'm just enjoying this breathtaking view." *As the blood rushes to my head.*

"It is quite beautiful. Well, I'll let you get back to it. Have a good day."

"You, too." As I hung up, I twisted to assess the damage the best I could. Besides a most definite bruise forming on my lower back and a dirty smudge on my white shirt, nothing was broken or ripped. I sighed. How the hell was I supposed to get out of this?

As I saw it, I had three options:

a) pray that I suddenly developed telekinesis

b) somehow induce an adrenaline rush that would give me Hulk-like abilities

c) beg the Chewbacca spider to bite me so I could die a quick, painless death before one of Jason's employees found me and reported back to him that I was completely incompetent

The first two options seemed a tad unattainable at the moment. The latter option erred on the side of melodramatic, even if this was a sucktastic situation. A tickle webbed across my calf, but I brushed away my paranoia. This would be totally fine. In the meantime, I'd just enjoy the beautiful scenery. While cursing this whole place.

After fighting a few more seconds and failing, I resigned myself to the fact that not even Crisco would get me out of this jam.

I did the only thing that seemed appropriate. Texted my best friend.

Zoey: *SOS*

Lainey: *What's up?*

Zoey: *I have a situation.*

Lainey: *…are you going for the suspense factor, cause it's working.*

I took a selfie and hit send.

Lainey: *OMG. Are you…uh…stuck in a window?*

Zoey: *Yup.*

Lainey: *What the hell happened?*

Zoey: *This resort is alive and is actually trying to kill me. Tell my dad that I love him.*

Lainey: *Only if I get to keep the couch and your Chanel purse once you pass.*

Zoey: *You are ruthless.*

Lainey: *I can't help myself. For real though, do you need me to come get you?*

Zoey: *No, one of Jason's guys will be here later today. It'll be embarrassing AF, but at least it's not Jason, right?*

Lainey: *#truth Also, WTF is on your leg, dude?*

My leg? I spread my two fingers over my screen, enlarging the picture I'd sent Lainey and froze at the sight of my hairy foe on my left calf.

No, no, no!

I thrashed and screamed in the sill, the window not budging even a millimeter. My scream echoed through the canyon, and if there was enough snow on the mountain, an avalanche would soon follow. Then, at least, I wouldn't have to worry about the fact that Chewbacca was picking out china patterns for its new home. Sweat beaded on my brow as I continued to struggle.

Just as the initial sting of tears invaded my vision, the distant sound of gravel crunched from the direction of the parking lot. Thank the lord, my savior had arrived.

I could play this off as a total accident, right? Maybe bribe him not to tell Jason?

A tall, broad-chested figure limped down the path on a pair of crutches, and my stomach bottomed out.

Shit.

It looked just like…no…it couldn't be.

My pulse pounded triple time in my temples as the *crunch tap crunch tap crunch* of gravel under his tread drew closer.

"Zoey?" a low, gruff voice asked.

No.

I'd recognize those wide shoulders anywhere. The backs of my legs knew them intimately.

Ryder. Freaking. Covington.

Okay, Chewbacca. Any time now. Sink those fangs into my leg and end this Valentine's Day from hell already.

Ryder stopped a few feet from the window, looking like he'd seen the Ghost of Christmas Past coming to bite him in the ass.

"Yup. It's me," I said.

He quickly recovered, his lips curling into a smile I'd once found charming. "You know, there's this thing called a door. Some people use it to go in and out of buildings."

I flipped him off. Immature? Most definitely. I blamed it on the blood rushing to my head. And the fact the one-night stand I had with him was the reason for my current string of sexual encounters of the lackluster kind.

He'd ruined me, in the worst way, for all other men. I hated him.

He chuckled and the deep bass of his voice shook down my spine. "Fair enough. I deserved that. What are you doing hanging out of the window?"

"I'm stuck." Understatement of the century.

"I figured." He hesitated, looking unsure. "Want help?"

My first instinct was to blurt out "go to hell!" I didn't need a goddamn thing from this person who single-handedly ruined my sex life. It was petty and I knew it, but a girl could only go so long on crappy sex before she started to feel a little stabby.

I instinctively reached to pull my skirt lower with one hand, and hit glass. It was up to the clothing malfunction gods at this point whether or not this day could get any worse.

"You want to keep burning a hole through my head or do

you want me to help you?"

"Fine. But if you touch anywhere besides clothed areas I'm going to put my stiletto through your skull, *capisce*?" I managed to keep my voice authoritative and firm, nothing like the shakiness flowing through my body. That was how being around Ryder had made me feel from the first time we met—like I'd just come off an intense adrenaline high.

He put his hands up. "Wouldn't dream of it."

I sunk back down and rested my arms on the sill, waiting to be sprung from the window. I prided myself on being self-sufficient, never needing help from others, especially dirt-bag hookups. And yet here I was.

He moved closer until the soft fabric of his faded shirt brushed against my arm, and I bit back a gasp. His rich cologne mingled with his detergent, and my eyes rolled back in my head at the heavenly scent. Most men that I'd dated smelled good in that dude-musk sort of way. Ryder took it to a completely different level, one that induced visceral reactions such as drool and the sudden need to find something to do with my hands, anything so I didn't fist his shirt.

Within seconds, he had the window open, and a firm hand wrapped around my hips. A wave of goose bumps bloomed across my skin as he pulled me down, depositing me on the gravel path, supporting me with his arm. I wobbled unsteadily in my heels and looked up at my ex-hookup, and the breath rushed from my chest like I'd actually taken a physical blow. Ryder stood there, henley pulled tight across his muscled chest. The color matched his ocean-blue eyes. He'd traded his clean-shaven face of a few months ago for a neatly trimmed beard that ran along his chiseled jaw. Which, let's be honest here, the whole light-eyes dark-hair thing did it for me. A lot. I might dislike the guy, but holy hell, he'd gotten even hotter since I'd last seen him. He looked over me, assessing, and then quickly bent down and swatted my leg.

"Ow! What was that for?" I retreated a step, stumbling as I rubbed at the spot he'd hit. When my fingers hit a squishy mound, it took every ounce of self-control not to dry heave. "You killed Chewbacca."

His brows creased, and some of the tension eased as he visibly hid a laugh. "You named him after a Star Wars character?"

I shrugged. "It seemed appropriate."

I stood there for a few moments, unsure of what to do. Grab my keys from the lodge, book it out of here, and apologize profusely to Jason, or snap on the big-girl panties and continue taking measurements? Decisions, decisions.

I took another step back and bumped into the wall. I was just full of smooth moves today. "Well, thanks for that."

His big, calloused hand brushed a stray lock of hair out of my face, sending heat radiating between my legs. His lips pulled into a smile, one that deposited my undergarments straight into the panty incinerator.

Nope, panties, no time for vaporizing. You hate him, remember?

My body was a traitorous wench.

I crossed my arms, trying to hold my ground. "What are you doing here, anyway, Ryder?" When Jason said someone was coming to Divinity, I didn't think he'd meant his brother.

It was his turn to fold his arms over his chest. "Jason wanted me to check on a few things. I wasn't expecting to have company."

What he really meant to say: *I really wasn't expecting to see you.*

"Same." I stared down at my stiletto heel, digging it into the gravel. Birds chirped, wind rustled through the trees, and we continued to stand there in silence.

So. Freaking. Awkward. This could end any time now.

He cleared his throat and thumbed at the braided leather

bracelet on his wrist. "Well, guess it's time to go our separate ways." He reached for a set of crutches propped against the building. And just like that, his smile faded, dismissing the incident, like he often ran into ex-hookups and saved them from dangling out of windows. Who knew—maybe he did.

I glanced at his leg, taking in the black boot encasing his leg.

Mr. Pro Snowboarder on crutches?

If I weren't fighting the intense urge to impale him with my stiletto, I'd maybe consider doing the polite thing and strike up conversation. Ask how he hurt himself. But let's be real, that wasn't going to happen without the aid of *a lot* of alcohol, or a lobotomy. "Well, thanks for that." I hitched my thumb toward the window. "I think you've achieved superhero status for the day."

He grinned. "Good to know there are two in the vicinity."

"Excuse me?"

He lifted a brow. "C'mon, I'd have thought the Flash would be better at getting out of tight situations. I'm a little disappointed."

What the…? Why would he call me that?

I winced and groaned as realization hit. My red-zone laundry situation meant I'd snagged the last pair of underwear in my drawer—the Flash undies that I'd used under my costume junior year of college. It even had a bright yellow lightning bolt across the ass.

Lord hath very little mercy for me today.

"Ass." I should have come up with a better comeback than that. I should have slapped that smug grin off his face. I should have done *something*. But all I could do was think about his bare chest hovering above me, his eyes blazing into mine as I lost myself in his touch back in November.

"Is that a reference to me or your underwear?"

Oh! The nerve of this guy.

By the time any semblance of a response surfaced in my mind, he'd already made his way up the path toward the front of the building. "It was a pleasure, Flash," he called, waving one crutch, not bothering to look back.

The sun had moved and was now hidden by the tree line, forming shadows over Ryder's retreating figure. A gigantic rain cloud glided across the sky with alarming speed, heading straight for the resort. Nothing on the weather forecast called for rain, but then again, when did I ever fully trust the weather app?

After I'd finished taking pictures and measurements of the main lodge area, Ryder had disappeared somewhere deep in the resort, and a storm had rolled in on the mountain. When I peered out the coke-bottle glass windows, snow came down in sheets, creating white-out conditions. There was no way I was leaving the resort tonight.

And Ryder's car was still in the parking lot.

Chapter Two

Ryder

The first time I met Zoey Reynolds, she ripped my brother a new asshole. Over furniture selection. It wasn't obvious to the average observer—in fact, my brother didn't even seem to notice. He'd suggest something and before he could take two bites of his chicken parm, he'd switched his opinion to agree with her.

There were two things that remained constant in my life:

1. The world revolved around the sun.
2. Jason Covington *never* compromised.

He didn't show mercy. Hell, he still held a grudge over the fact that I melted his favorite GI Joe in a campfire twenty years ago. But he gave in to everything this blond woman that barely came up to his shoulders said.

It was her eyes, I'd decided, four months back. Everything about her was fascinating. She talked a good game, but I'd decided right then and there Zoey Reynolds didn't even need to open her mouth to bring someone to their knees. One glance would do it.

In fact, just five minutes ago, I'd been on the receiving end of one of her stare downs, a look that promised I'd be spoon-fed my own balls. Did I deserve the silent threat that had my lower region ducking for cover? That'd be a resounding yes.

In most aspects, I'd classify myself as a good guy. I opened doors for old ladies, gave most of my sponsorship money to charity, and paid my taxes.

Relationships were a different story. I loved women. I respected the hell out of them. But, I still had a while until I was ready for someone else's toothbrush in my bathroom. My schedule was the same every day—get up, train, train some more, eat, pass out, repeat. The most committed relationship I'd ever been in was with my manager Andy, and he didn't require a lot of maintenance besides the occasional commission check.

A few months back, Zoey and I hung out a couple of times. I even spent the night once after a few too many drinks. We clicked. She was cool, someone who I could actually joke around with. But after we slept together, she got this look in her eye, and I'd realized I made a mistake. The sex itself was incredible—that part I didn't regret. But Zoey was *that* kind of girl. White picket fence, home-baked apple pie, two-point-five kids...all that shit.

So was I surprised to find the one girl who'd haunted my thoughts for the past four months flashing her underwear to the walls of my brother's new resort? Let's just say I had a better chance of nailing a Double Mctwist 1260 on my broken leg than running into her again. And I just played it off like nothing had happened between us, because what was I supposed to do? My default was going for the quick laugh.

I pulled out my phone and dialed Jason's number. It went straight to voicemail. I waited for the automated message to end and then spoke. "Hey, J. A storm's about to hit, and I'm stuck up at the resort. I'll keep you posted once I get back into town." I hung up, tossed my phone in my bag, and moved as fast as I could with crutches.

My clothes stuck to me in odd spots as I hobbled back into the building. Snow dumped onto the ground, thick and heavy, and I would have decided to screw grabbing my overnight bag if it weren't for the fact that I'd packed a couple of sandwiches and bottles of water.

Zoey stood in the middle of the great room, her teeth grazing her bottom lip as she studied the archway and the large, charred brick fireplace. Her blond waves curved down to the middle of her back, giving way to a dark smudge running the width of the white shirt tucked primly into her black skirt. It reminded me of something a librarian would wear, if librarians looked like Instagram models.

I shook the snow from my hair and brushed the remaining powder off my shoulders, leaving a trail of wet spots on the orange carpet.

"It's really coming down," I said, breaking the silence. If we were going to be stuck here all night, it was better to patch things over than to just ignore each other.

She looked up from her notebook, did a full-body sweep of my disheveled state, and frowned. "Did you come to that conclusion all by yourself?"

"I had to carry the one and do an impressive amount of long division in my head, but I finally figured it out," I shot back.

She broke into a slow clap that echoed in the cavernous room. "And here I was thinking you only thought with your other head." Her lips twitched in the corners.

It was hard to tell which I'd get frostbite from first—the weather outside, or Zoey's attitude. Even though it was clear her main goal tonight was to eviscerate me, I still found it sexy as hell.

"I didn't hear any complaints from you when I used that one." I raised my brow, a silent challenge.

Zoey was a box of TNT. Brilliant, intense, dangerous as hell. I'd just lit the fuse and would soon be suffering the repercussions.

Her skin flushed, and I should have been ashamed at how much I liked riling her up, especially after how I'd left things.

Before she could say anything else, I quickly added, "The master suite is down the hall and to the right. It's the most spacious, and if I'm correct, it has body wash from this century stocked in the bathroom."

She shivered, and if I didn't think she'd follow through with her threat to put a stiletto through my skull, I'd wrap her in my sweatshirt. "Good to know," she said.

I'd never had an issue with one-night stands before, due to the fact I never ran into them after parting ways. Everyone got what they wanted out of the deal—a good time, no harm no foul. But seeing her, the hurt in her eyes, made me feel like I'd hit a new level of scum.

"I brought an extra pair of sweats if you want something warmer to wear," I offered.

She shook her head. "I'm fine, thanks." The goose bumps pebbling her skin told a different story. The message was received loud and clear: she'd rather freeze her ass off than take anything of mine. I had a lot of work to do tonight if I wanted to wake up tomorrow morning.

"Okay..." The silence stretched between us and I decided not to press further, shoving down the irritation of knowing she was suffering to spite me. "I'll be down the hall if you need me."

"Right." She went back to her work, her hazel eyes ten seconds away from lighting her clipboard on fire.

I planned to grab the room next to hers, purely out of convenience. In case she needed anything. That was the story I was sticking to. After finding the breaker box and the thermostat to the place, I made my way to my room. Zoey had left the main area. With the shitty lighting, I assumed she gave up for the night and disappeared to the master suite.

I opened the door and grimaced. Words such as *décor* and *color palette* rarely crossed my mind, but even my design-inept self knew that the guest room was a goddamn abomination. With mustard-yellow sheets, faded wallpaper, and a bald eagle painting hanging crooked on the wall, it would be better to steamroll the place instead of wasting time and money on a remodel. Tear down the building, add a few new ski lifts, and it'd be good to go.

Dropping my bag onto the bed, I stripped off my soaked clothes and made my way to the shower. Between the snow and Zoey's arctic stares, the ancient heating system wasn't doing much to warm this place up.

I limped across the bathroom tile, and my hand stopped on the faucet when I heard a voice resonating through the walls. Every word echoed in the shower. From what I could tell, it was an audiobook. Something about a duke, or maybe an earl, although I couldn't be sure, since kings and queens were the extent of my knowledge on royal lineage. The water in the next room turned on, and the spray tapping against the porcelain floor muffled the voice on the audio.

Once I started the shower, I grabbed Saran Wrap out of my bag and wound it around my cast. Only a few more weeks of this hell and then everything would return to normal. Back to my team, my board, my life.

The narrator's thick British accent carried the story through the wall as I stepped in the shower. And then I heard it. A groan and a thump. Followed by a "*Why, God? What did I ever do to you?*" Along with a few creatively crafted expletives. There was a good chance my name was thrown in there as well.

I fisted my hair and sighed. Even if we were both in agreement about wanting to be anywhere but here, it didn't feel right going the rest of the night pretending she wasn't there. I also might have had a death wish, because I couldn't seem to keep my damn mouth shut around her.

"The accent's probably fake," I said as I worked a bar of soap over my chest.

The audio stopped. "I didn't know you took the time to get a linguistics degree in all that spare time of yours?"

"A self-educated expert, but I'm sure Harvard would mail me a degree if you require evidence."

"You should get right on that. Maybe add on a minor in manners while you're at it, because then you'd know it's not polite to eavesdrop."

Even with a wall between us, her glare pierced through my chest. "I can't help it if the walls are thin."

"Funny you chose that room when there are ten others in the vicinity that don't share a wall with mine."

"I figured it'd be convenient in case Chewbacca had family that will want to avenge his death."

"If I remember correctly, it was his blood on *your* hands. I'll make sure to send the eight-legged mafia your direction."

"So harsh," I said, smiling.

"Well, you're coming between me and my audiobook time."

"Let me sum it up for you: the Earl of Yorkshire is trying to get in the handmaiden's pants."

The book did actually sound kind of interesting, not that I would ever admit that in a million years.

She scoffed. "His name is Duke Renau. And he is trying to earn the love of Lady Eddington." She paused and then mumbled, "Some men understand basic human decency," and I had a feeling those words weren't meant for my ears.

I scrubbed my hands over my face. I'd been an idiot for

thinking I could have a civil conversation with her after how I'd acted. "I'm sorry about November and not saying goodbye."

She paused for a long time, and I resigned myself to the fact that she'd shut me out for the rest of the night.

"I'm gonna get back to my story now," she finally said quietly.

"Duke is better company than me?"

A deep, throaty laugh came through the wall. I loved that damn sound, even if it was currently at my expense. But it was better than silence. "Wait, you want me to answer that honestly? I mean, if we're ranking on a one to ten scale, you're at least a solid four. Admirable effort."

"If I had a heart, I might actually be offended." I was a little bit, but she didn't need to know that.

"Careful, Ryder. Your ooey-gooey center is showing." And with that, she restarted her audiobook.

I dipped my head under the warm spray and laughed. Zoey Reynolds didn't hold any punches.

• • •

ZOEY

Hour five of the white-out conditions.

Status: No food and only a few swigs of water left in my bottle.

Boredom level: the DMV now qualified as a magical oasis.

According to my weather app, I had another few hours until the storm system moved out of the mountains. Not that I trusted the forecast to begin with. Even worse, I was at 7 percent battery, and I'd forgotten my charger. I silently shook my fist at the weather gods. Seriously, a night without my ebooks? With *him* next door? Let the torture commence. I could practically feel his arrogance radiating through the walls. I might have been a little harsh with what I'd said, but I wasn't about to play it off like we were BFFs just because he wanted to clear his conscience.

I shot a quick text to Lainey explaining the situation and shut off my phone.

"How's it going over there, Flash?"

I gritted my teeth. Nope. Wouldn't give him the satisfaction of knowing he was getting under my skin.

"Fine." My stomach growled. I was such a wimp. In fact, there was a distinct possibility that I'd be going Hannibal Lecter on my arm by the time dawn rolled around.

"Liar. I can hear your stomach grumbling from over here."

I didn't doubt this because these walls were toilet-seat-cover thin.

"I have an extra peanut butter and jelly sandwich over here," he offered.

Food. Sweet, delicious food.

My stomach grumbled again.

This guy was deep down in the depths of my shit list at the moment, but he just might have moved up a few pegs. I didn't say anything, weighing my options. Suck it up for a few minutes and eat his food, or be stubborn and possibly resort to self-cannibalism—a tough decision.

"C'mon, Reynolds. I know you have to be hungry. Why don't you come over here and I'll share my sandwich with you?"

"Is that a euphemism?"

"My peanut butter is completely platonic. Scout's honor."

I smothered my laugh. Damnit, why did he have to be funny? I was supposed to be hating him, not smiling.

I considered his offer again. How hard could it really be? Small talk for a few minutes, eat Ryder's food and then sneak back into my room and pretend this whole being stuck in the creepy lodge thing wasn't happening. Seemed like a solid enough plan.

"Were you even a Boy Scout?" I asked.

"For a whole forty-eight hours."

"Couldn't handle the uniform?" I rolled over, staring at the divots in the ceiling, bracing myself for another face-to-face interaction with Ryder. It was easy to rip him a new one when we weren't in the same room, but when I had to look at him, those blue eyes watching me, assessing me, it frayed every single nerve in my body.

"No. Decided I wanted to get my fire badge early and burned down a tent."

A smile twitched at my lips. "Somehow, that doesn't surprise me in the least bit." I scooted off the bed and straightened my skirt, making my way out of the suite. I took a deep breath before knocking on his door.

In, out, keep it quick.

The door swung open, and Ryder smiled down at me, his blue eyes twinkling in the dim light. My stomach plunged. Really, the whole hotness factor was a distraction. Nothing short of a lighting strike to the head could deter me from my food mission, though. Peanut butter or bust.

I cleared my throat as we both stood in the doorway. "Did you at least get the badge?"

"No." He hesitated, but then gave a smile.

My gaze followed the curve of his lips, the way the deep pink faded on the outer edges, giving way to tanned skin and a neatly trimmed beard that I bet would give my cheeks road rash if I brushed up against him.

Down girl. Food. Focus on food.

I'd spent the past months cursing him, and now that he was in the same room, it was like my mind had been wiped clean. Poof. No recollection of waking up and being utterly humiliated by picking another wrong guy.

"Thanks for coming over. I was starting to get a little stir crazy."

"I only came for the peanut butter." As if on cue, my stomach let out another growl.

"Then I won't keep you waiting." He motioned with a crutch to the table across the room where two sandwiches sat stacked atop each other in plastic baggies.

Ryder sat down. The table overlooked the view of the mountain—or what would have been the view if it weren't completely white with blowing snow. He pushed a sandwich across to me, and I stared at the door longingly, debating to make a run for it. Even in an extreme state of hunger, I retained an iota of manners. I dropped into the chair across from him, tore off a piece of sandwich, and popped it into my mouth.

Sweet baby Jesus in a manger, this was the best thing I'd eaten all day. "Thank you," I said.

"No problem. My brother wouldn't be too happy if his designer died on the job. Liability and all."

"Good point." I took another bite.

He placed his sandwich on top of the plastic bag and looked at me, his expression turning serious. "I know you want to be here about as much as I do, but let's make the best of it?"

Fine. Civility wouldn't be too hard to manage for a couple of hours. That, and the fact that after this, I most likely wouldn't see him again, so what the hell?

I raised my sandwich. "To stupid weather."

"To stupid weather." He clinked his sandwich to mine and we both took a bite. The wind howled against the window pane and I shuddered again, cursing myself that I hadn't even packed a sweater.

Ryder pushed away from the table, grabbed a crutch, and strode over to a black duffel bag sitting on the bed. "I can't watch you shiver," he growled, the sound going straight to the space between my thighs. "Just take this." He pulled out a pair of gray sweats and handed them to me.

I hesitated for a moment, then took them, thumbing the soft material. "If I hear one joke about being in your pants, I'm leaving."

"Wouldn't even think about it." He pulled off his hoodie and held it in front of me, leaving him in his henley. "I don't need this, either."

I swallowed hard and pointedly ignored how the shirt clung to him, tapering at the waist. "Aren't you going to be cold?"

He shrugged. "I'm used to the snow."

Right. Snowboarder. One that was currently on crutches. I wondered what that meant for his career, but didn't feel comfortable enough to ask him. People in professional sports were injured all the time—this probably was just a minor setback.

"Thanks," I said, pulling the sweatshirt over my head. The material brushed over my nose and—oh my—hello, delicious cologne. The smell brought a flashback of tangled sheets, sweat-slicked skin, and fingers running through my hair. My eyes fluttered shut and I fought back another shiver—this one having nothing to do with the storm outside.

Do. Not. Go. There.

Again.

Okay, safe topic. I needed to find a safe topic so I didn't make an ass out of myself and say something like *your scent calls to me more than a Cinnabon kiosk at the mall—oh, and hey, can we, um, fix the four-month dry spell you've caused? K, thanks, bye.* "I can't believe the weather turned so ugly."

He shifted his gaze to me, his deep voice cutting through the silence. "Anything can happen on the mountain."

I swallowed hard. Looking at his leg, I didn't doubt that.

Again he thumbed at the bracelet on his wrist, his jaw tensing. He'd worn that bracelet when I first met him, and from the ragged state, it appeared that it never came off. Ryder didn't strike me as the accessorizing type, unless you counted his gear. He was like a Snowboarding Ken doll, though an anatomically correct one—seriously, I couldn't have been the only one that peeked as a kid and was completely disappointed with the whole mangina situation going on in Ken's pants.

He scrubbed his palms over his face and rested his elbows on his knees. "This was not how I saw this night going."

"Big Valentine's Day plans?"

He lowered his hands and looked at me like I'd just claimed I single-handedly caused the storm raging outside. "I didn't even know that was today. Does this mean we're each other's valentines by default?"

I scoffed. "Not a chance."

He chuckled. "Always so blunt. I like that about you." He quickly cleared his throat as if he hadn't meant to say that. "Well, non-valentine, looks like we're going to be stuck here a while. Have anything in mind?" he said.

I decided against packing on another insult. He was being nice, and this sure as heck beat staring at the wall the rest of the night. "My form of entertainment is at 6 percent battery, so I'm open to suggestions."

"Mine is fully charged. Want to watch something?"

"Sure." What else did I have to do? Before I knew it, I was sitting on the bed next to him, leaning against the ornately carved headboard.

Snow gusting against the window was the only sound in the room as he searched for a show for us to watch.

So quiet.

Way too quiet.

I fidgeted with my necklace, moving the small diamond back and forth on the chain. The last time I was in bed with

Ryder… I didn't even want to finish that thought, because it'd do nothing but make this situation worse. I chanced a peek in his direction.

He chewed the inside of his cheek, swiping through our options. "This is awkward, huh?" he said.

"We've achieved Urkel status."

He chuckled and scrolled through the show queue. "Would you rather watch *Law and Order: SVU* or *Criminal Minds*?"

"That is quite possibly the worst Would You Rather question ever asked."

His eyes cut to mine. "I didn't know I was playing a game."

"You've never played it?"

He shook his head.

Lainey and I played this game all the time in college, and when we'd take road trips together. She always came up with the grossest ones. "It's simple. All you have to do is ask the person which horrible thing they'd rather do. The harder the question, the better. Like would you rather lay in a pit of snakes, or eat questionably dead roadkill?" I pointed to his phone. "Oh, *John Tucker Must Die.* I like that one."

"Negative, ghost rider." He scrolled past my suggestion. "And what the hell does *questionably* dead mean? Is it still twitching, or are we talking suspicious cause of death?"

I shrugged. "The interpretation's up to you."

"You're absolutely no help." He swiped his thumb across his beard and contemplated. "I guess I'd go with the snakes."

"Okay, now it's your turn," I said.

"Do I really have to play? I thought we were picking a show."

I shot him a look.

"Fine. Would you rather have me or Chewbacca as your valentine?"

"Too easy. The spider."

He put his hand to his heart. "You wound me."

"Stop being such a baby." I swatted at his chest and immediately pulled my hand back. Nope. Would not go there. "Okay, would you rather not be able to see or talk for a month?"

He answered instantly. "See."

"Right. You'd probably go nuts if you couldn't open that big mouth of yours."

His lips twitched. "You're one to talk."

"Excuse me?" Okay, I did have a tough time keeping my thoughts on lockdown outside the office, but that was my own cross to bear.

"Don't even try to play it off like you're innocent."

I'd dated a lot of losers in the past, most who hadn't even bothered to get to know me, but even after only hanging out a few times, Ryder had me pegged. He was perceptive. I saw the look in his eyes whenever I dealt with Jason. His attention focused solely on me was unnerving. "Jerk," I sputtered.

"Now I know you're holding back. You can do way better than that." He scrolled through his phone again. "How about *Die Hard?"*

"Are all your show selections about death? I'm starting to worry I made a mistake coming over here." My lips pulled into a smile and I quickly extinguished it. God, I wanted to hate him.

"Fine." He continued looking at the Netflix queue. "Would you rather eat sushi from a taco stand, or lick an airplane armrest?"

"Good one. Sushi." I pointed to his screen. "How about *10 Things I Hate About You?"*

He shook his head and chuckled. "Are all of *your* suggestions going to not-so-subtly tell me you hate me?"

I smiled sweetly. "Maybe."

"Just think, most people would find this to be a romantic

escape. Two people, stuck in the mountains on Valentine's Day," he said.

"We're Hallmark movie material, all right," I deadpanned.

"Okay, fine. How about *The Walking Dead*?"

"Your show picking powers have been officially revoked." I grabbed the phone from his hand.

"Hey!" He grabbed for the phone, and I held it out of reach. "You're going to regret that." Within seconds he was on top of me, playfully pinning me to the bed, his strong hands circling my wrists. Air evaporated from my lungs as our gazes connected.

I was immediately transported back to that night.

Tell me what you want, Zoey. Tell me what you need from me.

I swallowed hard. That was months ago, and those words still haunted me from time to time. Because he did exactly that, gave me what I wanted and needed. Repeatedly.

We were frozen there, him hovering above me, the heat between us burning a trail through my veins, from head to toe. I ached for him all over again.

His voice came out gravelly as he said, "You have peanut butter on you."

Before I could swipe away the food, he bent down and his tongue swept along the curve of my neck. A groan escaped my lips before I could check myself. Lights exploded behind my eyes, and I melted into the mattress as he continued working his way down to my collarbone feverishly, like he was getting lost in himself. His fingers left my wrist and fisted my hair. My body arched into him. I needed him. Needed this so badly. One time wasn't enough.

I froze at that.

Last time.

Oh no.

I was not going through that again. He ruined me once,

and I wasn't sure I'd be able to survive a second time, no matter how bad my body begged for it.

I pushed at his shoulders. "Stop, Ryder."

He immediately pulled away, his face flushed, blue eyes wild and unfocused.

The sight was enough to make me second-guess my decision.

"I—I need to go." I rolled off the bed and made my way to the door before I could do something stupid like remove any clothing. "Th—thanks for the sandwich," I called before shutting the door, not daring to look back.

I made it to the safety of my room and tore off his sweatshirt, not wanting to be reminded of his smell, of anything of his that would change my mind and pull me back to his room. I lay down on my bed and moments later, the shower started up in Ryder's suite.

No cold shower would extinguish what my body craved at the moment.

Chapter Three

Ryder

Snow clung to every tree lining the mountain floor outside my window when I woke up the next morning. I pulled on my shirt and jeans and made my way to Zoey's room. An apology was required for last night—I'd taken it too far. Something about her just drove me to the point where I wasn't in my right mind.

At least one of us had common sense, because in that moment I would have given my left hand to finish what we'd started. She'd done us both a favor.

I knocked on her door. "Flash, you in there?"

No answer.

I tried again, which proved to be a fruitless effort. I pulled on my shoes and went out into the parking lot, where I found a fresh set of shoe prints and departing tread marks disturbing the otherwise pristine snow.

Dammit.

Karma was a cruel bitch.

Unease settled in my gut. I'd like to say it was because I was hungry as hell after having a measly PB and J sandwich for dinner, but I knew better than to kid myself. I never expected to be in the same room with Zoey again. Now I remembered why I wanted her in the first place. I swiped a hand over my face. It was that mouth of hers, that damn attitude that drove me half up the wall.

Jesus.

That woman had been my undoing without even trying. Which was why I needed to stay away from her. Far, far away.

My phone buzzed on the nightstand, pulling me out of my thoughts. I clicked the call button. "'Sup?"

My brother's voice boomed through the speaker. "How is the resort? Did you see Zoey?"

"The resort is—yeah." The only thing worth keeping was the land it sat on.

"How does it look?" Jason repeated.

"If you want to keep tabs so bad, you should've taken up my offer to drive you yesterday."

"I'm…not ready for that yet."

All smartass remarks died on my tongue. At the moment, we were both injured; I'd broken my leg two months after his accident, but while my tanked run down the mountain led to a career hiatus, Jason's accident changed his life forever, leaving him paralyzed from the waist down. Even if Jason handled everything with Superman stoicism, he was only human. And even tyrants needed a day off.

"I need to ask you a favor," he said.

• • •

ZOEY

Breathe in.

Your body is a crime scene. Slap on the caution tape,

close that shit up for business. I liked to get creative with my inner mantras. Temple? So cliché. Plus, there were so many more murderous thoughts than peaceful ones going on that I couldn't really classify it as a sanctuary anymore.

Breathe out.

Bitable scruff so scratchy and delicious against my skin.

Shit. No. Bad, Zoey.

Breathe in.

Can't forget that tongue. Oh, girl. Spread the peanut butter on thicker next time.

Good. Lord.

I fell out of Half Lotus Crow and face-planted into my yoga mat in the middle of my living room. Screw this noise. I lay there, sprawled out on the floor. What the hell? Why was I so flustered? I *never* screwed up my poses. Not when I totally bombed stressful meetings. Definitely not after breakups. Though, nobody had caused my mind to strike a line in the sand with my body before, either. It was WWZoey. First showdown—Battle of Hornysburg. Mind won, just barely. Multiple casualties.

Even if my body was cuing up the sad trombone at my refusal to end my current dry spell, I had bigger things to focus on. Namely, making sure my client was happy. All this sexual frustration could be channeled into making a fabulous resort.

It didn't matter anyway, because I'd never see Ryder again. Sure, leaving without saying good-bye *might* have been a bit insensitive, but it also earned me a delicious slice of payback for how things went down in November. Who cared? I was working with his brother, who could have written a textbook on how to be professional. Someone who would never lick *anything* off my neck.

I ignored the shiver winding down my spine. Time to get into business mode and shift my focus to something worthwhile. Goose-feather bedding. Much more fascinating. Yep.

I peeled myself off the floor and made my way to the kitchen to pour a cup of coffee. Lainey was just coming out of her room when I dropped a dash of cream into my cup.

Without so much as bothering to keep both eyes open, she shoved her mug across the counter like our kitchen was now a saloon and said, "Coffee me."

Lainey was one of those people you made sure not to breathe the wrong way around before she'd had her daily allotment of caffeine. If the average person drank the amount of coffee she downed in the a.m., they wouldn't even be able to write their own name by noon. I'd tried substituting the pot with half-caf one time. I'd never make that mistake again.

I slid her favorite mug her way and shuffled out of the kitchen, taking a seat at the breakfast bar. "Take a lot of work home with you this weekend?" I asked. Dark rings etched the skin below her eyes, and I'd woken up a few times last night, tossing and turning, thinking about certain jerk men, and had heard the clicking of her keyboard. Last time I checked before zonking out, she was still up at three.

"Yeah, just a ton of paperwork for Brogan's new company."

Her boyfriend, Brogan, or as I had officially dubbed him, Mr. Broody Billionaire, is the owner of a social media management franchise. Lainey had been his second assistant, and then they started the whole *bow chicka wow wow* office romance thing. I liked the guy once he took his head out of his ass and realized that Lainey was essentially the catch of the century. After a few hiccups (which is to say, a helluva lot of them), he turned into good boyfriend material, made her the manager at his new company, and they've been attached at the lips ever since. It was both sweet and nauseating.

She scowled at her mug and took a deep pull. "We're

coming up with a new employee manual, and you know how Brogan is with all his rules."

I choked on my coffee. The dude had more rules than the English language. Not that I couldn't relate—I tended to keep my own set of rules, but with about a tenth of the neuroses.

"It'll get better, especially with you there to keep him in check." Hopefully. For her sake.

Luckily, the rules were fairly lax at my firm. Follow the five commandments, and I was in the clear.

I took another bite of my yogurt and granola, thankful that Lainey had distracted me from thoughts of the meeting I had with Jason later this morning.

Lainey dumped Lucky Charms into a bowl and scooted up beside me at the breakfast bar.

"Sugar and caffeine. Looks like you're off to a great start."

She side-eyed me. "Whatever. I have two food groups covered. My grains and dairy."

I just shook my head and laughed. Even though I liked the occasional splurge, Lainey still had the college student diet going on. Ramen, cereal, and anything that ended in "itos."

She pointed her spoon at me. "I have to admit that the marshmallows totally don't taste as good as they did when I was a kid."

"Same goes for TV shows. Nothing is ever as good when you re-watch it."

"What about *Gilmore Girls*?" she said.

"That's the exception, and you know it." Nothing would ever beat that show. Except for maybe *Game of Thrones* and my beloved Jon Snow.

"Truth. I bet we couldn't even make it through thirty seconds of *Hannah Montana*."

We used to love that show when we were in middle school, something that I'd never admit to anyone but, well, Lainey.

"You're just bitter because she got all weird with the

Home Depot products."

"She did make for a good Halloween costume," she said wistfully.

Lainey looked at her phone and jumped off her stool, almost knocking it to the ground. "Crap. Gonna be late. I'll catch you later, Z."

"Later."

I watched as she disappeared into her room and came out ten minutes later, jacket in hand, rushing out the door.

Taking one last sip of my coffee, I made my way into my room, grabbed my favorite blouse and pencil skirt, and fixed my hair in the bathroom. Call me superstitious, but I always wore the same outfit when meeting clients for a new job. It hadn't failed me yet, and gave me the extra boost of confidence to propose my ideas. I'd worn it when I took Jason to lunch at Giovanni's and convinced him to go with a sectional rather than the eyesore of a futon. I'd seen him several times after that, so I wasn't worried he'd catch on to my recycled outfit choice. Plus, he was a guy. I couldn't name a single one who'd notice stuff like that.

I moved to my desk to grab my computer and the designs I'd printed out last night. Jitters, my cat, lay on top of my laptop, his tail swishing the designs off my desk, the papers fluttering to the floor. He looked up at me and seemed to smirk.

I picked him up and placed him on my bed, then bent to grab the papers strewn across the hardwood. "Not you, too. You're supposed to be the one man that doesn't disappoint me." Besides my dad, anyway, who was every bit of a superhero as I'd believed him to be since I was six. Except, instead of a cape, he donned an apron, and his weapon of choice was a crème brûlée torch.

He owned a bakery in downtown Portland called The Way the Cookie Crumbles. Shortly after my mother's death it had been featured on the Food Network, and he'd spent the past ten years overseeing the franchise's expansion throughout the U.S. If he'd taught me one thing, it was to follow your dreams. Sure, he had been gone a lot, but his determination was something that I could relate to. I loved my job. Quite possibly more than most things in my life.

Jitters managed a meager meow and began cleaning his fur, giving zero craps about anything but a comfy spot.

I feigned a glare, even though we both knew I could never be mad at him. The only time he'd been on my shit list was when he'd used my new leather boots as a personal scratching post. "Okay, I forgive you just this once because you're so cute." I scratched behind his ears and then packed my papers and laptop into my bag.

By the time I grabbed my smoothie off the counter and my purse from the coatrack, precious time to prepare for this morning's meeting with Jason had dwindled.

I parked in the underground garage of our building with thirty minutes to spare.

At the entrance, though, a shudder splintered through me, and I paused with my hand resting on the handle. Game time. Seven months into the job, and talking to clients should be as easy as resting in Child's Pose. My brain had other ideas, though. Mainly thoughts of binging on Nutella and Netflix.

You've got this on lockdown. Pencil Skirt. Blouse. Cat eyes on point. Time to hike up the big-girl panties, a pair that did *not* have the Flash emblazoned on the butt.

I pushed through the door to the building and took the elevator to the sixteenth floor, the main headquarters of Bass and Goldstein Interior Designs. The elevator doors opened, giving way to a reception area filled with plush leather couches, spotless glass tables, and abstract oil paintings created by a local artist.

I strode out of the elevator and gave Mary, our receptionist, a quick wave. "Morning, Mary. How's it going?"

A warm smile spread across her face as I walked closer. Mary was in her late seventies and embodied the grandmotherly vibe. She loved pearls, chunky yellow gold rings, wore way too much perfume, and *sometimes* smelled of moth balls. Strike up a conversation with her, and unsolicited (and often cray cray) advice was sure to follow. Her flaws were easily overlooked, though, because she made an apple tart that rivaled my father's. Her goodies magically appeared on my desk on a bi-monthly basis. My taste buds adored her; my waistline did not.

"Morning, sweetie." She pointed her pen at the second door on the left and said, "I sent someone into your office. He seemed a little perturbed." She leaned in and whispered, "My guess is he's low on fiber. Needs a good push to get things moving, if you get my drift."

I smothered my giggle. "Did you get a name?"

"A Mr. Covington."

"Wow, he's"—I glanced at my watch—"really early." More so than I expected. Jason had punctuality down to the millisecond. But he wasn't one to be early, especially if it meant he'd have to wait.

"I told him he was more than welcome to sit in the waiting area, but he refused. Said he'd feel much more comfortable in your office." Mary clutched at her pearls and bristled in her seat.

"No problem. Thanks for sending him in there."

"Sure thing, sweetie." She went back to clicking away at her computer, and I stared at my office down the hall.

Nothing to worry about. Jason Covington was about to get his damn mind blown by my designs.

The elevator door dinged and moments later, Lance Bass, not the early-nineties boy band one, mind you, but the one who owned Bass and Goldstein Design Firm, entered the office and came to stand near me at Mary's desk. His stubby arms were crossed, pulling the seams of his suit jacket tight across his shoulders. He was the human equivalent of a Shar-Pei with small dog syndrome. I'd trained under him personally during my six-month probationary period, so I was lucky enough to be in his good graces. He was kind to most people up until the point where someone pissed off a client or broke one of the office's five commandments.

The Client is always right.

Don't piss off the Client.

Don't sleep with the Client

Always remain professional.

The Client needs to be 100 percent in love with the finished product.

So far I was batting five for five.

My boss eyed me suspiciously, which wasn't any surprise as I was ten seconds away from sweating through my bra. Did I mention I hated meetings?

His forehead creased in valleys so deep they might very well have their own topographical map. Seriously, though, pens could get swallowed up in those wrinkles. I'd been half tempted during *very* long staff meetings to test out that theory, but I loved my job way too much to get on his bad side. "Everything all right, Zoey?"

I cleared my throat once more, my voice scratchy and forced as I said, "Good, just about to meet with Mr. Covington."

Lance glanced down the hall to my closed office door. "I saw the email from Jason on Friday. Nice work," he said. He flashed a smile and I nearly choked. Those tended to make an appearance as often as Punxsutawney Phil before Groundhog's Day.

"Covington is a huge client. You're doing a great job, Zoey. Another couple of years, and you could really move up in the firm."

Inside, I indulged in a victorious booty shake. On the outside, I kept my features subdued, only allowing a small smile. "Thanks, Lance." I'd just passed my probationary period and was now considered a full-time employee. More than anything, I'd love to work my way to a senior-level position. Bass and Goldstein was considered a top-tier design firm on the West Coast. I was being trained under the DaVinci of designers, and I wasn't above any amount of ass-kissing to keep it that way.

"Let's make sure Mr. Covington stays happy. I'll assume you'll go above and beyond, just like you always do."

Meaning: *Don't screw this up. This is a huge paycheck for the firm.*

I nodded. "Of course. I'll do whatever it takes."

Meaning: *My lips will be numb from the amount of times I will kiss the ground upon which Jason Covington walks.*

He rapped his knuckles on Mary's desk. "I knew I could count on you. Let me know if there's anything you need."

The only things I might need were a Costco-size wine bottle and maybe some Xanax.

As Lance disappeared into his office, I stared at my own door, the only barrier between me and the oddity that was Mr. Covington. I braced myself for the weird requests I'd come to expect from him. He wouldn't make my job easy, but if it were easy, where would be the fun in that? I loved a good challenge, and Jason would definitely deliver. Lance was right—I could do this.

Bring it on, Covington.

I grabbed my water bottle from my bag, took a sip of water and jiggled the door handle.

The door swooshed open and my eyes locked with a pair of familiar bright blue ones.

No.

Water sprayed out of my mouth as I saw a different Covington occupying the chair across from mine at my desk.

Ryder. Freaking. Covington.

Oh hell no.

He smiled at me, that same cheeky grin he'd managed when he pulled me out of the window the other night. My toes curled into the soles of my stilettos, and the taste of peanut butter ghosted over my taste buds.

"Flash! So good to see you again."

Nope. Nopity nope. Where was Jason? Was this some sick joke?

I had my power outfit on. I was impenetrable. This was not supposed to happen.

"Mr. Covington," I said in a cordial tone, one that hid my DEFCON 1 meltdown status. "I thought I was meeting with your brother this morning."

His smile faltered for half a second before he fixed it back on his face. He cleared his throat and said, "You were, but Jason asked me to step in. I'll be taking over the renovation project from here on out."

He was talking. Words. Quite a few of them, in fact. Some were even strung together in complete sentences. But all I could think about was his tongue on my neck. About how it'd felt months ago with his fingers skimming across my exposed flesh. His mouth. Everywhere.

So screwed. So utterly screwed.

I'd been in bed with this man, and now he was technically my client? It wasn't a big deal before, because there was nothing in the bylaws that said anything about one-night stands with a client's brother, but if I took him on, this was a whole next level of wrong.

"Is Jason okay?"

I'd take weirdo Covington over the drool-worthy one any day of the week. For my job's sake.

His expression darkened. “He will be. Eventually.” He stroked the pad of his thumb across his lips and leveled me with a gaze that told me not to push him any further on the topic.

“Eventually? How long has he been ill?” It made no sense. He’d hired me three days ago. If he was unwell, why was he buying properties?

He looked at me, eyes wary. “Since November.”

November. Jason had been my client the majority of that month. I would have known if something was wrong. Unless…

I shook it off. Nothing good would come of me thinking back to that night.

All speculations came to a screeching halt when he said, “We have a lot to discuss, so let’s get to it, minus the mind-control crap. That won’t work on me.” He smiled, toying with me.

“Mind-control crap…” Did it make me a horrible person that the sole reason I wanted Jason to get better ASAP was so I didn’t have to look at his smug, self-assured brother? Yep, I was going to hell.

He huffed out a laugh. “I saw the way you got him to agree with whatever you said. That never happens.”

“I don’t know what you’re talking about. Jason liked my designs, and I can’t help it if he sided with my ideas.” Okay, it’d taken a *teeny* bit of persuading, but nothing I’d be ashamed to admit. It was all for the sake of the design. Sometimes a client just needed a push in the right direction.

“Listen, you can cut the crap with me, Zoey. You may have everyone else fooled, but I know your type. You’re methodical and superstitious. You wore that exact outfit at Giovanni’s.” He paused and did a quick assessment. “Well, you had a red necklace, not the one you’re wearing now. Gift from a boyfriend?”

“I—what? No. This is all ridiculous.” No way. This guy had

not just figured me out in two point four seconds. Was I really that transparent?

He must have seen that question on my face, because he continued, "Go on—tell me I'm wrong about the outfit, and I'll walk out the door right now." He arched a brow.

This…was not how the meeting was supposed to go. What happened to the cordial nodding? The *oohing* and *ahhing* over the plans I'd angsted over for the past two days? On top of that, he'd debunked my power outfit.

The right thing to do would be to pass him off to another designer. All I had to do was keep it professional for another few minutes while I brought Lance in here. He'd be more than happy to help out a Covington.

"Mr. Covington." I dropped my bottle of water, briefcase, and purse on my desk and smoothed my sweaty palms over my skirt before taking a seat. "As much as I'd love to design the resort, I think there is now a conflict of interest. I'd be more than happy to pass your project to another designer in the firm." Anyone who could remember the exact detail of what I wore *months* ago crossed a professional line.

There. He couldn't argue with that. I could avoid this whole mess from the start and still keep true to the code of conduct.

He shook his head. "That's not going to be possible."

"Why?"

"Jason said he would only work with you, no one else."

"I'm sure he would be perfectly happy with Mr. Bass. His experience is unrivaled by anyone at this firm."

"You really think dumping Jason as a client would make him happy?"

Lance's words played in the back of my head. *Do whatever it takes to keep the Covingtons happy.*

Dammit.

Ryder's voice lowered to that deep, gravelly tone that

tugged at my gut. "Unless you're worried you can't keep things professional. Is that why you left so quickly on Saturday?" His gaze slid toward the curve of my neck, to where his mouth had been not even three days ago.

Gauntlet thrown down.

I eyed him. He had no right to throw shade when he'd done the same thing to me first. "I didn't know I needed your permission to leave a public place."

I bit down on the side of my cheek until the ache in my mouth overpowered the ones in other spaces.

"You're right," he said.

Our gazes met and the energy between us crackled.

This was quite possibly the worst idea I'd ever had, playing mind games with the man who had set the sexual satisfaction bar to Olympic heights.

I bristled. Game face. No freaking out allowed, not at work. And definitely not in front of *him.* Even if I wanted Ryder out this door in the next thirty seconds, I would not let him know that. "And to answer your other question, everyone at Bass and Goldstein embodies professionalism. Myself included."

"Then I don't see a problem. We need a resort renovated, and you are a design firm."

You are a professional.

That had broken the thou-shalt-not-bone-thy-client commandment.

I cleared my throat, shifting in my seat. "You're right. Not a problem at all." I smoothed an invisible wrinkle on my skirt, stalling for a moment to focus. "Would you like to see the designs?"

Game plan: stay polite. Stay at arm's length.

He shrugged. "Sure."

I pulled the designs out of my briefcase and slid them across the surface, making sure not to come anywhere near his hands, splayed on the other end of the table. My body heated, pulled to his massive frame as if by a magnetic force. I cleared my throat.

Reality check, girl. He tapped you harder than a fraternity kegger and fled before he could even warm the other side of your bed. Not exactly job-losing-worthy material.

There. That put things into perspective.

He took one quick glance at the drafts, frowned, and pushed them back toward me.

"I have to be honest with you. I think this is the worst business decision my brother has ever made. This is nothing against you or your firm, but I fully plan on convincing him to sell the resort as soon as he's feeling better. In the meantime, we can discuss new designs. For his sake."

Oh-kay. A client who didn't actually want my services might pose as a roadblock. A large one. "For *his* sake, you'd better give it proper consideration. We do charge by the hour." If he thought I'd just roll over and take this, he was messing with the wrong person.

Lance expected me to make this project work. Ryder didn't know who he was dealing with. What I lacked in experience, I more than made up for with my inherited determination. I'd change his mind, and we'd find something that would make this resort fantastic.

"Of course. But would you rather strong-arm me into liking these designs I'm not crazy about, or wait until you come up with something that'll blow my mind?" His lips curved into a smile.

Oh! My vision hazed over, and it took everything in me not to reach across the table and throat-punch him. Using my own game against me. Despicable.

"I would never want you to 'settle' for something you don't care for. I'll rework the plans."

"If you come up with anything new, I'm free Friday night

to discuss it. Over dinner, if you prefer."

"I-I don't think that would be wise."

"Why? You took me and Jason out to lunch." He lifted a brow. He'd baited that hook with expert precision. Of course he knew that I took my clients out to eat. "Or do you need him as a referee?"

"Well, yes. I mean, no."

"For someone who claims to be professional, I'd think you'd want to treat all of your clients equally. Unless working with me makes you nervous?" His gaze moved from my waist and slowly made its way to meet mine in a challenge.

I ignored the heat pooling in my cheeks, and other places much, much lower. We were walking a fine line. One I wasn't comfortable toeing, not when it involved my job. Especially not when it involved *him*. So, for the sake of my career and personal sanity, I pushed all thoughts of Ryder to a far recess of my mind, the same place that held forgotten passwords and the whereabouts of the TV remote.

"Of course not. You're right. If I come up with new plans before Friday, I will set up a company dinner." Yeah, not a chance in hell.

We both stood at the same time, and I smoothed the wrinkles on my skirt before extending my hand. "I look forward to working with you, Mr. Covington."

He took my hand, the pad of his calloused thumb sliding across my skin. "Same here. Good luck with the new designs." He leaned down and pressed his lips to my fingers.

Oh boy. Oh crap.

They were soft and warm and something I should not be thinking about. "And for the record, I still think I'm more interesting than that duke of yours." He smiled and grabbed the crutches propped against my desk, then made his way out of the office.

I didn't know how he managed this, but even with a

broken leg, he swaggered out of the room like something out of a Bond film. And of course, what was I looking at? How his pants fit snug against his supremely fine ass. Really, in terms of guy butts, his was up there with Charlie Hunnam. I mean, it'd be a crime against all women not to appreciate that sculpted beauty. Not like he could see me anyway, since he was facing the other way.

"If you stare any harder, I might burst into flames." He turned around and shot me a smile before I could avert my eyes or even pretend I wasn't ogling the shit out of him. "Looking forward to exploring our professional relationship."

Boom. Battleship sunk. S.S. Lady Bits obliterated by enemy torpedo. "G-good-bye, Mr. Covington," I stuttered.

What the hell just happened?

Chapter Four

Zoey

Rule #13: Tamales can cure everything

I sat back down at my desk, dazed. How had this happened? Not only was it a bad idea to work with him, but he explicitly said he didn't want to see this project through. I didn't know which was more disturbing. Give me a challenge and I rise to the occasion, but even this seemed foolish.

A tap on the doorframe snapped me out of my thoughts.

Lance stood at the door, beaming from ear to ear, carrying a large pink box. He opened it and said, "Doughnut?" Something very good must have happened if he was buying sweets for the staff.

I grabbed one with bright red frosting and sprinkles, because really, who could pass on these? "Thanks."

"How did it go?" he asked.

"Jason's brother is taking over the contract."

His forehead wrinkled. "Jason Covington? Putting his

brother in charge?"

I waved my hand and quickly put it down because not only did I hate the blouse I was wearing, it now had the added accessory of perspiration. Jesus. Even yoga didn't make me sweat this much. "I know. Completely crazy."

"Well, it's nothing you can't handle." He looked at me as if to ask, *right?*

To tell him or not to tell him… If I said something, that made it seem like I couldn't solve my own problems. That wasn't what Lance had come to expect of me, and it wasn't what I would accept from myself. I'd make this work or give myself a brain aneurism trying. "He might prove to be harder to work with than I anticipated."

"If anyone can do it, it's you. A few more projects of this scale under your belt, and you'll be on your way to senior designer status in no time."

I smiled. It was comforting knowing that my boss had so much faith in me. I wouldn't let him down. "Thanks, Lance."

"My door's always open if you need anything." And with that, he exited my office.

I stared at the doughnut on my desk. A sweet, unnecessary temptation. Much like another one.

I wouldn't give in to this. With a sweep of my hand, the doughnut landed in the trash.

Yep. I'd do a great job at ignoring him. The best thing for me to do now was put all my focus into my work and do yoga later as penance. Ten Sun Salutations for every time I imagined Ryder's rough hands sliding over my skin. Could I even do that much yoga? I might not be able to walk in the morning.

I sat down at my computer and pulled up my drafting software. To get my mind off what had just happened, I spent the next few hours redesigning each space in the resort. Ryder wanted something amazing? I'd give him just that.

By the time two o'clock rolled around, my stomach was threatening mutiny if I didn't stop for lunch. I texted Lainey and asked if she wanted to meet up at the taco cart on Adams. Since she'd started her new position early this year, her building was only a couple of blocks from mine. We were able to get lunch together a few times a week, and I liked this setup, since she spent most nights at Brogan's.

Zoey: *Lunch?*

Lainey: *You read my mind. I'm needing tons of guacamole to make up for this shitastic day.*

Zoey: *Dude. I feel you. Meet you at Pepe's.*

Lainey: *Last one there buys empanadas.*

Zoey: *You're on.*

Ten minutes later, I was in the heart of downtown Seattle. Lainey beat me there, already sitting on a picnic bench in front of the taco stand, wolfing down a taquito. I ordered two tamales and empanadas and went to join her. She beamed at me, her signature red lipstick glinting in the sun as she chewed. "How did the meeting go this morning?"

Horrible?

Disastrous?

I want to dry hump my client and kill him at the same time? Yep. I definitely needed a little retail therapy tonight.

"Not as planned. You remember Ryder, right?"

She leveled me with a look. "Um, you mean Shirtless Dude? The one who has put you in a funk for the past few months, and with whom you suddenly end up stuck in a resort over the weekend, sending me frantic texts and then leave me in the dark until the next morning? Nope, don't remember him, whatsoever."

"Your sarcasm is so appreciated right now," I deadpanned.

"Okay, sorry." She took a large bite of chips and guac, chewed, and said, "Carbs are being ingested, hangry crisis averted. What's up with Shirtless Dude?"

Ryder would forever be known as Shirtless Dude to Lainey because she'd interrupted us by coming home early one weekend. If only she'd had that same great timing the night I slept with Ryder—then I wouldn't be in this mess.

"It turns out he's my client now."

Her mouth opened, chips and guac in full view. "Shut the front door."

"Front door is wide open and Ryder is a knockin'."

"Wow. He's really messed with your head if you're pulling out the dad jokes for me."

I threw a chip at her and it landed in her cleavage.

She grabbed it from her shirt, glanced at it, shrugged, then popped it in her mouth. "Are you going to take him on?"

"What else can I do? My boss is banking on this huge client—" I groaned. "You should have seen the way Lance looked at me. Like a proud dad. What was I supposed to say? 'Actually, sir, I've turned into a thirteen-year-old when dealing with my client'?"

She took a bite of empanada and groaned. "Do you have a plan?"

"To not kill him?"

Her mouth twitched. "That's a start. Is it going to bother you that, you know…?"

No, it would not bother me that I'd hooked up with him. I had no intentions of making that mistake again. After our night together, I made it a point to avoid men like him—ones who probably stood in front of the mirror and grunted as they curled a pair of forties. I cleared my throat, trying to wipe the image of Ryder's biceps bunching while lifting weights, his shirt soaked with sweat, plastered to his wide shoulders and broad chest. Nope. Not going there.

I'd do us both a favor and work efficiently so we'd never have to see each other again.

"Hell no." I stabbed a chip into the bowl of guac. "All I have to do is find a design that works for him, get it done as quickly as possible, and then this whole thing will blow over." Said that way, it didn't sound too hard.

If I were delusional.

Lainey blinked hard and didn't say anything. Her bullshit meter was even more refined than my own.

"Okay, fine. We did it. It was a mistake. I can handle this," I said.

"*Did it*? Dude, he really has taken you back to your middle-school self."

"At least I have a better bank account. And better skin."

"Amen to that." We clinked our plastic water cups together.

If I wanted to keep my cushy job at my firm, I had to put this grudge behind me and move forward.

Design. Implement. Get the hell out. That was my plan, and I was sticking to it.

• • •

Ryder

Thirteen. Fourteen. Fifteen.

I pressed my nose to the floor and then pushed myself back up, my arms still shaky from four sets of incline bench presses I'd performed in quick succession.

Sixteen. Seventeen.

Shake it off, man. You don't do girl trouble.

That was the issue—Zoey wasn't just any other woman. It wasn't a date gone wrong, or a girl swiping my gear to sell on Craigslist to the highest bidder. No, she sat across from me today expecting to roll through that meeting, bending me to her every whim. But what I lacked in decorating knowledge, I more than made up for by keeping Jason's best interests front and center. Because no matter the situation, we always had each other's back. That included me telling him he'd made a huge mistake buying that dumpster fire of a resort.

Did I have to be a dick to her in the process and tell her that her designs sucked? No, but what was I supposed to say? "Your vanilla shampoo is now engrained into my sinuses, and I couldn't even drink my protein shake this morning without thinking about you." I'd rather free fall down a black diamond run than admit I lost half my wits when I was around her.

So, yeah, I'd dialed it back a few notches and put on the dismissive front.

As soon as I finished my last push-up, I collapsed on the ground. My Bluetooth beeped in my ear, and I clicked the accept-call button.

"Hello?"

"Ryder, man, how's it going?"

"Hey, Andy." I hadn't heard from my team manager in over two weeks. He'd been radio silent since my injury. "Just working on rehabbing my leg. Want to be ready for next season." I propped myself onto my weight bench, carefully maneuvering my leg.

"Great." He let out a strained laugh. "Good, good, good."

Fresh sweat beaded at my hairline. Whenever Andy rambled, it always followed with bad news. "What's going on?"

"I don't want you to freak out or anything, but I just got a call from WildNFree."

WildNFree was one of the many sponsors I had plastered

all over my board and helmet. They'd given me a generous endorsement this year.

"What about them?" He paused for long enough that I had to check to make sure the call wasn't disconnected. "Andy?"

"They dropped you."

"What?" Holy shit. I'd been out for twenty-eight days, not even a full month. "I said I'd be back before the start of next season."

He cleared his throat. "They said they'd reconsider once they saw you strapped back on a board."

I thumbed my bracelet, staring at my cast. "They don't think I'm coming back?"

He sighed into the phone. "Listen, Ryder, it wouldn't be a bad idea to start looking into your plan B. Just in case things don't…you know…work out."

I clutched the edge of the bench, fighting for calm. Was my manager really telling me to give up? Hell, I was twenty-five, not seventy. Things would work out. They had to.

Snowboarding had been my identity since I was ten, and I wasn't about to give it up because of a busted leg. "Andy, that's bullshit. I'll be back up on the mountain, and screw those sponsors. I'll get there myself if I have to." I'd managed to live my dream for nine years now. I wasn't about to piss it all away because of my tibia.

"You know I'm in your corner, man. But it's my job to give you options."

"There's only one option. I'll keep you updated on the rehab." I hung up before I had a chance to really let this conversation sink in. I'd lost a sponsor. A big one. Money was never an issue, but it helped having a company actively promoting my brand. If my other sponsors caught whiff of this, who knew how many would get spooked. I scrubbed my hand over my face and went to stand, then almost face-planted on the floor when I realized I couldn't put weight on my left side. Damn leg.

My earpiece beeped again, and if Andy called to add on more bad news, I'd need to do another three sets to blow off steam. I clicked on the Bluetooth and said, "What now?"

"Is that any way to greet someone over the phone? Really, Ryder, I thought we taught you better manners."

My spine stiffened. I'd prefer another sponsor loss to this.

I braced myself for the wrath of Beatrice Covington, the real balls behind the Covington empire, aka my grandmother. Baking cookies and coddling didn't fall under her job description. Causing migraines sure as hell did.

They say personality can be inherited. Well, Jason didn't fall far from the ruthless and determined tree.

"Sorry," I said, pain flashing behind my left eye. Migraine was right on cue today.

"I was beginning to worry you were avoiding me." She was right. I had. Seven calls in one day might seem excessive, but that was child's play. If I hadn't answered, thinking she was Andy, she'd have abused that redial button until I finally broke down.

"Never, Grandma. Just busy. What's up?" What kind of dick ignored his grandmother? One who couldn't last two minutes in the same room with her without having an existential life crisis, that's who. Could I have answered earlier today? Sure, but I liked to go a few days without being reminded of my every mistake since age six.

"Have you heard from your brother? He hasn't been answering my calls."

Smart man.

"Maybe I can help?" I was supposed to be acting on his behalf right now. Taking one for the team and refocusing my grandmother's wrath decidedly fell under these duties.

"You've been to that dumpster of a resort, haven't you?"

"Divinity. Yes, I was there last weekend." Last I'd heard, that was what Jason intended to name it once it reopened. When we visited there as a kid, it was called Brushtail Resort. Back then there were stables, a gym with a basketball court, and a restaurant that made the hottest wings my ten-year-old tongue had ever tried. They held one of those contests where if you finished ten wings in five minutes, you got a T-shirt and your picture on the wall. My brother and I both won the contest, but my dad had to tap out after the third wing. I couldn't taste anything for a week after that.

I remember my mother sat back and watched us with deep amusement, especially when my father chugged four glasses of milk and drooled like a bullmastiff for twenty minutes. She rubbed his back, and even then it was so damn clear they were in love with each other. The kind of love promised in those chick movies Zoey liked. If I hadn't seen it with my own eyes, I never would have believed that kind of love existed. The only type of girls I seemed to attract were after new purses and fifteen minutes in the limelight. I'd learned that one the hard way.

"I told him it was a mistake to buy it," I said. And I'd keep telling him until he came to his senses.

My parents would have been celebrating their thirtieth wedding anniversary next month. Instead, they were buried together on a plot of land in Bellevue.

I visited them once a year on the anniversary of their death whereas Jason clutched every last memory of our parents. I had one picture of them in my wallet, because anything more would just drag me back into the dark time right after their death. I worried it might do the same for Jason. Which was another reason why I thought this whole idea to buy and revamp that pile of garbage was such a shit idea. An impulse buy backed by emotion was destined for disaster.

"I agree," she said.

"What was that, Grandma?"

"I said I agree." She huffed. "Maybe you need to book an appointment with an ENT to get your hearing checked out."

"No, I just wanted you to say it again." I smiled. I couldn't resist a chance to irritate her at least once during a conversation.

"Your joking is not appreciated. Jason funneled a lot of money into this resort, and your grandfather is worried about the return on investment."

"For what it's worth, I told him he should sell it. The land is worth more than the property."

"Then we need to make that happen."

"What?" I scrubbed my hands over my face. Once an idea took hold, there was no stopping her. The last thing my brother needed was our grandmother scheming behind his back.

"We need to convince him to sell it. You know he hasn't been right since the accident. This will only drag him down further."

"He put me in charge of the designs until he's up and running, so maybe I can try to talk to him."

"He *what*?"

Damn. Her low opinion worked under my skin like a splinter, adding to the irritation of the news from Andy. "Is it that surprising that I am helping out?" I may have been new to the business aspect of things, but I always kept my promises.

"Ryder, I've never seen you follow through with anything when it gets tough."

I squeezed my eyes shut and took a deep breath. My career as a pro snowboarder earned zero consideration in her book. I didn't hold this against her—she'd never understand my world—but for once, I'd have liked for her to think I was semi-competent. "I appreciate your vote of confidence."

"Listen, you are great at your little snow sport endeavor, but when have you really shown any initiative to something that isn't all play? The only thing it has done is ruin your brother's life."

She was right. Jason was out of commission because *I* begged him to participate in a snowboarding fundraiser a good buddy of mine had sponsored. I knew he was rusty, but I didn't think he'd try any crazy stunts. It was for charity—he could have carved his way down the mountain without doing a single trick and it would have been fine. I'd gotten the call the night I'd been with Zoey.

Normally, I'd push my grandmother's comments aside, but with my sponsor just dumping me, and my manager's faith dwindling, I was more than a little on edge. In her eyes, except for my riding stats and the near-death of my brother, I had zero credit to my name.

"Tell me how you really feel, Grandma." I grabbed my crutches and made my way to my bedroom. "If you need me, I'll be working on the resort." I ended the call and tossed my earpiece on the bed.

This was much more than just healing a broken leg or a run-down resort. I wouldn't let my brother down a second time.

Chapter Five

Zoey

To Do List:
• Stop buying all the leggings

By the time I got home that evening, I still hadn't been able to sort out my thoughts on the project. I'd prepared two more mock designs for the resort and emailed them to Ryder, ignoring the fact that he'd asked me to share them over a dinner that would never happen. Lainey arrived home around the same time as me, which was a rarity these days. I had takeout pizza ready on the coffee table when she plopped down and snagged a slice.

"How was the rest of your day?" she asked.

"Quiet." Too quiet. I didn't know what I was expecting when I sent the plans to Ryder, but it wasn't radio silence. More like Ryder making me regret agreeing to work with him for the umpteenth time today. I bit into the slice of pepperoni and checked my phone again. Nothing.

Okay, maybe he wasn't as much of an email addict as the rest of the world, but could a guy really stay off the grid for five hours?

Lainey cleared her throat, arching a brow in my direction. "Wow. What did that pizza do you to, Z? Third degree assault on anything from Giovanni's is a criminal offense."

"Sorry, just frustrated." In so many ways. There were only so many times I could analyze what happened up on the mountain before I drove myself absolutely insane. The guy pissed me off. He was a risk to my job. I should not be thinking about him as anything else but enemy number one.

She put her slice down on her plate and turned to me, sitting crisscross on the couch. "It'll all work itself out. I've never seen a challenge you couldn't handle. Other than…" She trailed off, smiling, a gleeful glint in her eye.

"If you bring up the toaster-oven incident again, this pizza's not the only thing getting assaulted." I shook my slice at her.

"What about the time you tried to cook pasta?"

"How was I supposed to know you can actually burn water? Seriously, it should come with a warning label." My dad had tried to teach me to cook throughout my childhood, but I had a mental block against it. I saw a pot or a spatula and all logic and reason went out the door.

"Right. Because it's not user error at all."

I nudged her with my foot, but we both laughed because, yeah, she was right.

Superman had his kryptonite, and mine came in the form of a cooking utensil. Any of them. I managed to turn anything that needed a heat source into a charred mess. Lainey had limited me to the use of forks, knifes, and spoons—the rest were off-limits after that *tiny* kitchen fire last year. Seriously, a girl melts a countertop and that's grounds to revoke a cooking license. I hoped my hypothetical future spouse could handle kitchen duties or else we'd be eating yogurt and granola and Hot Pockets for the rest of our lives.

So, for my sake, I hoped dealing with Ryder was nothing like my terrible kitchen experience. I'd never had the added challenge of being grudgingly attracted to a man before—not to mention the little fact that I had shared a bed with him. But hey, there was a first for everything.

She giggled and took another bite of pizza. "I just tell it like it is." Her phone buzzed on the coffee table and she snapped it up. Her smile grew. "Gotta take this. It's my mom."

Lainey and her mom had a really unique relationship. I'd never, to this day, seen anyone as close with their parent as she was with hers. Sometimes on visits to her house over college breaks, she'd pull us both in for hugs and I'd get this intense moment of missing my own mom. Obviously there was no way of knowing if I would have been as close with her as Lainey was with Mrs. T, but I'd like to think so. Gloria Reynolds was a fabulous woman who was taken from me way too early.

Mrs. T had claimed me as a second daughter well before my mother passed. But it was after my mom got in the horrific car wreck that I realized how much I needed another woman in my life. The week after my thirteenth birthday, two weeks after my mom's funeral, my period started. Lainey's mom took me shopping for pads and showed me the ropes, since my dad, though well-intentioned, was clueless in that regard.

When we were in college, she made sure my favorite peanut butter was in the care packages she sent to our apartment. We may not have been related by blood, but Mrs. T was as much my mother as my own. So when she was diagnosed with cancer last summer, and then proceeded to go through a horrific battle with chemo treatments over the following months, it was a profound relief that she was now in remission.

Lainey disappeared into her room, and I decided to go back to my email-stalking to see if my *client* had looked at my plans yet.

Nothing.

I went online and perused my favorite stores. I *may* have had a teensy addiction to leggings. So far I owned enough pairs to warrant buying one of those plastic shoe racks that you hang from the back of a door. Except instead of shoes, my thirty-six pocket temple was filled with buttery soft perfection for my legs. And today's events called for a few additions to my collection.

By the time Lainey came back out of her room, I'd ordered a pair of orange spirals, black cats wearing aviators, and sheep. I was in the depths of contemplation between a pair of bicycle leggings and pomegranate ones when an email from my work account popped up across the screen. Ryder.

I'll get back to you.

I clicked back into the shopping site and bought both pairs.

• • •

Tuesday: Refresh. Refresh. Refresh.

• • •

Wednesday: Panic refresh. Bought two more pairs of leggings.

• • •

Thursday: Fear of thumb falling off from refresh button overuse.

• • •

Friday: What the hell?

I'd prepared myself for massive revisions to my plans. For him to be an ass about the whole thing. What I wasn't prepared for? Complete and utter silence for four days.

Which was how I'd come to be wearing a path into the living room rug on Friday night.

Lainey popped out of her room, her curls swishing from side to side in her ponytail as she readjusted her shirt. "Are you ready yet?"

"Yep." I'd been ready for the last half hour. I hadn't bothered to change from my work attire, since my outfit included the infamous eyelet skirt. This time I'd made sure to wear panties that didn't have any comic book heroes on them. It was safe to say, though, that there'd be no intentional undie flashing.

We grabbed out jackets and made our way to Dean's, our favorite pub-chic club a couple of blocks from our apartment. It was in the center of downtown and had the best of both worlds—cozy alcoves for people who wanted a low-key affair, or karaoke and dancing for action-seekers. I definitely fell into the latter of the two categories tonight, especially since yoga and morning runs were doing zero to alleviate my pent-up irritation at the fact I was being ignored. Whether it was on purpose or not, who knew, but with all of my other projects wrapping up this past week, there was a hell of a lot of thumb twiddling and Candy Crush playing going on right now.

Arms linked, we made the walk in the blistering cold. Lainey's boyfriend Brogan said he'd meet us at Dean's once he was finished with a meeting.

The same as on any Friday night, the line to get into the place wound around the building. A chill clung in the late winter air. Clouds puffed out of peoples' mouths as they stood waiting to get in. Girls in short dresses and no jackets rubbed at their bare arms as they clustered together in groups. I was past the point of caring if I brought a jacket to the club. I'd rather be comfortable for thirty minutes than freeze my ass off.

Before we had a chance to take our place at the end of the line, the bouncer called out to Lainey.

"Miss Taylor?"

Her head whipped around to him and then she smiled. "Yeah?"

"Mr. Starr is here already. Told me to keep an eye out for you." He unhooked the velvet rope from the pole and motioned us in.

"God, I love your boyfriend." And the fact that I did not, in fact, have to stand out in the cold for thirty minutes.

She gave one of the sighs that I'd become accustomed to ever since Brogan had entered her life. "Me, too," she said.

Their relationship started out a little rocky, but I had to hand it to Brogan. He'd gotten his shit together, and it'd been smooth sailing ever since.

The bass beat of a rap song bounced through the club, so loud that each note pulsed under my skin. As we ascended the stairs to the main area, each step brought an onslaught of thick air filled with sweat and the promise of a good time. We made our way through to the upper level, looking for Brogan. I glanced at the bar and saw Ian, our favorite bartender, shaking and pouring out mojitos. Drinks—now that would do the trick of dulling the edge of this crap week. A Tom Collins and dancing. Yep, perfect. Maybe I'd even flirt with Ian. Anything to get last weekend off my mind. "I'm going to grab a drink. I'll meet up with you and lover boy in a minute."

She smiled. "Sounds good."

She beelined to Brogan's booth in the back as I tracked to the bar. Ian's face lit up as I took a seat on one of the stools. "Where's your partner in crime?"

I pointed toward the back of the club. "With her boyfriend."

He gave a dimpled grin. "Guess that means I get you all to myself tonight."

"You and however many people are in the club." I motioned around me.

"The usual?"

Even with this crappy week, I found myself smiling. "Yeah." This was why I liked Ian. He remembered my drinks. He was cute, if maybe a little tacky with the flirting, but I knew what to expect with him. He wouldn't up and leave me before the crack of dawn after an incredible night of sex. Probably. Then again, any guy I'd ever been remotely interested in turned into a douche.

In less than a minute, a Tom Collins was sitting in front of me. I went to dig for my wallet in my purse, but Ian waved me off. "This one's on the house."

I took a sip. "Thank you." Okay, this was the part where I was supposed to flirt. The man had essentially paid for my drink, and all that came to my mind was a procession of crickets. Maybe I really *was* out of practice.

He looked at me expectantly.

Awkward…

Go go gadget flirting. Nope.

Go go gadget smooth-talking. Nada.

I took another sip of the drink and made an exaggerated groan. "Mmm, so good."

Jesus. *Why not get a damn room with the drink, girl?*

Ian was polite enough not to laugh. "It's one of my favorite drinks to make."

"A-plus. It's going down really smooth tonight." I drummed my nails on the counter. "So smooth."

Just. Stop. Talking. This was an embarrassment to all lady-kind.

I was all for the well-timed double entendre, but I was starting to sound like I was starring in my own soft core porno.

"I mean you did a great job shaking it." I stopped myself again. "I'm going to stop right there because this is getting way too awkward, and I haven't had enough to drink yet."

And now I was pretty sure I would never be able to show my face at Dean's again.

"You know I'd shake it for you anytime, Zoey." He winked.

I snapped my gaze to his. That was such a Ryder-like comment that I had to make sure I was still talking to Ian. If it were Ryder, I probably would have had a decent comeback. Instead, there was nada. Might as well cut my losses before I made any other stupid comments.

I managed a polite smile. "Thanks again, Ian." I saluted him with my drink as I scooted off the stool.

Well, if I didn't know it before, I just confirmed my skills with the opposite sex had succumbed to the "use it or lose it" curse.

I made my way across the bar, through the packed dance floor, and into the section with booths lining the wall. As I neared the table, Lainey looked at me and gave a quick shake of her head.

The hell?

I continued toward the table because, really, where else was I going to go? No way in heck I was going back to the bar.

She gave me another look, jutting her chin toward Brogan and whoever he was talking to. I couldn't tell who it was because the lighting in this place sucked.

I sidled up to the table just in time for a familiar voice to say, "Flash!"

• • •

RYDER

If I thought Zoey had perfected *the glare*, her roommate

Lainey was her sensei. My body temperature dropped a good two degrees each time she shot me a look. One parka minimum to sit in this booth.

"When do you go back on tour?" Brogan asked me.

Lainey lifted a brow. "Yes, when do you go?"

I looked between the two of them. Brogan and I went way back. He was my first friend at Culver Academy, one of my only friendships that had lasted over ten years, besides our buddy Jace. When we first met, he could barely manage two words when talking to the opposite sex. Looked like he was doing just fine now. In fact, that was what we met about today. Before Lainey'd come in, he asked me to go ring shopping with him. The irony did not escape me that he'd asked the person with the worst luck with women to pick out the most important gift of his life. Even so, I couldn't say no to him.

"A few weeks. As soon as I get the cast off and get back to training."

"Good," she said. When Brogan gave her a questioning look, she said, "I mean, it's good you'll get back to your snowboarding. I bet you're bored here. I hear snowboarders can't even manage to stay in one place very long because of commitment issues."

"Lainey." Brogan chuckled but squeezed her a little tighter. "What is with you tonight?"

"Nothing. Just stating something I heard through the grapevine." She shrugged and then discreetly slid another glare my way.

I expected Zoey to be annoyed with me after leaving her in the middle of the night. It seemed pointless to call her the next day and explain, especially when it'd been a one-time thing, but now I wasn't so sure I'd made the smartest choice. My chest tightened to think she'd been so upset that her friend now ranked me as enemy number one.

"I should probably—" Before I could scoot out of the

booth, I spotted Zoey staring at me, her fingers straining white against her glass. "Flash!" I gripped the table, steadying myself as I became the sole focus of her sudden irritation. It'd be best to grab my crutches and get out of here, but I found myself reaching for my beer instead, taking a deep pull. I wanted to be near her, even as the target of her wrath.

She stiffened as she realized I wasn't moving to leave. "Mr. Covington. What a surprise."

A series of looks passed between her and her roommate. I wasn't fluent in girl eye-speak, but I figured none of it was a testament to my character. I regretted that night back in November, if only because I'd obviously caused her pain.

"I thought we were on a first-name basis by now," I said as Zoey slid into the circular booth next to her roommate, directly across from me.

She didn't say anything, just took a sip of her drink.

Lainey glanced over at me and narrowed her eyes. Then she cleared her throat and said, "Did you know that Ryder and Brogan used to go to school together?"

"Almost got me kicked out with the pranks we pulled," Brogan added, pulling Lainey closer.

I thumbed the bracelet on my wrist, remembering Jason's pleas to not fuck up anymore. I may have kept my promise to remain in school, but it didn't mean I quit doing stupid teenage shit entirely. "I was a bad influence on you, Starr," I said, and took a sip of beer.

"Not surprising," Zoey cut in.

As much as I enjoyed the hole Zoey and Lainey were burning through my skull, I decided this was a good time bow out. I tapped my mug on the tabletop and said, "I should be going."

"C'mon, man. Sit a while. At least finish your beer."

Lainey smacked him in the chest.

Brogan looked at her, wide-eyed, not even noticing the

tension in the booth. Some things never changed. "What?"

Zoey let out a long breath and closed her eyes. "It's fine," she said, but it was clear she was only saying it to be polite.

I looked around the group. It'd been a while since I'd hung out with anyone, not since my accident. "Okay. For a few more minutes."

I took another swig of my beer.

Brogan's phone buzzed on the table. His brows pinched together as he looked at the screen. "I have to take this." He kissed Lainey's forehead, and I stood to let him scoot out.

And then there were three.

Lainey drummed her fingers on the tabletop and then cut her gaze to me. "So, Ryder, I hear you're working with Zoey to fix up a resort in the mountains."

"We're in negotiations." I'd been a dick and ignored her email all week while I tried to figure out a plan to convince Jason to sell the place. Jason remained adamant about keeping it. Looked like the resort would be happening after all.

Zoey lifted a brow. "Oh?"

"I was just going to email you tonight."

She frowned. "I see."

Yeah, she didn't buy my bullshit.

Lainey's phone vibrated along the surface of the table. "Crap. It's my mom." She bit her lip and looked from me to Zoey.

"Go ahead. Take it," Zoey said.

"You sure? I can call her back later." Lainey clutched at the phone, clearly warring with herself.

"No big deal."

Before scooting out on Zoey's side, Lainey leaned in and whispered in my ear. "I can get very creative with a ballpoint pen. Or any office supply, really. Don't screw with my friend."

And with that, she smiled sweetly at me. Zoey slid out of the booth to let Lainey out and then resumed her position across from me.

After she settled into the seat and took a slow sip of her drink, she said, "Really? Negotiations?"

I moved closer to her in the booth, and the intoxicating scent of her vanilla shampoo hit me like a blow to the face. She always smelled so damn good, like a cupcake, or an expensive pastry at one of the specialty shops downtown.

"I've been thinking all week about your email," I admitted. Correction: *she'd* been on my mind all week. I'd pulled up that email at least a dozen times but couldn't find it in me to reply.

"And?" she prompted.

I shrugged. "The designs were okay." I knew nothing about design elements, but everything seemed to be there. Beds, tables, dressers, even a mini fridge.

Her eyes bulged to cartoon-level proportions. I had a feeling I'd misstepped. "Okay?" Her voice climbed an octave. "Okay is for mediocre food and subpar sex. Heck, it's used to describe Nickelback music."

"Hold up there. That's being very generous to Nickelback."

She scoffed. "Exactly, Ryder. My work has never been described that way. Ever. Tell me—what do you need me to change so we're on the same page with this project?"

Shit. I never said the right things around her. The last thing I wanted to do was insult her skills. "Maybe *okay* was the wrong word to use." I kicked back the rest of my beer. "I've never done this before. I know you're ready to go, but I still have reservations."

"Can you please fill me in? I'm here to work *with* you. Not against."

I debated confiding in her. Those hazel eyes willed me to tell every damn thing to her. If I didn't know better, I'd believe she really did possess mind-control abilities.

"Jason bought this resort after his accident. For reasons I

don't agree with."

Her brows pinched together, and she shook her head. "I'm sorry, you lost me. What's going on with your brother? I haven't seen him since November."

"That night we were together?" Recognition flickered in her eyes, but I continued before she could get too pissed off. "My grandparents called to tell me he was in the hospital. He was boarding at a fundraiser and hit his neck on a rail. He's paralyzed from the waist down."

Her expression went from irritated to crestfallen in under a second. "That's horrible."

"It is." My jaw tensed. After the accident, Jason closed up completely. It killed me to see him suffer and not be able to do anything about it.

The music changed from a slow song to a fast, Top 40 beat. "I figured if you had to choose between me coming clean or keeping you in the dark for even longer, the answer was clear," I said.

"Answering a Would You Rather question for me? Doesn't seem fair." Her lips pulled into a smile. "Does that mean I get to ask one?" She looked at me as if to say *if you dare.* I liked that about Zoey—she knew how to read people. Like the fact that I really didn't want to talk about my brother's accident.

"Fine." I'd play this game with her all night if it meant that smile would stay on her face. Enough thinking about depressing shit.

"Hmm..." She swirled the straw around her drink in slow, methodical movements.

"Going to keep me waiting?" I said.

Her eyes cut to mine. "Would only be fitting after how long you made me wait for an email response."

I put my hands up in defense. "Touché."

"Okay, I got it." She took a sip of her drink. "Would you rather live without the internet, or modern heating and AC?"

"Depends. Do I have someone to keep me warm?"

She flushed at this. "The questions are subjective. It's up to you to decide that."

I moved closer to her, and the heat from her body radiated against my side. "Then I'll believe there is someone and pick no internet."

"What happens when it gets too hot?"

"C'mon, Flash. Never gotten creative with ice cubes?"

"Right." She fanned her face. "Wow, is it hot in here? I think I need another drink."

I pointed to the one in her hand, condensation trickling along the length of the glass. "You still have half of your Tom Collins left." I liked the fact she turned into a fumbling mess around me.

She cocked her head. "How do you know what drink this is?"

The fact was when it came to Zoey, I remembered everything. I remembered the first words she spoke to me besides an introduction: *I like your shirt.* I remembered the first time I heard her laugh—she liked my joke about the Oregon Ducks; Zoey was an OSU girl after all. I remembered how soft her hair was, brushing against my chest as she fell asleep in my arms. Suffice to say, everything about her was memorable.

"Would you rather take a year off designing, or a year off using your phone?"

"Those really go hand in hand. I'm even really good at sending work-related emails from my phone. You should try it sometime." A ghost of a smile worked across her lips.

"Answer the question, Flash."

She let out a dramatic sigh. "Fine. I guess I'd have to give up my phone. I love my job too much. Okay, my turn."

"Fine. Shoot." I sunk into the seat and propped my arm against the back of the booth. My fingers brushed the exposed skin of her shoulder, and she shuddered beneath my touch, her hazel eyes hooding. Always so responsive. It took every bit of my restraint to not sink my hands into her hair.

"Would you rather keep your bracelet, or win the Powerball?"

"My bracelet." The answer came out so quickly, I barely let her finish her question.

"Thought so." Her lips pulled into a full, satisfied smile.

"Oh yeah?"

"You're not the only observant one. You don't take it off, do you?"

"No. Never. It's a reminder, I guess." I thumbed the frayed material. Jason had always been my touchstone, but now he seemed to need one more than I did. "I did a lot of stupid stuff when I was younger. My brother pulled me out of a really tough time." I owed him my life. Who knew where I would've ended up without him kicking my ass into gear.

A beat of silence passed between us. She hadn't expected that answer; I could tell by the part in her lips.

I mulled over my next question, deciding to push it further. "Would you rather have Jason as a client, or go on a date with me?"

"Oh, um." Red bloomed across her cheeks, and she went to stirring her drink again.

Hell. The answer was written clear on her face. I'd messed up so badly that she'd rather have my brother dictate an entire renovation than spend a night with me. So, I bit the bullet and tried to make this situation less awkward for the both of us. "I'm just kidding around, Zoey. We already know I'm the way better option."

She rolled her eyes, but her relief was palpable. "Right."

I cleared my throat and drummed my fingers on the table. "I really am sorry for not saying good-bye a few months ago. I never felt right about that. I just wanted you to know that."

Her teeth raked over her bottom lip, and she broke our stare-down, suddenly very interested in the napkin on the table. "Thank you."

Lainey dropped into the space next to Zoey. "Seriously, why does the ladies' room always have such a long line? I mean, does everyone have to pee—" Lainey looked from me to Zoey. "Oh, am I interrupting something?"

"No, I was just heading out. It was nice seeing you again, Lainey." I looked to Zoey, who still wouldn't meet my gaze. "I'll email you tomorrow with my choices."

Chapter Six

Ryder

I had to admit, Zoey was talented. The plans that she sent on Sunday were even better than the originals, better than anything I'd seen her design at Jason's previous business. Even though Jason put me in charge of the remodel, it'd be good for him to have a little involvement. He'd been holed up in his house for too long, and making a few decisions might get him back into the swing of things.

Zoey sure as hell would rather have him on the project.

I groaned thinking about the other night at the club. I thought we were getting somewhere—I was getting a vibe from her. And then after asking her out again, there was no turning back. I didn't even know why I'd asked her in the first place—I didn't do second dates. But that look in her eyes, the hurt. It sucker punched me in the gut, and I'd do anything to make that look go away.

Maybe that was the issue. After sleeping with her, it just felt different. Whether I liked it or not, I was drawn to Zoey.

Her smile, her laugh, the way her hooded eyes burned me alive during the one night we'd shared together…

I shook my head and focused on the road, weaving my way in and out of traffic.

Shit, there was obviously something wrong with me, more than just a broken left leg, if I was getting philosophical before ten in the morning.

I pulled into the parking lot of the doctor's office, and the weight of the past few weeks eased off my chest a fraction. Finally, I'd get this damn cast off my leg and resume training with my team. A little rehab, and the leg would be as good as new.

After cutting the engine, I grabbed my crutches from the backseat and wound my way up the path to the building. The final minutes of unscratchable itches and uncomfortable showers. Thank fuck.

A few signed papers later, I was escorted back to a tan exam room where I waited, sitting on the crinkly paper on a table, staring at the human anatomy poster plastered to the wall. Dr. Edmond walked in, wielding a small circular saw and my chart.

He smiled at me as the door swung shut. "Mr. Covington. How are you feeling today?"

"I'll be a lot better after the cast comes off." I gave an easy smile, even if my nerves were shot to hell. It was the moment of truth, to see if I would ride again. To see if I'd be losing even more sponsorships in the weeks to come.

He applied foam hand-sanitizer and reached for a set of latex gloves from the container hanging on the wall. "Then let's get right to it."

After a quick examination, he pulled out the saw.

I closed my eyes and lay back on the table as he turned it on and began to cut through the plaster.

Don't be screwed up. I need this.

I would never describe myself as the praying type, but I sent a few desperate wishes to any deity who would listen.

As he finished cutting the material, he snipped at a layer of wrapping and opened the cast. I glanced down at my leg, so much paler, my calf muscle significantly smaller than the one on my right side. The first few rides down the mountain were going to suck, I could tell already. The only positive in this situation was that this wasn't my dominant leg, meaning I wouldn't have to change board stances to accommodate.

"How does it look?"

Dr. Edmond took my leg in his hand, examining it carefully. "We'll have to take another X-ray, but it looks like it's healing nicely."

I allowed hope to slide out from where it'd been holed up and hiding for the past couple of months. "Does that mean I can go back to training?"

"It means you should avoid any extreme sports for a while." He eyed me seriously. "You were lucky this time, but if you take another bad fall on it, there could be permanent damage."

I slid off the table and tried to apply weight. Screw more time off. I needed to train with my team. Seattle's walls were closing in on me at the thought of spending an indefinite amount of time here.

As my foot hit the floor, stars lit behind my eyes and I sucked in a sharp breath. "Shit." I fell back against the table.

Dr. Edmond steadied me and handed me the metal crutches. "You'll need to get used to walking on it. Your crutches will come in handy for the next couple of weeks while you continue to heal."

Everything in my life had always moved at bullet train speed, and the glacial pace I'd been at for over two months now was enough to drive me mad.

A few X-rays later and the doc confirmed that the bone

had healed into place correctly. I limped back to my car, still using my crutches. Pain shot up my leg and I winced with every step, cussing under my breath. I thought for sure when I got the cast off, everything would magically be healed. Just like with a lot of things lately, it was another unexpected outcome.

As if on cue, my phone buzzed in my pocket. I shuffled my crutches around, propping them against my car, and then answered my manager's call.

"'Sup?"

Andy said, "How's your leg doing? What did the doc say?"

I grabbed my car keys from my pocket and opened the door, sliding my crutches into the back seat. "He says I need more time." I winced as I put pressure on my left leg and hobbled to the driver's side door.

"Good. Okay, okay, okay," he mumbled.

Shit. Another sponsor? "What is it, Andy?"

"I got a call from Haywire. They were just checking up on you, but they sounded a little spooked you weren't back on the mountain yet."

Hell, it'd only been two months. What did they expect from a broken leg?

"I'll be strapped back onto a board in no time." That or I'd be back in the emergency room. Because there was no way I'd be taking more time off.

"Great. You're going to miss out on Chile this week, but we'll be back in the States at the end of the month. You think you'll be ready by the season opener?"

That bought me a few months. Even if I was a little rusty, I could manage. "Yes." I had to be. There was no other option.

"That's what I like to hear. Let me know if there's anything I can do on my end."

"Keep my endorsements and my spot on the team." I hung up and tossed my phone into the cup holder.

Only a few more loose ends to tie up, and everything would be ready for my departure.

I drove through downtown and parked in Jason's office building, seven blocks from Zoey's work. I wondered if she was working on drafting new plans for the resort. I wouldn't blame her if she was getting frustrated. She had a job to do, and I was stalling. With Jason so adamant about this project, I shouldn't hesitate, but just because he was enthusiastic didn't mean it was good for his bank account.

As I slid out of my truck, I craned my neck at the towering building that Jason had abandoned for a quarter of a year. I could count on my one hand how many times I'd been in his office. All I remembered was his office assistant, Heidi, who kept that place on a tighter lockdown than a prison yard.

Heidi sat behind a large oak desk, glasses hanging low on her nose as she read through paperwork. A picture of her husband and her son was placed next to her computer, along with pens, manila folders, and an ungodly amount of staplers.

"Mr. Covington. So nice to see you." She smiled. Heidi had to be in her early forties but didn't look a day over twenty—except for the silver streaking her hair.

I walked toward her, trying my best to put weight on my left side. "Thought I'd drop by and see the person who keeps Covington enterprises in one piece."

"You came to the right place, then." She winked. "Looks like you're getting around a lot better now."

"Thanks. You have Jason's mail? I'm meeting up with him tonight."

She mashed her lips together and pointed her pen to the large stacks of letters piled into two boxes. "That's just from this week. Do you know when he's coming back?"

"I planned on asking him that tonight."

"Can you also have him sign these? I need to send them out by next week." She grabbed the mountain of manila folders on her desk and handed them to me.

"No problem."

I looked around the office again. Too stuffy, too formal. My grandfather had offered me a job during my second year of college, but I'd taken one look at his office—almost an exact replica of the one where I currently stood—and declined. Five minutes here and I could already feel corporate life sucking up my soul.

"Have you seen him lately? Is he doing all right?" Heidi had left her station and leaned against the doorframe, her eyes sweeping over the room with concern.

"As well as expected." I didn't know if that was true. I had no comparison with this level of injury. But four months seemed like long enough to avoid people. "Do you know if he had anything else in the pipeline before his"—I paused—"leave of absence?"

She shook her head. "The acquisition of the resort was the first I'd heard in months. Honestly, if a paycheck wasn't deposited in my account every month, and a few sporadic emails didn't land in my inbox, I'd assumed he'd dropped off the face of the planet."

I ran my knuckles along the empty desk, noting how even in Jason's absence, the wooden surface remained shiny and dust-free. Everyone was waiting for him to come back to his old life. "That's what I was worried about."

Enough. Jason wasn't about to piss away his career because of an injury. He just needed a push in the right direction.

Chapter Seven

Zoey

Rule #17: Never trust pigmy goats

It was the Mondayest of all Mondays, I'd decided. What started off promising—yoga and a smoothie—soon went downhill when my car wouldn't start. I had it towed to the mechanic and then Lainey dropped me off at work. On top of that, I'd sent Ryder new plans and heard nothing, not even a confirmation he'd received them.

Fresh projects normally gave me those same butterflies as I got when I met a cute guy. Bubbles in the stomach. A million ideas bumbling around my head. Fabric swatches and furniture catalogues were my eye porn.

The giddiness factor was at an all-time low, seeing as my client avoided me like I was carrying a highly infectious disease. Except for the other night at the club, which I didn't even want to think about unless I had a punching bag readily available.

Lance stood at the end of the hallway as I entered work.

"Just the person I wanted to see," he said. His forehead had an additional crease today, which either meant he was *really* jazzed about something, or he was going to fire my ass because he'd just found out I'd been fantasizing about my client all weekend.

"Really?" I straightened the papers on my desk. There wasn't much to tidy since Ryder's resort was my only project at the moment.

"I wanted to check in with you on the Covington account."

"There's not much to say at this point. We're still negotiating designs."

He frowned. "Is everything going okay? If that family didn't bring in so much revenue, it'd be more trouble than they're worth."

No kidding.

Hmm, how to answer this… *No, Lance, the whole working with my ex-fling is a complete mindfuck because instead of worrying about my designs, I'm overanalyzing every word he says. Oh, and I think I might be having a quarter life crisis and have doubled my leggings collection in the past two weeks. No biggie.* "Fine."

"Good, because I have news." He stood there, practically dancing in place. Who was this, and what had they done with my tiny, grumpy boss?

"I'm hoping this is celebratory news?"

"I just got a call from HGTV. They're interested in filming the resort once it's finished."

Good thing I was sitting down, because I was pretty sure I'd have face-planted at his feet otherwise. "You're shitting me." And then I remembered who I was talking to. "I mean, are you serious, Lance?"

"Yes. They heard that the Covingtons had acquired the place and want to feature it on a winter resort getaway episode."

"Wow. I don't know what to say." Besides the obvious, because I couldn't really say *shit, there is literally nothing in the works at the moment and can you please move to the side so I don't vomit on your shoes?* Continue the leggings splurge tonight? Yep, it was happening.

He beamed a shark smile, all teeth exposed, gleaming in the fluorescent lighting. I had a feeling those teeth would go straight for my jugular if he found out how bad I'd been tanking on this project.

"This'll be huge for the firm. Think of all the new clients we'll get from this." He continued walking down the hall then turned back around, throwing his hands out to the sides. "Talk it over with Mr. Covington, and we'll get a date nailed down with the production company."

I sat there in silence. A television show wanted to showcase my designs. I was definitely going to vom. "On it, Lance." Right after I went and rocked in the corner for a solid fifteen minutes.

It was game time. Bases loaded. And I was counting on a guy who wouldn't even attempt to hit a foul ball.

So Ryder wasn't going to play nice with the email game? I'd take it to the next level—the phone. I stared at my cell. Yep. All I needed to do was put his number in there and then hit the send button. That seemed easy enough. And yet my fingers refused to close the distance.

This is your career, Reynolds. Some asswipe snowboarder who is sometimes charming and most-of-the-time infuriating is not going to get in your way.

Right. I was so, so right. This was HGTV we were talking about. I'd torch my entire life savings before I let this opportunity slip away.

I took a deep breath, snatched my phone, and dialed his number before I could chicken out. As the phone rang, I gave myself a pep-talk. "Seriously, you're a big girl, get your shit together. He has no hold on you. Just another gorgeous face." That was all he'd be, because even if he was funny, the stakes were different now. My work would get national recognition.

"Hello?" his deep voice warmed my body like a shot of tequila.

Crap. Had he heard that last part? "Ryder?"

"Speaking."

"It's Zoey."

"Ah, I figured you might call." His voice was like the richest cashmere against my ear.

I shook my head, deleting that thought from my brain. "What? Why?" Before five minutes ago, I didn't even know I'd be doing this.

"Just a feeling. I'm going to go out on a limb here, but seeing me at Dean's reminded you why I am your favorite client. How close am I?"

My clients who called every twenty minutes talking in the equivalent of shouty caps ranked higher than him. "I can't give a fair assessment if you won't let me do my job." I cleared my throat. "I was wondering if you wanted to get together and discuss plans for the resort."

"You're in luck. I'm downtown right now taking care of some things for my brother. I'll be over in a few."

"Oh. So soon?"

"Unless you want to do sometime next week, right now works best."

Was I prepared? With plans for the resort, yes. Mentally, no. The guy was harder to track down than my unicorn leggings. "Sounds great to me."

"Oh, and Zoey?"

"Yeah?"

"I appreciate the compliment, but I'm more than just a pretty face." Amusement laced his voice.

Where was my letter opener? Maybe if I jabbed myself in the eye a few thousand times, it'd make me forget that this conversation was happening. "That, uh, wasn't about you." I smacked my palm against my forehead.

He laughed. A rich laugh that turned coherent thoughts into mush. "You're still a terrible liar." And with that, he hung up.

Well, there went the whole professional facade. I groaned and laid my head down on my desk.

Time with Ryder was what got me into trouble in the first place. The best approach to keeping on track was to put a time limit on our meeting. We couldn't argue too much if I booked an Uber ride for twenty minutes from now. I pulled out my phone and made a reservation. There. That gave me approximately ten minutes, give or take, to discuss the new designs. Barely any time at all to humiliate myself.

A throat cleared across the room.

No, please let that be my boss. Or one of my coworkers.

I looked up to find Ryder in the doorway to my office, and fought the urge to cringe.

His brows creased together as he palmed the doorframe. "Did I come at a bad time?"

"No, please, come on in and take a seat." I motioned to the chair in front of my desk. A quick peek at the clock on my desktop told me I had twelve minutes. "Have you thought more about the plans I sent you? Did you like any of the designs?"

He was dressed up today—a nice pair of slacks and a light-blue button-up shirt. I snapped my gaze to his face. Professional. Career. HGTV. As much as I enjoyed our ongoing game, Ryder was officially no looky, no touchy.

He slid into the chair and steepled his hands together. "I appreciate you thinking outside the box with the designs. The snowboards lining the exposed beams were a nice touch."

"I thought you might like that." I tapped my pen on my desk and then set it down. What was it about him that made me so nervous? It took every ounce of energy to string together my thoughts. I shook my head, trying to jar myself back to a higher level of cognitive function. "I wanted to run something by you."

"Yeah?" He looked so comfortable in the chair, like this was his own office, with none of that vulnerability he'd shown for a split second last night. But I knew it was there. There was something deeper to Ryder, but it wouldn't be up to me to scratch the surface.

"My boss got a very interesting phone call today. Apparently, a TV show wants to feature the resort—if you're okay with that, I mean."

"I'd have to run it by Jason, but I'd say that any publicity is good publicity. When do they need to do the shoot?"

"Six weeks."

"I see." He frowned. "That doesn't give us a lot of time."

What was that? The sky parting? Angels serenading me with sweet, sweet music? The man finally understood that weeks of dicking around finally had caught up to us.

"To save some time, how about I find a few samples at the fabric store and send them to your office later this week?"

"Do you have any samples here?"

I did, but none that I'd use on a luxury lodge. Swatches of peaches and spring tones didn't exactly scream *come spend the entire day snowboarding and then snuggle up next to the fire with a mug of cocoa.* "No. I'm scheduled to leave for the store in"—I looked at my desktop clock again—"six minutes."

"Great. I'm meeting up with Jason tonight for dinner. I can show him the swatches and get his opinion."

"Yes, I'd love Jason's opinion."

His smile faded a bit, and I was brought back to Friday night and the question he'd asked. The truth was, I *would* rather work with Jason. I didn't have stupid things like *feelings* for Jason. Or the urge to slap him. Or kiss him. Jesus, this was so confusing.

Six more minutes and I wouldn't have to worry about it. I'd be in a car, on my way to a fabric store, my Mecca. Hell, maybe I'd even peruse the leggings store on the ride. Now *that* was multi-tasking.

"Should we head downstairs, then? Wouldn't want to be late to our appointment," he said.

"*Our*?"

"Yes. You're picking out samples for the resort, so I'd like to be involved."

"Of course." I swallowed hard. From a designer aspect, I should be elated that he wanted to be involved. It'd make the process that much easier. Instead, every inch of my body went on high alert, waiting for the next disaster to strike. Because when it came to Ryder, nothing would ever be *easy*. "The car service should be here any minute. Ready, Mr. Covington?"

I'd had pretty rotten luck the last few times I'd used the app—either they didn't show up, or they did but I felt I needed to have 911 on speed-dial just in case they decided to pull down a dark alley. Probably a sign I should have waited until my car was out of the shop to make a trip to the fabric shop.

"Ryder." He looked at me more earnestly this time. "Please."

I sighed. "Fine, Ryder." Just because I called him by his first name did not mean anything. A lot of clients preferred this. But his name on my lips was like the first sip of coffee in the morning—rich and mouthwatering.

I got the sense he was here to make a peace offering, which was nicer than anything he'd done this entire project. If I could only focus on his shallow aspects—because really, he filled out a pair of Dockers *very* well—I'd move through the next six weeks without any hesitation. But I couldn't shake what he'd said at the club, giving me a sliver of the puzzle that was Ryder Covington. There was a nice guy under there. It was under a tangled web of sarcasm, but it was there.

I motioned to his leg. "I barely recognized you without your cast."

"Got it off this morning." He smiled, but something was off about it, almost forced. "I'll probably lose the crutches within a week or two."

"That's great. When I broke my leg in middle school, it hurt almost as bad walking after I got my cast off as it did when I broke it." The guy had to be in a lot of pain at the moment, even if he was hiding it behind that smile of his.

"How did you break your leg?"

"An unfortunate escalator accident."

"Now, this I have to hear."

"There's not much to tell. I tried to jump off the side of an escalator and tanked the landing." I left out the part where it had been a guy that'd dared me to do it. Seemed like all the stupid things I'd done in my life had one common denominator—men. So there it was. Men turned me into an idiot. Awesome. And the weather forecast called for another stupid front blowing in from the east. From what I could tell, it was the storm of the century.

He shifted his gaze to mine. "You don't strike me as the daredevil type."

"And why's that?"

He shrugged. "I've seen your office. And your apartment. The scariest thing in there was your beverage selection."

We continued our way to the elevator and waited for it to hit our floor. "What's wrong with my drinks?"

"La Croix? Zoey, that shit's an abomination."

"What's wrong with my flavored water? It's better than drinking soda." I crossed my arms.

"It tastes like socks." He paused and grimaced. "Hell,

that's even an insult to socks. Seriously, how do you not dry heave when drinking that?"

I stifled a smile and managed to pull my features into some form of indignation. "Because it's delicious."

We walked into the elevator and the doors slid shut behind us. As luck would have it, we were the only two in there.

He was talking. There were words coming out of his mouth, but as I looked at Ryder leaning against the elevator, his broad shoulders nearly taking up half the wall, his cologne filling the space, all my brain could think was *abort mission.*

My body had a funny way of showing its appreciation for my brain's warning. It flipped my brain the bird and started the whole sizzle from head to toe.

Brain: *But he's your client.* And *you know exactly what will happen if you sleep with him again.*

Body: *I do what I want.*

Brain: *Seriously? Are you an idiot? The dude is a player and this could jeopardize your job.*

Body: *Dayummm. Did you see those forearms flex when he grabbed the elevator rail?*

Brain: *Stawp.*

Body: *I'll just be plugging my fingers in my ears. Lalalalala.*

Apparently my body had turned into a petulant teenager.

"Zoey?"

I snapped my attention back to him. "Yeah?"

"You coming?"

It was only then that I realized the elevator doors had opened and he was holding one side, making sure it didn't close on me.

"Yeah, sorry. Zoned out." I was in so much trouble.

"I didn't know my tirade on flavored water was that boring."

"It was fascinating. Really."

Just as I was about to continue my point, the Uber driver pulled up in a beat-up minivan. The pocked doors had more dings than actual smooth surface, which didn't exactly give me the most confidence in this ride. But it was either that or stand here on the street, spending more time than necessary with Ryder, and a potential door-ding incident seemed like a much better option.

"Are you sure you don't want to take my truck?" he offered. "It's in the parking garage down the street."

"No, I'm sure this will be fine." I hoped.

"You know those look like bullet holes in the side, right?"

"I'm sure it's just a rock chip."

He gave me a look. Okay, they totally looked like bullet holes. What the hell was I getting myself into? Like I said before, my brain went into idle mode when it came to dealing with men.

"Did anyone ever tell you that you're stubborn?" He let out a low chuckle, that deep voice tugging at the seams of my resolve.

I had to stay strong. Sharing a car with someone smelling of delicious cologne would not be my professional undoing. "Driven would be a better term."

"So you're driven to be as far away from me as possible? I didn't realize riding in a *client's* car made you that nervous."

It was eerie how perceptive he was. No one besides Lainey and my dad could see through my crap.

"Since you're my client, I'm looking out for your well-being. What kind of designer would I be if I made you drive on a hurt leg?" I smiled at him. Wait. Was I flirting?

He looked at me, his lips curling into a sincere smile. "That's really nice of you."

Those lips. So soft. So unrelenting.

I shuddered.

Down, girl. I had fabric prints to focus on, not the possible pattern of Ryder's bedspread. Which, by the way, I totally pegged him as a steel-gray comforter guy.

"Ladies first." Ryder waved his hand toward the van.

As soon as my butt hit the seat, an overwhelming stench of garlic, refried beans, and…barnyard animal hit me like a tidal wave.

The driver gave me a sheepish smile through the rearview mirror as Ryder slid in beside me.

"Does it…smell bad in here to you?" I whispered.

He leaned in, and I was momentarily thankful for the decadent scent of his cologne. It was a mixture of sage with woodsy notes. The scent snaked its way through my central nervous system, constricting vital processing functions, such as thinking and the ability to scoot farther away from him.

"Yes," he whispered back.

I decided against plugging my nose because I didn't want to insult the driver. After all, the smell was the least of my worries. Getting to my destination in one piece took precedence. I looked sideways at Ryder again, waffling on my decision not to take his truck. But we were in here, so this was happening, even if it did smell like Old MacDonald and his farm had taken up residence.

"Second and Adams, right by the bookstore." As I gave him the address for the shop downtown, a weird bleating sound came from the back of the van.

"What the—"

I turned around and stifled a scream as I found myself face to face with a tiny goat, who stared at me over a makeshift cardboard barrier between the middle row of seats and the back, chewing on a piece of hay.

The driver and I connected gazes in the rearview mirror. He said, "That's Bertha. She's due to have her babies any hour now, so she's hanging out with me in the meantime."

"You're driving with a pregnant pigmy goat?" Did that

phrase just come out of my mouth? The Pacific Northwest was known to be a little eccentric, but this was just bizarre.

The driver arched his brows as if to say *you're the one who needed a ride, so I guess you're stuck.*

"Are you sure you don't want to take my truck? Or reschedule for another day?" Ryder offered. That would be just what he wanted, to delay this even further. He'd been doing his best not to make this project happen from the start. I needed to remember where my priorities lay.

I darted a glance at him, playing as coy as I could manage with pregnant goat smell doing a full-on assault on my nostrils. "Aren't you up for an adventure, Ryder?" When, inside, my thoughts were *get me out of this vehicle!* and *OMG, I have eighteen city blocks to pray that I will not have to help deliver a goat.*

"It's better than her being alone for the birth," the driver said.

The urge to eye roll was strong. Very strong. But I managed to cast my gaze down and fiddle with my phone instead. "Right." I didn't know much about farm animals, but I was fairly certain they'd been birthing babies since, well, the beginning of goat time.

The goat bleated and nosed the back of my head.

"Aww, Flash, I think she likes you."

I scooted closer to the window, trying to get as far away from it as possible. Cats and dogs? Loved them. But I drew the line at anything that could be listed in an Old MacDonald song. I turned and pointed at the goat. "You keep that baby goat inside you for twenty more minutes, missy."

The goat bleated in response.

Ryder patted the goat's nose and cooed. "It's okay. Mean Zoey was just kidding. She'd love to meet your baby." Those big strong hands moved in gentle strokes along the goat's head, and my brain fuzzed over.

"Pro snowboarder and a goat whisperer? Is there anything you can't do?"

"I'm only fluent in Goat. If she were a sheep, all bets would be off." He looked over and smiled at me. "And I am horrible at table tennis and always manage to overcook my scrambled eggs, in case you were thinking I was too perfect." He winked.

"Subpar Ping-Pong skills and rubbery eggs. Definitely a deal breaker for most people."

He rubbed his lips together, almost like he was nervous. "Are they for you?"

I froze. He'd jokingly offered to take me out again while we were at the club, but this time it didn't seem like he was playing around.

Was it hot in here? So, so very hot. Before I could say something stupid like *you can overcook my eggs any day of the week,* I popped open the window and the noise of traffic boomed through the air.

I was just scraping the surface when it came to him, and my whole body physically ached to know more. To find out what made this guy tick. Someone that was so protective of his brother but got kicked out of boarding schools, and was able to woo women and then disappear overnight like he'd never existed. So many puzzles that I hadn't solved yet.

Client. He is your client. There will be no thoughts of breakfast or anything else other than complete professionalism.

Just as I composed myself enough to not fall under the spell of his words, there was a tug at my braid. A fissure of irritation spread through me. Asking me if I'd like him to cook eggs and hair touching were on two different levels. The only people I let touch it were Lainey and my hair dresser. I tried to swipe Ryder's hand away and was met with fur. And teeth. The tugging grew stronger.

No.

A prickle ran down my spine, and I turned my head slightly to find a pair of beady little eyes glaring at me. Her mouth worked as we endured a stare-off, pulling my head slightly to the side each time she chewed.

Holy crap.

Holy crap!

My hair, which took seven times of watching a YouTube tutorial to do this morning, was in the mouth of a goat. She eyeballed me.

Out of the corner of my eye, Ryder tensed. "Flash, don't move," he said in a calm, slow voice.

"Help," I squeaked. Hysteria bubbled up in my voice. There was no keeping my cool. This was my hair. *My* hair. I spent more money on hair products than I did on food each month. And it was in the mouth of something that stepped in its own feces.

The driver looked in the rearview mirror and he cringed. "Holy shit. Just sit still." He pointed a finger and glared in the mirror. "Bertha. You let the woman's hair go."

The goat continued grinding her teeth and my hair, ignoring the cab driver's warning.

Sweat beaded along the driver's forehead, and he swiped at it with his sleeve. He cut his gaze to me, his cheeks flushed. "I'm so sorry. Bertha has a thing for flowers. She especially loves scented shampoos. Bertha, let go!" he screamed.

Of course my shampoo happened to be made of tea tree oil mixed with vanilla and lavender.

No. This was not happening. A goat wasn't munching on my hair because of my choice in products.

"Yes, Bertha, drop the hair, good girl," I tried in my best soothing voice.

She butted my head with her nose. Damn goat.

"I think she's bitter you ignored her earlier."

"It was warranted." If this goat ruined my hair, she was as

good as dead to me.

He gave a gentle reassuring squeeze to my thigh. "Just hold on a sec. Let me see if I can distract her. Do you have any food in your purse?"

"I think I have a granola bar. Just take it." I kicked him my purse, and he picked it up, gingerly going through the contents.

He dug deeper, almost to his elbow, searching. "Jeez, how many tubes of lip gloss do you need?"

"Food, Ryder."

"An Allen wrench? What is this, the Mary Poppins bag?" He paused and dug a little deeper, unearthing a granola bar. "Aha."

"C'mon, hurry up." I tried to shoot him a glare for taking his good ol' time, but Bertha continued to use my hair as a chew toy. I bit back a sob climbing up my throat.

Keep it together. You can cry in the bathroom later.

He unwrapped the bar, and the goat immediately dropped my braid in favor of a sweeter treat. I slumped into the seat and let out a whimper as my fingers circled the sopping mess that was my hair.

My lips quivered as I hit a jagged piece. "How bad is it, on a scale of one to utterly destroyed?" Getting an appointment with my stylist took weeks in advance.

Ryder moved in closer and sucked in a breath. "It's not as bad as it could be. Don't freak out, okay?"

Why is it that whenever someone says to not freak out, the first instinct is to lose your shit? "Um, okay?"

He swiped his hand across my braid and grabbed a small chunk, at least half the braid, and held it in front of me. "I, uh, think you got a haircut from a goat."

"Oh my God." My hair. My hair that had taken months just to grow out long enough to even *put* into a braid. Gone in sixty seconds, thanks to a damn goat.

He gave a strained smile. "It's not that bad."

"Not that bad," I repeated. My vision blurred with red as I grabbed my fistful of hair out of his hand and shoved it toward the driver's face. "See what your goat did? Do you see this?"

The driver paled and averted his gaze to the road.

"I am not paying your fare. And you can write me a check for the haircut I need to have now that your goat gave me a makeover."

"And you." I turned to Ryder, who was chuckling softly. "Don't even get me started on you."

He held his hands up. "Me? I helped distract Bertha. That earns me some points."

"Then why the hell are you laughing?"

"I'm not laughing because it's funny. It's just so damn ridiculous. This type of shit could only happen to you, Zoey. You're a magnet for disaster." He laughed again, and I smacked him with the piece of braid in my hand.

And then looked down at the hair, wet and matted, completely shredded. A hysterical bubble of laughter caught me off-guard. He was right. This really was the most insane thing. Before I knew it, I was doubled over, tears streaming down my face as I cackled, the goat still working on my granola bar.

The driver looked at both of us in the rearview mirror, eyes wide.

"I like when you laugh," Ryder said. "You have a nice one." Then he stiffened, like he'd meant to keep this comment to himself.

The driver took that moment to pull over and let us out at our destination, awkwardness hanging heavy in the air. He apologized profusely and handed me a few twenties to pay for my hair appointment. I gave the goat one more glare before I slid out of the van, fisting my braid in one hand and my purse in the other. She continued working on the food, giving zero shits about what had just gone down.

I wiped the tears from my eyes and straightened, a gust of wind ruffling my frayed, goat-chomped locks against my cheek. "Thank you—for saving the rest of my hair."

"At your service. Just like that duke of yours." He smirked.

"Right." My skin prickled as memories from our night stuck in the resort washed over me. I'd been so close to letting go, putting my trust into this man who had done nothing but proven he was going to leave again. No matter how pretty his words were, I had a job to do, one to keep. "Ryder, I have to ask, would you like me to pass your account to one of my other partners? I think you might feel more comfortable with another designer." Even if it killed me to pass up a TV segment on one of my designs, it was the right thing to do, to offer this. My common sense was the eye of the storm, and these feelings were the debris and clouds swirling around it, blinding me.

His expression softened, and the smile faded from his lips. "I'm sorry, Zoey. Seriously, I was just trying to make light of the situation. I don't want to work with anyone else from your firm."

I shifted my gaze to the storefront ahead of us, not trusting myself to look in his eyes. "This job in particular means a lot to me. There's a lot at stake with getting ahead in my career—I can't let anything get in the way of that." Especially not someone who had a track record of disappearing, and who was already wishy-washy about the project in general.

"I said I'd give this an honest chance, and I meant it. I'm prepared to be wowed by the wonder that is fabric samples." He gestured to the building. It could be taken as smartass, but he seemed genuine.

I made the mistake of looking at him, seeing the heat in his eyes, the pure intensity in the way he regarded me…

Nope. Would not go there. Just because he did the chivalrous thing saving my hair—mostly—from a goat did not mean my body needed to react to him in *that* way.

"Great. Let's do this."

"Ladies first." He pulled open the door and motioned for me to go first.

• • •

RYDER

As we walked into the fabric store, I was sure of two things: Zoey was so incredibly sexy when she was pissed off, and even if it went against the ingrained need to keep things simple, I couldn't stay away from this woman. One night had always been enough with other girls. With Zoey, I wanted to know more than what she liked in the bedroom. I wanted to know what the hell she was thinking every time she looked at me, and why she shut me down consistently. Her determination and focus in everything she did was the sexiest thing I'd ever seen. Someone that was so proud of her work, that fought for what she believed in.

"Okay, should we start with window treatments?" She tucked the piece of hair behind her ear and cleared her throat.

I tore my gaze from her. Ever since we started this project, I'd acquired a problem. I seemed to be going through a second round of puberty where I stared a beat too long, reduced to a complete jumble of raw sensations. *Need. Want. Must have.* Words that only made an appearance when I was around Zoey. Or *thinking* about her.

"Lead the way." I gestured to the aisles upon aisles of the most boring shopping trip of my life. Jason would probably shit himself if he found out I'd voluntarily offered to go on this excursion. Even I didn't completely understand why I was here.

As we made our way through the maze of fabrics and swatches, my eyes glazed over at about the fiftieth sample. This had to be the driest job ever. Worse than heading a company. From what I'd seen of Jason's office and his insomnia ever since he joined my grandfather's firm, it'd be a cold day in hell before I chose a corner office with a view over something with more freedom.

"How about this one?" She held up yet another flimsy blue piece of fabric.

"I don't know. Is that the same one you showed me a couple of swatches ago?"

"Are you even paying attention?" She swatted my chest. The gesture caught us both off-guard, and her hazel eyes widened. If she wasn't so clear about her boundaries, I'd call it for what it was—flirting. She cleared her throat and quickly apologized. "The last ones I showed you were white and cerulean."

"Is that even a color? Or is that one of those made-up names like in the crayon boxes?"

She groaned. "For someone who was so adamant about picking out samples, I don't think your heart's quite in it."

"You're right. It's not. I hate this." I grinned at her.

She blinked rapidly and sucked in her cheeks. Her eyes narrowed as she clutched the fabric sample in her hand as if imagining it were my neck. "Then why did you ask me to take you?"

She was two seconds from kicking me out of this excursion, and I said the first thing that came to mind. "Because I like being around you." My own words surprised me, and I quickly looked away. What the hell was this voodoo magic?

Pink tinged her cheeks, and she was getting riled up again. Something about her ripped open a primal part inside of me.

Want.

Need.

Must have.

It overrode my number one rule. Something told me, though, that she'd be worth breaking the rules.

Screw it. I'd break five hundred rules to have her lips on mine again.

"Ryder..."

Her mouth opened and closed, and I could tell she was trying to come up with a polite way of telling me off. Dammit, all I wanted to do was back her up against the shelving unit and fist my hands in her hair, to kiss her mercilessly until she realized just how wrong she had it. We already knew our chemistry was off the charts.

"Ryder what?" I prompted. "Tell me, Zoey."

She shook her head. "I'm obviously not thinking clearly." She lifted the jagged braid. "I think I still have goat PTSD."

"You're blaming the flush trailing down your neck on a pregnant pigmy goat? You can do better than that." I moved a step closer to her, bridging the gap.

"No." She swallowed hard, looking up at me with desperate eyes. She'd given me that look before, though that other time she'd been more focused on getting closer, not farther away. "But I wouldn't have been distracted if you weren't"— she motioned to me and scoffed—"there. My hair might have lived to see another day."

"I'll take my power of distraction as a compliment." There was no going back now. I'd fought this, ignored this feeling for weeks now, and it wasn't getting any easier. I was not going to piss away a chance with her just because I was her client.

"Can't focus on anything else when we're in the same room, can you?" I moved in closer, and she backed up a few steps, bumping into the shelves. All it would take to kiss her would be me caging her in, pressing my body against hers.

I bet she'd whimper if I touched her.

She cleared her throat. Her teeth dug into her bottom lip

as she stared at me, assessing. Always assessing—everything was so calculated with her, and a need to be a part of this equation ripped through me with enough force that if I hadn't been on crutches, I'd be knocked on my ass. I was intoxicated by her, every goddamn thing about her. My need for one more taste, one more anything when it came to Zoey, had skyrocketed exponentially as her chest rose and fell, inches from mine. "That is definitely not the case," she whispered.

"Is that why you can't stop staring at me when you think I'm not looking?" I moved in even closer. "Either your body or your mind is lying. Which one is it, Zoey?"

She let out a shuddering breath. "I-I don't know."

"I think you want to try again. To see what this is between us. Tell me I'm wrong, and I'll back off."

Her mouth worked. I knew the answer before the word came out of her mouth because this was all part of the game. I asked her out, she said no. The outcome wouldn't change unless the rules did. "No," she said. "It isn't worth risking my job, Ryder. It'd be my position on the line." She meant it. The sudden fear in her eyes shone clear.

"Then go to dinner with me. As your client." She was hiding behind the excuse of her job, but it was obvious there was more to it. She didn't trust me. And I wanted to kick myself in the teeth because I'd created this doubt in the first place. I'd never jeopardize her job or try to hurt her.

"No," she said, this time more firmly.

"I thought you said you meet with clients over meals all the time."

Her face turned an even deeper shade of pink. "I'll think about it."

"All I'm asking is to share a meal with you. Nothing more. Clothing mandatory." I didn't even know what the hell I was doing. I'd never asked this of someone before, the platonic meal thing. But I did know I'd give my right hand for even a dinner with her. She wasn't taking me seriously, though, and I didn't know how to change that.

She straightened, squaring her shoulders. "I know your games—been through it before. I also know how it ends. You don't think past one night, but I do."

I opened my mouth to argue…and then quickly closed it.

Shit, she was right.

This entire month, I'd had one thing on my mind—my training. Once this project was done, and I finished rehab on my leg, I was gone, no matter how differently I felt about Zoey. I'd be as big a dick as she accused me of being if I pursued whatever this was between us, because it'd be the same outcome, no matter what. She'd done me a favor by calling me out for what I really was—someone who didn't have time to commit.

I backed away, letting the topic fade into awkward silence. We wound our way through the store, and I decided that I never wanted to deal with picking out upholstery for furniture ever again. It was stupid that I'd come here in the first place.

Zoey busied herself with sifting through material, placing sample after sample on a table. "You seriously don't agree with any of these fabrics?"

I focused back on her question. "No. They're horrible."

"What is so horrible about this one?" She held up a colored swatch labeled *dusty rose*.

"It's too feminine. We have males staying at the resort, too, you know."

She let out a frustrated sigh, and I could tell she was fighting to hold on to every last shred of patience. "Who do you think we're trying to impress here? Most men won't give a shit about the chair colors."

I put my hand to my chest. "Why, Ms. Reynolds, that is awfully sexist of you. I happen to care deeply about this."

She side-eyed me. "My bullshit meter is off the charts

right now. Listen—" She sighed. "I'll get back to the office and come up with a new plan, and then I'll shoot you an email with some new designs either tonight or tomorrow. Sound good?"

There was nothing to argue with. She'd drawn the line, and I wouldn't be crossing it again. "Okay."

By the time the cab dropped us off at her office building, the air had turned crisp. Her breath puffed out in front of her as we exited the sedan. "Have a good night."

Before I could stop myself, I tucked a strand of hair behind her ear. My fingers grazed her cheek, and she leaned into the touch, her soft skin burning an imprint into my hand. I physically ached with the need to devour every inch of her with my mouth. "You, too, Ms. Reynolds."

She shuddered as she slowly moved away from my touch. "Bye, Ryder."

And with that, she turned and walked into the building. I watched her, that confident sway in her hips, the way her coat hugged her curves, the way she put me in my place for being an asshole. This woman would be the end of me.

Chapter Eight

Zoey

To Do List:
• Fix goat-chomped locks

Two days had passed since the hair debacle. I'd managed to book an appointment with my new stylist when she'd had a last-minute cancelation. There was just something about a hair dresser's chair that acted like a therapy session. The second I plopped my butt into the black swivel seat at Monique's station at Bend and Snap Salon, I couldn't stop the words from pouring out of my mouth. The chair was my confessional and Monique my priest.

I told her about Ryder and the resort, what he'd said to me, the peanut butter incident, *and* the goat. Everything.

"So, I'm assuming you want a round two?"

I shot her a look in the mirror. "Of course not. He's a client!"

She pursed her lips. "Girl, sounds to me like you both just

need to get laid and get it over with," she said as she continued to work her magic with the scissors. Pieces of hair fluttered to the floor as I sat back and stewed about the situation. "Just sayin'. Sounds like you're obsessing about the dude. Might finally get you past the whole dry spell situation so you can move on. Unless it ended between last week and now?"

"Nope, still Sahara-level conditions."

"Is anyone going to know if you sleep with him again?"

"Besides Ryder?" I bristled at the thought of breaking one of Lance's company commandments, because, yeah, ethics and all that jazz. "No." Plus, Ryder was just as likely to up and leave this time around. I didn't know which one gave me more pause.

"Then what do you have to lose?"

She had a point. Maybe I was putting too much emphasis on a future. Hell, I didn't need forever; I just needed a night, something fun and freeing. The fact was there was absolutely no chance of a long-term investment with him, so why did it matter if I had one good night of sex? Maybe this was the key to getting back in the game.

I couldn't tell if my brain was saying this, or if my lady bits had finally claimed domination of the Zoeyverse.

"Maybe you're right," I said, but even I was having a hard time convincing myself at this point. Shit, I was going through the worst dry spell of my life, and if I waited any longer to find someone, the whole nether region area might dry into sandpaper.

"Girl, I'm always right." She gave a deep, throaty laugh. "You have *need to get laid* written all over your face."

"Yeah, no kidding," I mumbled.

She took out the blow-dryer and blew bits of hair off my cape and onto the floor. "Well, you're all fixed up, lady. Don't go pissing off any more goats, because I'm booked solid for the next month." She smiled at me in the mirror.

"I'll do my best to keep away from any animals besides my cat." After paying Monique, I jetted to my car to escape the torrential downpour outside and made it home twenty minutes later.

As soon as I walked through the door, Jitters hopped down from his scratching post and nuzzled against my legs.

"What do you think, Jitters?"

He meowed in response and let me scratch him behind the ears. After he was done with me, he trotted over to the container of cat treats on the coffee table and pawed at the top.

"Buttering me up to get treats. I see how it is." I loved my cat, but even he had ulterior motives. I rolled my eyes and opened the jar, extracting a fish-shaped goody for him. "It's a good thing you're so cute."

He gave another meow in response, and as soon as the treat was in his mouth, he scurried away to his scratching post.

I shook my head and laughed. User.

Before I had a chance to drop my purse on the counter, my phone beeped.

An unknown number with a Seattle area code flashed on the screen. Except it wasn't unknown when I read the message.

Ryder: *How is your hair doing?*

I bit at my thumbnail, deciding whether or not to engage. Email was one thing. Texting held a certain intimacy, with no professional email signature or cordial messages to hide behind. Just me.

Christ on a cracker, I was going to give myself a brain aneurism if I thought any harder about a damn text message. I clicked the reply button.

Zoey: *How did you get my number?*

Ryder: *You called me the other day. You should really be careful. Shouldn't use your cell phone if you don't want people to message you.*

Zoey: *You're right. What was I thinking, using my phone to call a client?*

Ryder: *Just watching out for you.*

I rolled my eyes. Ryder thought he was so smooth. And maybe he was, because my stomach was doing the flip-flop thing that I'd previously reserved only for swoony words that came out of Ryan Gosling's mouth.

Zoey: *My hair is good, by the way. My stylist was able to get me in.*

Ryder: *Do I get to see?*

I snapped a quick picture and sent it to him.

My heart raced the second I hit send. The hellhound better known as my conscience butted in next with *Ooh, girl, look what you just did.*

Yeah, where was my conscience twenty seconds ago when I was making that stupid duck face? I'd never send a selfie to a client. Ever. I paced the room, waiting for a response. I'd managed to lap the couch once when a text popped up on my screen.

Ryder: *Looks great. Although, I thought the goat did a decent job. Chopped was a good look on you.*

I stared at his message, trying to come up with a witty response. Nada.

Lainey walked into the apartment, tapping something

into her phone. She plopped down beside me on the couch and swung her legs onto the coffee table.

"Nice haircut. What's got you smiling like an idiot?"

Crap. Was I smiling? "Just something from work." I slid my phone into the pocket of my sweatshirt, deciding to text Ryder back later. I rubbed my hand over my mouth, trying to smooth out my features. Okay, maybe I was making this more complicated than it needed to be. I had a problem, and he offered a solution.

• • •

RYDER

An hour later and I was still checking my phone for a response from Zoey. The last thing I'd expected was for her to send me a picture, especially when she'd been so adamant on keeping things professional. Her lips were pursed in a pout, and there was a crease in the middle of her forehead. Only Zoey could make a duck face look sexy. I'd come to terms with the fact that she wasn't interested. Was I fine with that? Not really. But if she wanted to play the friend card, I'd take it.

This whole month had been a bizarre string of firsts. First time I couldn't do something that had defined my life for the past fifteen years. First time my brother needed *me.* First time I'd let a woman get under my skin. A normal life sat on the periphery, one where people expected to be entertained by my performance on the trails. In a few short weeks, I'd be back where I started, for better or worse.

At exactly eight o'clock, I rang the doorbell to Jason's Bellevue mansion.

I shifted from side to side as I eyed the gargoyle mounted atop one of the pillars outlining the entryway. Jason always did like to flaunt his status. Honestly, that much space seemed like a waste. When I wasn't on tour, I preferred my downtown loft—I had my TV, my bed, a fridge, and a stove. The essentials. My mother would be appalled by his blatant display of wealth.

The door opened seconds later, to my grandmother doing her silent inventory.

"So nice of you to be on time for dinner, Ryder." Grandmother glanced at the loosened tie around my neck and frowned. Beatrice Covington lived and breathed propriety. Growing up in the South, she had kept true to her Virginia roots when they made the move to Vermont.

Before she could say anything about redoing my tie, my grandfather marched through the entryway, his chest puffed out, holding his customary glass of scotch. "See, Beatrice, I told you he'd be on time." He gave me a tip of the chin and took a sip from his tumbler.

I looked around the main living room area and the kitchen, scoping out where Jason was hiding. It'd been over a year since I'd visited him here since his work schedule and my training often clashed. And in a year, nothing about the place had changed. Still immaculate as ever. No indication that Jason was having a hard time adjusting to his new life.

"No traffic."

"That's a first. One of the reasons I hate this city," my grandmother said. "Good thing we're only visiting."

Yes, good thing.

Grandfather cleared his throat and took another sip of scotch. "Please, come join us for drinks."

My lips twitched. No amount of alcohol could prepare someone for an evening with my grandparents. But if there was the chance to dull the desire to hit myself over the head with a blunt object until unconscious, I'd take it. One drink wouldn't hurt. "Sounds good."

We made our way to the den, which was lined with floor-to-ceiling bookshelves, a drink cart, and a massive oak desk in the corner of the room.

Jason sat in his wheelchair next to a large L-shaped couch in the center of the room, sipping from a tumbler of amber liquid on the rocks. Dark circles etched the skin under his eyes, and his shirt hung loosely from his shoulders. Even though he'd been busy preparing to take over our grandfather's company for the past six years, he'd always found time to hit the gym, and could always go pound for pound when we'd lift together. An unexpected lump settled in the base of my throat seeing him like this. This wasn't my brother.

"Hey, J." I nodded toward him. My stomach clenched just thinking about how four months ago he'd been out on the slopes, carefree. And now here he was, paralyzed from the waist down because of some stupid trick he was trying to maneuver on a rail.

He smiled. "Ryder."

We both paused for a second, looking at each other. His eyes widened a fraction and darted toward my grandparents. I understood exactly what he was saying. What we always thought when we were all in the same room together. *Kill me with a hammer. Make it quick.*

I gave him a slow nod. *I hear you, brother. Loud and clear.*

Grandfather sat on the leather couch alongside my grandmother. I took my place on the couch opposite them and took a long swig of my drink. Let the games begin in five, four, three, two…

On cue, my grandfather started in. "Now that we're all together, we can discuss what needs to be done with Jason's recent investment."

Grandmother crossed her arms. A united front. A storm front might be more accurate. Category five hurricane. Record high winds with a side of pretention and snobbery. They'd done a similar routine each time I'd managed to get expelled from a boarding school. Granted, I was a little shit back then. But even now their high-horse mentality set my molars grinding together.

Jason let out an exaggerated sigh. "I'm right here, Grandfather. Not like I'm dead or anything," he deadpanned.

Clearly, this conversation was going to go as well as I expected.

My grandfather leaned forward on his elbows, steepling his hands under his chin. He had this way, ever since I was old enough to remember, of trying to intimidate people with his presence. "You've been out of commission for over three months. Did the doctor tell you when you'd be able to go back to work?"

"Rehab has taken up a lot of time. I've been working from home—Heidi is handling all the clerical issues at the office. Plus, Ryder is heading the resort project."

He motioned my way.

My grandfather bristled. "I'm fully aware of your purchase with the Covington account funds." He shifted his gaze to Jason, looking down at him over the bridge of his nose.

They were in fine form tonight. In fact, I hadn't seen them this concerned since high school, when I came home in the back of a cop car after a group of buddies and I left a lit paper bag of dog shit on the headmaster's doorstep. Yes, I was the kid who deserved a good ass-whooping. While I never had a hand laid on me, my grandparents took psychological warfare to the next level, loading me with more extracurricular activities at my boarding school, more tutoring sessions, until the day I graduated and high-tailed it out of there. But while I'd gone balls to the walls making my grandparents' lives miserable, Jason had always been the good grandson, the dependable one.

Jason squared his shoulders, sitting taller than he had moments before. "You've never questioned my purchases before."

"They've never been of a personal nature. I don't think

your head was in the right place during this acquisition."

I clutched the edge of the sofa, looking around the room. From my view of the window, there didn't appear to be an alien invasion. The world hadn't split into two. And yet doomsday must be fast approaching because I just agreed with something my grandfather said. I had the common sense and brotherly loyalty to refrain from sharing my opinion, though.

"I respectfully disagree," Jason said. "Snow sports and lodging are a great investment in the Northwest. You're just upset that it was Mom's favorite vacation spot."

He turned bright red and shifted on the couch. "That's not it at all."

My grandmother interjected. "I think what your grandfather is trying to say is that we're worried about you. We can still take care of this mess and sell the property to the highest bidder."

Jason lowered his voice, narrowing his eyes as he regarded our grandparents. "I can't believe you two. I've been essentially running this company for five years, without complaint. And now because of the accident, and me taking time off, you feel I'm too fragile to manage things?" There was an edge in his voice that stiffened my spine.

I'd never seen him disagree with my grandparents. Ever. That was always my job. Hell, maybe the world really was ending.

They both stared at him, blinking.

"I will go back when I'm damned ready. Ryder is in charge of my only project at the moment."

He turned to me. "I appreciate you helping me out."

"No problem." At the moment, my *help* seemed like the last thing Jason needed. I'd stalled on the project because I thought it was a bad idea. It was only this week that I decided to take Zoey seriously about renovations. I'd seen how important it was to her. And if Jason wanted to throw away his money? Fine. I'd go along with it because hell if I'd be the reason to get in the way of Zoey's career or my brother's happiness. They both seemed convinced this project was a good idea, so maybe it was me who was missing something. Maybe there really was more to this property than just the land.

My grandmother scoffed. "This has to be a joke. Really, Jason? Putting your brother in charge? Don't you see this will end in disaster?"

"Beatrice," my grandfather snarled.

"Go ahead, Grandma. It's nothing I haven't heard before." Her arsenal of potshots could put a thesaurus to shame.

"You've yet to prove you can handle money. What's to say you won't blow all of it on your silly snow sports?"

"Seems I'm doing just fine. Without your money, I'd like to add." That damn trust fund. My grandmother practically begged me to cash in, just so she'd have a little leverage over me. She'd be waiting a hell of a lot longer. "I get you think I'm irresponsible, and I don't know how to sway you to think otherwise, but I'm helping out with this renovation, whether you like it or not."

"If you'd like to hound Ryder some more, you can feel free to leave," Jason cut in, his tone lethal.

My grandparents sat there, shifting their empty tumblers, swishing ice cubes around. Finally, my grandmother stood and announced, "I'm going to see if Dora has dinner prepared yet. George?" She held out her hand, an order for my grandfather to follow.

I glanced over at Jason, at his tight-lipped smile, his hunched back. Before his accident, he was the life of the party. The type of guy that made sure everyone felt comfortable and happy to be there. I'd rather break my leg in five more places than see that light extinguished from his eyes.

My grandparents left the room, and it was just me and Jason.

"How is the project going?" He swirled his drink in his hand, regarding me.

"Zoey's sent me some great plans. I want you to come with me this weekend to finalize everything. Then we can start demo work."

He hesitated. "I don't know about that."

I could see it in his eyes—the same look I had after an extremely grueling practice and my coach tacking on two more runs down the mountain. Utter exhaustion.

Hell would freeze over before I let him continue down this path of solitude. He needed a reboot. Something to jumpstart his passion again.

"J, you need to get out. Come with me to the resort this weekend, or else I'll make Zoey paint the walls Pepto-Bismol pink." Not that I'd actually do this, but it seemed like a simple enough threat to be believable.

He smirked. "She wouldn't let you."

There we go. Keep smiling, J.

The brother I knew was still in there, even if he was hurting. I wasn't into the whole building a campfire and singing "Kumbaya" shit, but I could try to get his mind off his problems for at least a few minutes. "I can tell her you special requested it."

He took another sip of his whiskey, and after a few moments, he said, "Fine. I'll go."

"Good. Some snow will do you good." The final hint of winter clung to the slopes, trails that begged to be carved with my board. My legs ached to get back in the game.

Soon.

After I got this resort in order.

He cleared his throat and stared out the window. "I'm not ready to go back into the office." He rubbed his forehead. "I don't want people to see me like this. I don't want their pitying glances."

I'd never in a million years be able to fully understand how he felt, but this was Jason. He took life by the balls. He just needed a little push to get his confidence back. I refused to believe he'd spend the rest of his life avoiding something he loved. "If they look at you like that, fuck them. You're still the same, Jason. If they underestimate you, it's their problem. But hiding out here like you're Bruce Wayne is only letting them win."

"You sure you don't want a future in business?" A smile cracked the corner of his lips.

"Come with me to Divinity on Friday. Then you can go back to the office and show them you're stronger than whatever life throws at you."

"Does that advice apply to you, too?" He made a point to look at my leg.

I didn't know the answer to that.

Chapter Nine

Zoey

Rule #71: Don't fantasize about your client, even when he does something swoonier than a romance novel hero.

Ryder: *Join me at Divinity this weekend to finalize designs? Think you could manage Friday?*

Since the Uber ride incident, Ryder had moved from intolerable to somewhat manageable. He didn't shoot my ideas down within two seconds, and was finally answering emails. Whether that was because we were both walking a fine line, teetering on the edge of me losing my professional edge, or the fact he finally liked the designs, I didn't really know. Either way, I had a job to do, and he was finally allowing me to do it. At that point, I'd agree to almost anything to get this project finished.

I checked the weather app on my phone, and with a clear forecast for the next seven days, I trusted I wouldn't be met with another freak snow storm.

Zoey: *I'll meet you up there at 11.*

Ryder: *You can ride with me and Jason.*

Zoey: *Thanks for the offer, but I'll be driving on my own.*

Ryder: *You're missing out on a great Carpool Karaoke opportunity. I'm particularly fond of Adele.*

I rolled my eyes and smiled. When he wasn't being a pain in the ass, Ryder was a huge goofball. And I'd pay good money to see him belt out a few of her ballads. But I needed that time to think and prepare. If both Covingtons were there, I wanted everything to be perfect.

Ryder: *I felt that eye roll all the way at my apartment.*

Zoey: *There was absolutely no eye-rolling.*

Ryder: *You're still a bad liar over text message.*

I let out laugh. Seriously, the guy had me pegged.

Zoey: *I'll see you on Friday.*

Ryder: *Looking forward to it. Night, Flash.*

I smothered a smile and shook my head.
I was in so much trouble.

• • •

On Friday, I left for the mountains first thing in the morning to avoid the end-of-week traffic. This time I dressed appropriately for the brisk morning, with jeans and a zip-up, and decided to pack an overnight bag *just in case*. Even in March, there was a chance another storm could roll through, but it wasn't as likely. Most of the snow had melted on the sides of the pass, and by the time I reached Divinity, only traces of the storm the other week still blanketed the mountain.

I pulled into the parking lot of the resort, and parked under a large pine tree with flecks of powder dusting the branches. The clock on the dash informed me that I'd arrived twenty minutes ahead of schedule, so I hunkered down, turned on my audiobook, and ignored the fact that it was *really* quiet in this abandoned resort…all by myself. Freddie and Jason only came out at night, right?

Duke Renau had just said his vows to Lady Eddington. He'd gotten down on one knee, proclaiming his love for her with one single rose—the same color as her lips, he'd insisted. Um, sah-woon. Now there was a man who knew how to woo ladies. A guy doing that nowadays was about as likely as me successfully baking something. Didn't mean I couldn't crave brownie batter and burn the kitchen down while trying, though.

If I was comparing men to baked goods, then my hair stylist was completely right. I needed to get laid. They both might be yummy and drool-inducing, but that was where the similarity ended.

I closed my eyes, leaning my seat back to almost a full recline, listening to the narrator as the duke kissed down the heroine's neck, down her chest, to other parts.

Yeah, you get yours, Lady Eddington.

The heroine's eyes rolled to the back of her head as my new favorite duke did the wham-bam-thank-you-ma'am nineteenth-century style, and my mind started to slip back into the memory of Ryder's touch. His tongue on my neck. Him down on his knees.

I let myself take this opportunity to remember how his long lashes fanned over his cheeks as he kissed a trail down my body, and the way his tongue darted to places that hadn't been touched by another person in months.

Three taps rapped on my window, and I bolted upright, smashing my chest into the steering wheel. The horn's beep echoed through the bowl of the ski area, and my face flamed. Birds took flight from trees and a few squirrels darted across the expanse.

Ryder smiled at me as I put the audiobook on pause and rolled down my window, the icy air caressing my heated cheeks. "The duke have you all hot and bothered again?" he asked.

"He's not the one bothering me," I teased, and ignored the fact that though the narrator's English accent was on point, it was Ryder who was on my mind.

He clutched his chest. "My heart. It's wounded."

I tapped a finger to where his hand rested on his pec. "I still don't believe there's one in there."

"With the way my pulse races when I see you, I can safely say it's accounted for."

Holy hell. Seriously, what was I supposed to do with that? I wasn't usually the type to swoon over one-liners, but I had to admit, that one hit several buttons, including *do, me,* and *now*. "Did it take you all day to come up with that line?"

"Just the walk from my car to yours." He took a low, flourishing bow.

Before I could help it, a giggle slipped out. I liked this side of Ryder, the one that made it so easy to lower my walls. It was why I had been drawn to him in the first place, before we had our one-night stand, when we'd hung out, two people with their guards down. Above anything, there was a comfort in our back and forth. Up on the mountain, with enough space between me and my work environment, it was easy to fall into that easy, joking mindset like I had before.

"But who knew there was a secret romantic in there?"

His gaze cut to mine. "There are a lot of things about me that would surprise you."

Before I could ask what those certain things entailed, he strode to his car and opened the trunk of the SUV, extracting a wheelchair. After walking back over to the passenger side, Ryder opened the door, helped his brother into the wheelchair, and guided him to where I stood. Jason shifted uncomfortably, like he wasn't quite used to sitting in a confined space. He looked so different than when I'd last seen him.

The two brothers both had the same high cheekbones, dark hair, and charming smile. Which was to say, that family had a lot of great genetics going on. While Ryder was a little taller than his brother, from what I remembered when working with him on the last project, they both had that bulky build that screamed of hours at the gym.

"It's great to see you again, Mr. Covington." I didn't know whether or not to comment on his accident, but decided against saying anything because I didn't want to bring attention to what must have been a touchy subject with the injury being so fresh.

The tension fled his features. "Ms. Reynolds. A pleasure as always."

I looked between him and Ryder, debating if I should keep up the pretense of small talk, or dive straight into business. Jason was never one for wasting time, so I decided on the latter. "If you don't mind. I'm going to grab my mock-ups from the car, and then we can head in and look at the designs."

"Sounds like a plan. Ryder has been catching me up to speed with most of the changes," Jason said.

As Ryder wheeled his brother into the main lodge area, I made my way to the trunk of my car and took a minute to compose myself. I took a few deep breaths, letting the cold air sear down my throat.

Eye on the prize. Get them to approve the renovations, bring the demo team in here, and have this place looking brand-spankin'-new in time to be featured on HGTV. I'd claw my way to a promotion and wasn't afraid to get a little mud on my Alexander McQueens in the process.

Barring any unforeseen changes, I could get a crew up here on Monday to start tearing everything down. We even had a dumpster on the side of the building ready for all the seventies crap to meet its overdue demise.

All I had to do was not screw it up in the next thirty minutes. Completely manageable.

As if I'd summoned trouble himself, Ryder brushed through the double doors of the reception building and wandered toward me down the winding path. The sun streaked his dark hair, and even from here, his eyes glinted in the light. The sight completely robbed me of my breath. It wasn't even that he was attractive. Because yes, his attractiveness was completely unfair. Heck, even the scar on his right eyebrow was somehow sexy. It was more than that, though. Ryder drove me up-the-wall insane. He made me angry, made me want to slap the shit out of his artfully carved cheeks. He made me *feel* things, sent a procession of emotions volleying from synapse to synapse.

One hundred sun salutations wouldn't do jack crap to wipe him from my mind at this point.

A tight smile pulled at his lips. "I just wanted to apologize in advance if Jason says anything rude. He's not himself lately. The accident"—he paused, looking at the lodge—"really affected him. I thought maybe if he saw something from work, it'd get him interested in the things he loves again."

"It's understandable. He's been through a lot."

After a long moment he closed his eyes and slowly exhaled. "Thank you for not saying anything about his injury. He was nervous about that."

The protectiveness he had for his brother melted any icy remnants I'd felt toward him.

"I'm not going to look at him differently just because of an injury. He's still ruthless, I can see it in his eyes."

"Takes one to know one, huh?"

I decided to ignore that. I did whatever it took to get the job done, and I'd bring out the boxing gloves today if needed. "I'll bet you'll be happy to relinquish your CEO duties." If he was already out of his cast, it meant he must be well on his way back to training and snowboarding. In fact, he wasn't even using his crutches, which was impressive in itself.

"Not exactly my dream job. Anything involving a suit and tie is too stuffy for my taste." He gave one of those smiles that made my whole body tingle in response.

"That's too bad," I said, before I could reel it in. At least I hadn't added *you fill them out nicely*. I bit the tip of my tongue and winced.

"Which part? That I won't be doing business full-time or that I'm not in a suit right now?"

Both.

I stole a glance his way, which was a mistake because his blue eyes liquefied what was left of my insides. I cleared my throat and clutched the printout of my sketches. "We should get in there before your brother starts to wonder."

The heat in his eyes dissolved. "You're right."

I locked my car and we made our way into the reception area of the lodge. I had so many things I wanted to do. I'd keep the natural beauty of the columns and exposed beams, but I'd take this from hokey rustic lodge to winter-escape chic in no time.

The heat had been turned off except for the night we'd spent here, and the lodge was almost as chilly as the crisp mountain air. I rubbed my arms, trying to keep the last of the feeling in them while I walked next to Ryder.

Jason sat there in the middle of the room, examining it from floor to ceiling.

I spread the plans across the oak table, and both men studied them. There was nothing quite as nerve-wracking as people critiquing my work. When I first started the job, I barely managed to keep down my breakfast before client meetings. Now, it was more like butterflies in the stomach—ones hopped up on venti quad shot lattes and hooked up with grenade launchers.

I planted myself next to the table, fighting my urge to pace around the room.

After a few minutes, Jason asked, "Which one do you like better, Ms. Reynolds?"

Ryder cast a glance my way, and I knew what he was thinking without him saying a word. He was expecting me to manipulate Jason's opinion. He'd said so our very first meeting together. I encouraged clients, yes, but I'd never make Jason do something against his will. Sometimes it felt like Ryder equated my business techniques to that of a used car salesman. It seemed our trust in each other fluctuated. Frequently.

I took great care to keep my comments as impartial as possible today.

"Personally, I think the one with the neutral color palate will bring out the richness in the cherry wood."

Jason nodded, still looking at the images I'd created with my modeling software.

I continued on. "If you're okay with it, I'd like to keep the exposed beams. I'd take the wall out over there." I pointed to the space sectioning off the main lodge and what appeared to have been at one time a large storage closet. "It will open up the space, creating an airier atmosphere and better functionality."

"I like it." He turned to Ryder. "What do you think?"

He shrugged. "You know my opinion on this whole thing."

It was a minor miracle Jason was up here to get the ball rolling. If it were up to Ryder, I was sure this place would have been bulldozed already. In fact, given his track record, it was a minor miracle he was still in town.

Jason shot him a look, and Ryder's shoulders sagged a fraction.

"Fine. I like the open concept one as well," he said.

What was that? Just me doing an internal twerkathon followed by running around the room with my hands above my head shouting *yes* at the top of my lungs. My thoughts were so professional.

Outwardly, I gave a small smile. "If you're both happy with that, I can start as soon as Monday with the demo crew. We'll get this up and running before summer hits. And with the feature on HGTV, I'm sure you'll have this place booked in no time."

"I like your ambition, Ms. Reynolds. I'm excited to see the finished product." His eyes seemed brighter than when they'd first pulled up to the resort. Ryder had been right to take him up here.

It took everything in me not to give an audible sigh of relief. Finally. Victory.

Ryder stood behind Jason and caught my eye, mouthing a silent thank-you.

I gave him a quick smile and focused back on my plan of attack. There was no wasting daylight when it came to this project. It was go-time. "I'm going to make a few calls. I'll be around if you need anything," I said.

I made my way into one of the guest rooms, sat down

in the chartreuse tufted chair, and propped my feet on the oak desk. The sun glinted off the snow-coated ground, casting a glare into the room. I'd spent more time around snow in the past few weeks than I had my entire life in Portland. The novelty had officially worn off, and I'd need at least a month on a beach to remove the chill from my bones.

Just as I pulled my phone out to call one of the vendors for the window tapestries and my demo guys, Ryder and Jason came out of the lodge across the way, Ryder pulling his brother in a kind of sled with skis on either side for stability. Jason was yelling something at Ryder, but from this distance, I couldn't make out the words. Ryder continued to pull the sled up a decent-sized hill with a rope slung over his shoulder. He'd taken his jacket off, and the muscles in his biceps bunched together.

Weather forecast: partly sunny skies with a good chance of man-candy precipitation.

At the top of the hill, he turned Jason's sled to face the slope. To my small knowledge of everything involving snow sports, I believed this to be a bunny hill, but I wasn't up to date with ski lingo.

Ryder stepped onto the back, took a firm grip on the handles, and pushed off. Both of their faces lit up, and their elated *whoops* tore across the lodge area as they swooped down the hill. Within seconds, they were at the bottom. Ryder bent to say something to Jason, and his brother's face puckered. He pulled Ryder into a hug, and the sweet gesture formed a lump in my throat.

I moved away from the window, an outsider to this very private moment.

Every now and again, after I finished making a call, I'd take another peek. They went down the hill and Ryder would pull them back up to the top. The pattern continued until I realized I had reached every vendor I'd needed to contact.

Jason's smile grew wider with every run down the mountain. I couldn't hear anything through the thick windows, but it was clear he was laughing as he threw his head back, his arms in the air.

Ryder smiled at his brother and dutifully stayed close by his side through the whole process. Boom. Sucker punch to the feels. The flood of feelings washed over me so quickly, I didn't even have time to brace for the impact. I knew deep down Ryder was a decent guy. But this amount of kindness was far beyond anything I'd expected from him. It was hard to believe this was the same guy that had left in the middle of the night a few months ago.

Chapter Ten

Ryder

Three days later, Jason ventured back into his office. I drove him and then made my way to the resort to oversee the gut job.

Did I need to be there? No. But a certain designer would be, and that was enough of a reason to make the two-hour trip.

When I parked my truck in the lot, I saw a large dumpster in the middle of the courtyard lawn, three men carrying an old, dusty sofa out to it. Zoey circled the men, directing them, waving her hands wildly. Her hair was pulled back today, and she was dressed casually in jeans and a hoodie. She'd be beautiful dressed in a garbage bag, I decided. My chest tightened as I took in the sight of her, so confident and at ease in her domain.

I made it halfway up the path before she zoned in on my presence.

She put her hands on her hips, but a smile graced her lips.

"What are you doing here?"

"Wanted to make sure everything's running smoothly for you."

"We've hit a couple of snags with disassembling some of the furniture, but otherwise we're good." She swiped a strand of hair out of her face and tucked it behind her ear.

I jutted my chin toward the lodge. "Need any help?"

"Careful what you wish for." A rueful smile crossed her red lips, and I shifted restlessly.

Right now, I wished for a lot of things, none of them appropriate to mention to her. I'd respect her decision to keep things professional, even if it killed me.

After a beat of hesitation, she said, "You can help me sort through the clutter in the back closet."

We made our way through the resort to the back of the building where there were bookshelves overflowing with garbage, brass figurines, and books. Zoey pulled a large metal trash can into the room and began plucking unusable items off the shelves and tossing them into the receptacle.

After a moment, she paused, put her hands on her hips, and took a deep, bracing breath while she stared at the room. "I was surprised Jason picked this place. It's just so different from the building he had me renovate last year."

I ground my teeth, deciding whether or not to tell her the real reason we were all working on this crap hole of a resort. I'd already let on that he'd bought it for personal reasons. It only seemed fitting she know the whole story. "This was one of my mom's favorite places." It came out before I could put too much thought into it. Zoey was easy to talk to, much easier than most people.

A golf ball bounced to the ground as Zoey continued to rummage through the shelves. "Was?"

I grabbed a plaque for the 1997 Bingo Championship and palmed it. "She passed away when I was ten."

She frowned. "I lost mine when I was thirteen."

The pain of losing my parents was there, but it had dulled over time. I could see it in her eyes as well.

"I think she would have liked this place, too. It has a lot of character," she said.

I looked around at the ornately carved wood, the windows with wavy glass, the dust particles floating in the stream of sunlight. This place, albeit old as hell, was comfortable. In its prime, Divinity was a great vacation spot. It would still have been, current day, if someone had maintained it.

A memory of my mom pushing my brother and me down the bunny hill in our sled, her lips pulled into a smile, flashed through me. Her love of the snow—it was what got me into snowboarding in the first place.

I imagined Divinity as it could be, with Zoey's new designs and a ski school for the winter. More families could enjoy time together, sharing a love for the slopes. Maybe, just maybe, Jason had the right idea in buying the lodge.

We continued throwing stuff into the trash can in silence for a few minutes. By the time noon rolled around, most of the rooms had been cleared, aside from a few items Zoey thought might add to the rustic charm of the place, including a couple of desks and an armoire.

She laughed and unearthed a chart from the back of the room. "Look. They used to do a hot wings contest here."

Shit. No way they'd kept the same one I'd marked my name on over a dozen years ago. "Let me see that."

She handed me the placard. I scanned it, and sure enough, I found my name halfway down the list. "Tribute to my ten-year-old badassery. They also took polaroids of the winners."

"They have to be somewhere. Looks like they haven't thrown anything away." Within a minute, Zoey fished out a wire basket filled with photos, each person holding up the "We Survived the Fiery Five" shirt. "Oh my God, look at the 'stache on that guy," she said, giggling.

"There's still wing sauce in it," I said.

She laughed even harder at this and continued to sort through the photos.

"Oh, jackpot," she squealed.

"What?"

"A certain someone with a bowl cut." Her gaze cut to mine. "I also like the bleached tips. Very early two-thousands of you."

I groaned and reached for the photo.

"Oh no, we're going to frame this. Don't think for one second you're destroying this beautiful masterpiece."

"I was a masterpiece, wasn't I?"

"Were you always this modest? Or was it after you stopped using a mixing bowl as a haircut aid?"

"Hey, I put in the hard work. Just because my snowboarding career has been successful doesn't mean I'm not modest." I let my runs down the mountain speak for me and left the preening on live TV for my teammates. I'd made sure to keep true to what my mother taught me, even if my brother sometimes lost sight of it.

"I was just giving you a hard time. It must be tough being in the spotlight twenty-four seven."

I glanced at the photo still in her hand. "Yeah, my mom kept us pretty sheltered when we were younger. Didn't want us having anything to do with my grandparents' lifestyle."

"It must have been a shock living with them afterward."

"It was. I still won't take their money, even though they've been begging me for years to tap into my trust fund."

"Any reason? I'd kill to have money sitting around for me." She smiled.

"It just doesn't feel right."

A knock came from the entrance of the room. The foreman said, "Zoey, we're heading out to lunch. You want us to pick you up anything? We're going to that diner a few miles south."

"I packed a lunch. Thanks, Tom."

She looked back at me expectantly with those eyes. Those damn eyes that would make me confess every fucking thing I'd ever done. And I realized I wanted to.

I motioned to the trash can. "Let's haul this stuff to the dumpster and then take a break."

With her crew on lunch, we had the resort to ourselves. Zoey and I unloaded two large trash bags into the dumpster and decided that was enough until the demo team returned.

She swiped her arm across her forehead, her cheeks pink from the activity. This was the most gorgeous I'd ever seen her. Not because of what she was wearing, but because for the first time since I'd met her, she didn't have her guard up. I was seeing *her*—the real Zoey.

"It's so pretty out here," she said.

"It is. Great day for boarding." I still hadn't strapped onto one, mostly because I was scared as hell to tweak my leg again, but if I wanted to be on the roster for the season opener, I needed to get my ass into gear soon. It had to be a step in the right direction that I was walking around without my crutches, almost pain-free.

"I've never been," she said.

"Do you want to try it?"

"I guess someday, maybe." She shrugged. "I've never really considered it."

"How about now?"

She laughed. "I kinda need a board for that."

"I have one." She didn't know it, but I'd caught her watching Jason and me ride down the beginner's hill on Friday. Zoey tolerated me, at best, most days, but right now she didn't look like she wanted to throttle me. Yesterday at the local board shop I'd grabbed a pair of boots that looked close to Zoey's size. Presumptuous as hell to think that she'd agree to ride with me? Yes. But when it came to her, I'd shamelessly try anything to get an extra few minutes with her.

"With you? Right now?" She seemed surprised that I'd even ask. It should be obvious to her. I'd do just about anything when it came to Zoey Reynolds.

"Yes."

• • •

ZOEY

All aboard the Stupid Express. And there was only one passenger on this train: me.

I shifted as I stood on Ryder's board, cussing under my breath. Strapped in with a pair of boots that were one size too large, I wondered at this incredibly poor life choice. If he was a pro and broke his leg, that didn't exactly bode well for my six seconds of experience.

He finished fastening the bindings, checking over everything twice. His cheeks and the tip of his nose were tinged pink from the cold, and my pulse beat rapidly in my temples as I stared at the scruff on his jaw. I, Zoey Reynolds, payer of parking tickets and generally responsible citizen, was strapped to a death trap. And the reason for risking bodily harm? All evidence pointed to the person standing right in front of me. I could add another checkmark next to the list of idiotic things I did due to someone with a Y chromosome.

I stared at the board, which had a lime green background with a large skull covering the majority of the surface. Yep, total idiot. Feet buckled to a hunk of wood, unable to break free if needed. At least with skis, I could move both of my legs separately. This just seemed…unsafe.

"I can't believe you've lived in the Pacific Northwest your entire life and never snowboarded. Mount Hood is literally in your backyard."

"Crazier things have happened. Like the revival of overalls. Really, who saw that coming?" I looked up at him, panic starting to stiffen my muscles, despite my flippant words. "You're sure this thing is safe?"

He shook his head, smiling. "Nothing's ever a guarantee, but I'm here, and I'll do my best to make sure you don't get hurt."

He hoisted me to a standing position, taking my gloved hands in his. "Just don't try to catch yourself if you fall. Rookie mistake that breaks a lot of first-timer's arms."

He looked down at our intertwined fingers and swallowed, his Adam's apple sliding up and down his throat. Ever since the goat incident, he hadn't asked me out again. Maybe he finally took the hint, or lost interest and moved on. The thought of him being with anyone else sent a spear of jealousy flashing hot and intense under my skin.

Oh my God. Stop it.

This was just getting pathetic if I was irked by a potential other woman. I had no claim on Ryder. In fact, I'd told him the exact opposite.

"So, first things first. You need to bend your knees." He lowered into a loose crouch and tapped at the backs of my legs. "If you go down the slope with locked knees you'll fall on your face. The closer to the ground, the better."

"Okay." I bent even lower.

He chuckled and pulled me up slightly. "We're not doing power squats here, Flash. A slight bend in your knees should be sufficient for right now."

"Oh, right." I lessened my crouch and looked up to find him smiling at me. His black beanie came halfway down his forehead, and his dark hair curled around the edges of the cap.

"Next step: point your board down the mountain, left

foot in front of you." He pushed the board with his foot, positioning me toward the bottom of the hill.

"So it's almost like surfing. Only on snow."

His lips twitched. "Kind of."

I had a feeling that what I'd said had been completely off, but he'd been polite enough not to rub it in my face.

I shifted my board as he kept a gentle hold on me, our fingers still laced. "You don't have to keep holding my hand, you know."

Even if I do like it.

Being this close to him opened a floodgate of wants and needs. I wanted my nose buried against his skin, to commit his exact scent to memory. I *needed* to be near him, to lose myself in his warmth, his strong arms, his ability to calm me and put me on high alert at the same time. I'd gone mad with want.

"Would you rather fall on your ass a million times or listen to me for one second?" he said, pulling me back to the present.

"I'll take my chances." I did yoga on a daily basis. If I could handle a Firefly pose, I was fairly certain I could stand still on a board. This wasn't rocket science.

He let go, and I immediately lost my balance and dropped down onto the snow. Okay, apparently it was rocket science, and I was getting a crash course in the laws of physics. This snow wasn't as soft as the powder I'd encountered in other parts of the mountain, and my butt connected with what I found to be hard, compacted ice. Pain zinged up my tailbone, and it took everything in me not to wince. There'd be bruising there tomorrow, for sure.

I rolled my eyes. "Fine. You're right." I held up my arms. "Help me up?"

He grabbed both my hands and hoisted me to a standing position again. "Glad to see you're finally listening to something I suggest."

"Don't get ahead of yourself. You haven't taught me anything except that snow hurts way worse than water."

We started moving down the mountain, and Ryder kept ahold of me the entire way, which was only a few yards but felt a lot longer. A sloth might beat me down the mountain at this rate. My fingers clasped Ryder's as he moved me along the snow. Something about the way he held himself, so sure, so comfortable, caused a flicker of heat to spread through my freezing limbs.

I needed to take my mind off him. "Okay, game time. Would you rather swim in a shark tank with a gaping wound, or have creepy clowns follow your every move."

"The shark tank."

I looked at him.

"What? Clowns are creepy as shit."

I burst out laughing. Leave it to him to pick death over a carnival staple.

Before I knew it, we were at the bottom of the hill, and this time I hadn't fallen.

"You're doing great, Flash. A natural."

Ever since the day I met Ryder, I'd never doubted he felt secure in his own skin. Confident to a fault, he made it seem that everything he touched, everything he accomplished, was done with passion and power. Cocky. I used to see this as a weakness, but maybe I had it all wrong. Maybe it was all a front. On the mountain, he was an entirely different man. He wasn't pushy, just exuded quiet confidence that beamed like starlight in his eyes. This was his love, his life, and the way he moved in the snow with unexpected grace…I'd never witnessed anything so sexy.

Our boots crunched in the snow as we repeated the same loop. "Would you rather live the same day over for a year, or lose a year of your life?"

"Depends on the day," I admitted.

"How about today?" he asked, his gaze searching mine.

My board nicked something, and my legs gave out. My arms windmilled and I clutched at Ryder's jacket, my face smashed into him. My fingers gripped his broad shoulders, and it took everything I had not to let out a groan. Jeez, these were good shoulders. Capable, strong shoulders that I could lose myself in. We slowed to a stop, and Ryder pulled me closer, encasing me in his arms.

"Whoa. It's okay, I got you." His fingers stroked the back of my head in a comforting gesture.

Yes, Ryder. You totally have me with your hands that were forged from Thor's hammer with unicorn tears.

I realized, in that moment, I would do anything to relive this day for an entire year.

Oh dear. Oh no.

His offer to teach me to board had seemed innocent enough. Now I'd seen my mistake too late. I had an easy time saying no to him when we were feet apart, but when my body was pressed against his, there was zero chance I could deny what I wanted…another taste of him. I wanted to rake my hands through his hair, down his back. Hell, I wanted a lot of things right now, and it was not a safe thought. Not when I had so much to lose.

I cleared my throat. "Right, I think I'm okay now."

Slowly, reluctantly, he eased his grip from my arm and set me back on my own. He took a deep breath and looked down at me with an expression so tender that I momentarily forgot simple tasks such as breathing. And words. What use were vowels and consonants strung together, anyway?

He took my hands again, and even through the gloves, the heat of his skin, the gentle yet firm way that he held onto me, was a promise that he'd keep me safe. Trying new things, especially ones I didn't excel at, tended to spike my anxiety meter. But even if I sucked at this, hardcore, I was having fun.

He made this fun. "You're doing great. Fantastic, since this is your first time."

"Thanks. And you're right. This is nothing like surfing."

He didn't say anything to that, didn't crack one joke. He just continued to patiently work with me, giving pointers every once in a while. We did this a few more times, him helping me down the hill then unhooking my board and walking back up to the top to do it all over again. I'd fallen on my ass more times than I could count, but I had a smile plastered to my face the entire time. Ryder happened to be an awesome teacher, something that I wasn't expecting at all.

"You're ready to try it on your own now. I'm going to let go."

"Okay," I said hesitantly. I didn't quite believe him. Without Ryder to catch me, going down this hill seemed an impossible task.

"Remember, bend your knees, move with the snow," he said, his voice deep and reassuring.

"Be one with the snow; okay, Jedi Master."

As I started sliding down the hill, I gained speed and began to wobble. I leaned lower, bending into the curve, and managed to stay upright the entire way. My cheer echoed through the bowl of the mountain as I plateaued at the bottom. I gave a victory fist-pump and sank to the ground, unbuckling my boots from the board.

Ryder sped down and sat beside me. "You did great!"

I smiled. "Thanks. I had a great teacher." I bumped my arm against his. "Not every day I get instructions from a pro snowboarder."

He shrugged. "Always happy to convert poor, unsuspecting souls to the dark side."

For someone who loved the sport so much, it had to be hard to watch someone else ride while he sat on the sidelines.

"Are you going to start training again soon?"

His eyes searched mine, and a flash of pain radiated through his features.

Maybe it wasn't my place to pry. He'd just gotten his cast off a week and a half ago, and there must be someone putting pressure on him to get back on the slopes. There was always pressure when money was involved.

"Eventually. I'm taking it day by day at this point."

"Are you worried about your leg?" He seemed to be moving fine, but that didn't mean anything when it came to hard falls. My butt understood this personally.

His Adam's apple slid down his throat as he swallowed. "Yeah, I'm fucking scared. So are my sponsors. And my coach."

I swallowed hard as my gaze traced over the strong lines in his jaw, the tiny lines in the corners of his eyes when he smiled at me. "I have a feeling if you want it bad enough, you'll get it."

"Does that apply to you, too?"

His gaze searched mine, and for a second those blue eyes pulled me under, to a point where I wasn't sure what would come out of my mouth if he'd ask me out to dinner again. Okay, bullshit. I knew exactly what I'd say. *Skip dinner. Take me home. Now.* Heat flushed my cheeks even as the cold air bit into my skin. His thumbs stroked my arms, and time came to a screeching halt. The rush of my pulse throbbed in my temples, and each breath streaked the air with a tiny puff. My lips parted, and I moved toward him, giving him permission.

Do it. Lean down and kiss me. Before I change my mind.

His lips pressed together in response, as if he could tell exactly what I was thinking. Slowly he leaned in, his hands moving to my face, cupping my cheeks with his gloves.

"Dammit, Zoey. I don't know how much longer I can take not having you."

"Then answer this: would you rather have me now or

later?"

With that, his mouth was on mine. Strong hands coasted down to the small of my back, every inch of my chest flattened against him. More. I couldn't get close enough. The warm taste of peppermint bloomed in my mouth as his tongue swept across mine. Without his weight pressed into me, keeping me grounded, my body would float away in a boneless cloud.

He eased me back into the snow, and his hands were in my hair, running along my cheeks, gripping the back of my neck, and the tight grasp I'd had on reality slipped through my fingers like smoke. We'd danced around our attraction, using words as ammunition, and now that neither one of us was talking, we could finally hear one another.

I need you, my body screamed.

I'll give you anything, everything, his body responded, pressing against mine.

Cold seeped into my clothes, and a shiver ripped through me. He pulled away and wrapped his arms around me, tugging me out of the snow, cradling me between his knees. "Can I take you inside?"

"Yes."

Without a word, he stood, picked me up, and held me to his chest. His mouth was on me again, on my neck, nipping, sucking.

"The guys should be coming back any minute from lunch," I said, remembering where we were.

"Do you promise to be quiet?"

There was a logical answer to that. I'm sure there was. But all my mind could come up with was *Must. Have. Now.* I nodded.

In the span of three long breaths, Ryder had me inside the lodge and backed me through the door of the old storeroom at the far end of the resort. He pressed me up against the bookshelf, palming my breasts, his mouth devouring mine.

My mind went blissfully blank as he pulled my hoodie and my shirt over my head and continued feverishly kissing his way across my chest.

"I've been thinking about you for months, Zoey. I couldn't get you off my mind." Another kiss to the valley between my breasts. "One time was not enough."

The desperation in his voice had a direct line to the space between my thighs. One more time would never be enough.

His fingers dug into my hips as he ground into me, and I groaned as his erection pressed against my stomach.

More. Needed more. Faster.

I pulled his shirt over his head, and the fabric gave way to hardened muscle, ink splayed across his chest, down his arms. His breath hissed through clenched teeth as my fingers traced over each groove of muscle. This man, always so sure, so damn cocky, fell apart under my touch. His eyes squeezed shut, lashes feathering across his cheek.

"Zoey," he said, my name a plea.

I spiraled, cast out to sea, so far that I couldn't spot the shoreline anymore.

He brushed a strand of hair out of my face and tucked it behind my ear, his palm cupping my cheek. His thick, calloused fingers caressed my skin, and I whimpered, leaning into his touch, and slipped farther out to sea, each wave of need shattering reality.

His lips worked from my neck down to my stomach and stopped at the button of my jeans. I looked down at him, on his knees, his worshiping eyes dilated as they devoured me inch by inch.

"You okay with this?"

"Yes." But then remembered he'd just gotten out of his cast. "Wait, what about your leg?"

"Flash, not even a broken leg is going to get in the way of me tasting you."

Well, then. Who was I to argue with the man?

He unfastened the button and pulled my jeans to the floor. I hastily stepped out of them, and his hands returned, cupping my ass, trailing down the inside of my thighs, my ankles. His lips started at my knee and worked along the muscle of my leg until his mouth hit the edge of my panties.

My head knocked into a shelf as he moved the lace to the side and his tongue met the aching space between my thighs. Sparks exploded behind my eyes as I writhed against his touch. His thumbs dug into my hips, stilling me against the bookcase.

His tongue continued at a relentless, maddening pace. Heat spread from my core, scorching everything in its path as I floated on the edge. Only one lick stood between me and complete obliteration.

"I—oh God." A swirl. A single flick of his tongue and my world turned to a jumble of incoherent words, rough fingers digging into my skin, and my entire being hinging on his mouth's every move.

My fingers fisted his hair, yanking him closer, greedy to take everything he had to offer. When he groaned, reality sat ten miles below me as I floated, losing myself in his touch.

He sat back on his haunches and smirked.

Footsteps echoed through the empty building, pulling me out of my blissful state.

"Zoey? Are you here still?" someone called.

"Shit." I slammed back into Earth's gravitational field. "Shit, shit, shit."

Work. The resort. My client currently on his knees with my taste on his tongue.

Oh God, what was I thinking?

Chapter Eleven

Ryder

"Put your shirt on. Hurry!" Zoey whispered.

I'd never seen a woman dress so quickly in my life. She managed to get her jeans and shoes on before I'd pulled my shirt over my head.

"Stupid. So damn stupid," she kept muttering.

"Flash, it's okay. You're dressed."

"No, Ryder. It is not. We're at my work. What if my contractors had walked in on us?"

"I'm sorry." This was not how I pictured the aftermath of me getting down on my knees for her.

"I'm going to head out there and see if they need anything. I think it'd be best to take a breather for the rest of the day."

"Yeah, sure." I played it off as no big deal, but we had to talk about this. No way in hell would I take ten steps back when it came to her.

She barely waved good-bye as I made my way out to the parking lot.

• • •

Almost a week later and she hadn't texted back except to update me with resort progress. I kept mulling it over in my head, replaying the interaction. I still couldn't figure out what I did wrong. Maybe I never would.

I sat back in my recliner, clicking through channels, finally landing on a *The Walking Dead* rerun. My phone rang just as my mind began to drift.

I glanced at the phone and muttered under my breath before I answered. "Hi, Grandma."

"How is the situation with your brother going?"

Didn't even bother with formalities. All business today.

I paused my show and massaged my temple, waiting for the impending migraine to start. "What situation?"

"Convincing him to sell."

"If by convincing him to sell you mean starting renovations, then it's all going to plan. He seemed pleased with the design and made it into work last week."

Not that I'd admit it to anyone, but the resort was starting to grow on me. I'd made another trip up to Divinity the other day, and with everything cleared out, I was able to see Jason's vision for the renovations. Right now it was a shell of a place ready to store new memories.

"I'll believe that when I see it," my grandmother huffed. "I've talked to our lawyer, and he knows someone who is interested in the property."

"Then you'll have to run that by Jason." I didn't know why Grandma was coming to me with the scheming. I wouldn't turn on my brother in this lifetime or the next.

Did I want the resort to sell, now that renovations were underway and everything in my personal life was up in the air? Not really. Two months ago, the thought of investing this much time into a project with a woman who was only supposed to be mine for a night would have had me on the next plane to Chile. I waited for it—the urge to run—and nothing came. I wanted to finish this renovation, and I wanted to explore *more* with Zoey.

Now I just needed to get on the same page with her. My stupidity took us five steps backward in the progress we'd made.

"He won't return my calls," she said.

"I'll send a text. Is there anything else I can do for you?" Normally I didn't care about my grandma's antics, but when this directly affected my brother, it was a different story. Not to mention Zoey. If the place sold in the middle of renovations, who knew what would happen with the contract with Zoey's firm.

"Your grandfather and I will be back in town in the next couple of months. I expect this all to be sorted out then."

"Sounds good." My grandparents were delusional if they thought Jason would ever sell the place. It meant too much to him. I hung up and tossed the phone on the cushion next to me.

Today was the day. It'd only been a few weeks since my cast had been taken off, but I wanted to try a run on my board. An easy one, nothing involving tricks, just a little shredding on some powder.

An hour later, I dropped my board in the back of my truck and made my way to one of the ski lodges about fifteen minutes from our resort.

My temples throbbed as I strapped myself in, watching the people riding down the mountain as the lift took me to the top of the trail. I needed this to work, needed some sort of normalcy to return to my life.

I sucked in a shaky breath as I hopped off the lift and rode to the crest of the hill. I sank into the snow and took a second to peer down the mountain. Easy. This was a simple run. All

I had to do was manage not to fall on my face, which I hadn't done since I was just learning how to board. Granted, these weren't ideal conditions to get back into the swing of things. The snow was fairly packed at this point, especially with no new snowfall in the recent weeks, but I'd boarded in worse.

I was stalling, on something I had never thought twice about.

Before I could psych myself out any more, I pushed up and positioned myself to ride down the mountain. A couple of kids in beanies rode up next to me before I made my descent and said, "Hey, aren't you Ryder Covington?"

I nodded.

"We saw your wipeout on YouTube. Cool that you're already back on the slopes."

I swallowed. "Ride or die." That used to be my motto, but today I just wasn't feeling that sentiment.

"Good luck, dude." They both gave me a quick high-five, and with that, they were off, carving two paths through the snow.

When they were a safe distance away, I tilted my board and started down the mountain. Shooting pain spiked up my left side, and I gritted my teeth, pushing through it. If I fell, it'd only make it worse.

My whole world tilted as I made the descent. With no conditioning over the past couple of months, my legs wobbled, unsteady and unsure. Too much of my energy was spent babying my left side. Sweat rolled down my face before I even made it halfway down the trail, and I was so focused on my stance that I came within inches of a tree before cutting a hard right…and face-planting in the snow.

I pounded my fist into the snow and maneuvered my board over so I could sit up. Nothing appeared to be hurt besides my pride.

"You got this. You've done this a million times before."

Right.

The part of me I liked to keep hidden away from the rest of the world was freaked as hell that I'd just fallen while doing something that came more natural than walking.

First time back. Nut up.

Next run, I managed to make it to the end without falling.

Two more times down the trail and my jaw ached from clenching my teeth, and my leg throbbed, so I decided to call it a day.

Even though I'd survived, I was far from competition ready.

Snowboarding was my zone. I used it to tune out the world. I'd take anything as a distraction right now—anything in the form of a designer who had gone MIA.

As soon as I got back to my apartment, showered, and pulled on a fresh set of clothes, I texted Zoey.

Ryder: *You alive?*

Zoey: *Barely. Been swamped with renovations.*

Ryder: *I saw. It's looking great up there. About last week…*

Zoey: *Snowboarding was fun, but my butt still hurts.*

Ryder: *That sounds like a personal problem. I can think of a way to help you out.*

Zoey: *You are sick.*

Ryder: *Your mind is in the gutter. I was going to say ice*

for 20, then heat for 20.

Zoey: *Uh-huh. Right.*

Ryder: *My hands are available for massages any time you need, though. Just sayin'.*

Zoey: *Good to know.*

Ryder: *What's your schedule like for the rest of the week?*

A few seconds passed by then an image of a piece of paper popped up on my phone. It read: *To-do list: 9:30-10:00 whine to Ryder about physical ailments*. The rest of the week was blocked out with: *Spend week at spooky resort.*

Ryder: *I've made it in to your planner? I feel like this is a monumental occasion. Maybe we should celebrate with dinner?*

Zoey: *Ryder…*

Ryder: *I at least want to talk about what happened last week.*

I swallowed hard. Time to stop tiptoeing around this. I couldn't stop thinking about her, and I wasn't going to let my personal rule of no attachments get in the way this time.

Before I could change my mind, I dialed her number. She picked up on the second ring.

"Yes?"

"Do you like wine?"

"Does the Earth revolve around the sun?"

"From what I remember in my eighth grade science class, yes, but I slept through most of it. I had this spinster of a teacher with a hairy mole."

She giggled, and the stress of the day faded into the background.

"Would you like to go wine tasting with me? There's a vineyard opening up just outside the city, and I hear that their cabernet is amazing." I quickly added, "If you're into that sort of thing. Jason was thinking of serving it at the resort, and I could use a second opinion."

"Are you…asking me out?"

"Yes." For once in my life, I was so damn sure this was what I wanted. Just one more date. Everything about this woman drove me crazy, and to just be in the room with her was enough.

"I don't know…" She trailed off, and sweat beaded on my brow.

"Zoey, the last time I asked someone out I had braces and that bowl cut you loved so much, so can you cut me some slack?"

She sighed and her hesitation was palpable over the phone. "You said it has to do with the resort?"

"Technically." The new manager that I'd hired early last week would be in charge of picking the alcohol to dispense at the resort, but this winery was on the list.

Silence flooded the line. I braced for her to shut me down again. If she did, I'd stop trying, because there wasn't anything left in my arsenal.

An agonizingly long time later she said, "I'm in. When do you want to go?"

Victory. "Friday night," I said.

"Okay."

Great. "It's a date."

"Is not. Just wine."

"Call it what it is, Zoey. I'll pick you up at six."

My lips pulled into a smile as I hung up. This was uncharted territory, but for the first time ever, I was ready to explore.

• • •

ZOEY

Friday rolled around five excruciating days later.

Socks, shirts, and a pair of shorts flew through the air as I entered Lainey's room.

"Going to see your mom this weekend?"

"Yeah." She stuffed a rogue sock into her duffel bag. "She's redecorating her office for spring and wants me to help. Even promised me Greasy Guys as payment if I handle the glitter and glue gun."

"Sounds like a great deal." My stomach rumbled. Oh, how I missed Portland food. Seattle had its fair share of eclectic dining, but I hadn't found any restaurants that were favorites, those go-to places for certain moods. Like when I was a bloated mess, I'd always pick up gyros from the food cart in downtown Portland. Or if my favorite ship on TV sank, there was the Chinese restaurant in the parking structure off of Grant. They had the best pink egg flower soup.

"Did you want to come with? There's an extra glue gun with your name on it." She waggled her brows.

"Tempting, but I can't." I hadn't mentioned my date tonight because I didn't know what to think of it. Half of me was doing a victory dance, and the other half of me side-eyed the crap out of my decision. And last time I slept with Ryder, he'd disappeared without a trace. Sure, that had to do with his brother's injury, but what was to say he wouldn't leave again?

She slid her gaze to me. "I didn't know you had plans?"

"I have a date."

"Please tell me it's not with that guy on Tinder who sent you pics of his Star Wars figurine collection."

"Well, you do know how those battle droids really do it for me."

"Is it…?" She raised a brow.

I nodded. "I told him we're going as friends. We're going wine tasting."

She let out a squeal. "That is *so* not a friends thing."

I motioned between us. "We go wine tasting."

"Yeah, but I don't want in your pants."

"Don't deny you'd totally tap this if you didn't have Brogan." I shook my butt at her and she smacked it. "But for real, what do I even wear?" I dragged her into my room, and she stared at the options I'd laid out on my bed—a high-neck dress and my work slacks. "Which one would you choose?"

"Depends. Are you trying to send the message that you like to cross-stitch and watch *Wheel of Fortune*?" She laughed and threw both outfits on my chair. "And seriously, don't you wear those pants to work on laundry day? Last time I checked, you had a closet full of *fun* clothes, Z."

She rummaged through my closet and came out a few seconds later. "Jeans and a cute top should work. You can borrow my boots if you want."

"Thanks."

"And text me if you need anything. And for God's sake, don't bring up random trivia facts."

"What? It's a good ice breaker," I said defensively. I did that for *one* date, and she never let me live it down. Granted, the guy did make an excuse that he had to leave halfway through dinner, so maybe he didn't appreciate my knowing that when people blush, the lining of their stomach also turns red.

"I think the ice is more than melted between you guys."

"Right."

"And you can tell him that if he's an ass, I will personally throat-punch him when I return."

"Noted."

Lainey gave me a hug good-bye and then was out the door in a flash. I stood in the middle of the apartment wondering if I could Google what to wear on a non-date date.

Forty minutes later and my hair was in the middle of a throw-down with my flat iron. Half my wardrobe was on my bed or in a mound on the floor, and I was two minutes away from a minor panic attack.

After I pulled on a fitted cashmere sweater and jeans, I turned to my cat, who was sprawled out on my desk chair, cleaning his face. "What do you think of this, Jitters?"

He didn't even deign to respond, just kept licking his paw.

"Right. Cashmere is for luncheons with clients." He was such an ego booster.

I stared at my reflection in the mirror. Five outfits later, I'd decided on dark skinny jeans, a flowy top, and my hair was pulled into a loose bun. It said *casual, friendship,* and *I'm not trying too hard*. Right. Why was I doing this again?

Ryder knocked on my door the moment the clock on my phone hit six. My breath hitched, and a heat wave worked its way up my back, to my neck, and ended at my cheeks.

Stay cool. You kissed. He did amazing things with his tongue. And you're about to imbibe copious amounts of wine, but you have this under control.

Hell, I had jeans on, everything was on lockdown. Not that that had stopped him last week, but that was beside the point. I could handle myself like a responsible citizen. Whatever I needed to tell myself to feel better, right?

I kept my hand firmly planted on the door handle as I opened it. My breath rushed out in a whoosh as I took in Ryder's hulking frame in the doorway. He wore a pale blue button-up that brought out his eyes, a pair of jeans that hugged all the right places, and his hair was the same mussed mop as usual. He smiled and handed me a single purple calla lily.

"Gorgeous. Thank you."

He mashed his lips together and looked down at his hands. "I know your duke would have something perfect to say, but everything that comes to mind is cheesy as hell, so I'll leave it at I'm excited to have dinner with you, and you look beautiful."

Gifts didn't typically do much for me, but this one was especially sweet. It showed he was actually listening. "Wait, I'm pretty sure you weren't around when this happened in the audiobook."

He shrugged. "I might have sampled the audio."

Wow. He'd tried out a romance novel because *I* was interested in it. What happened to the guy who left me high and dry in November? Hell, even the guy from two months ago. I put the flower to my nose, inhaling the sweet scent. "Ryder Covington. You really are full of surprises."

I strode into the kitchen, grabbed a small vase, and plopped the flower in with a little water. As I shrugged on my coat, Jitters hopped down from his perch on the couch and wound through my legs, purring loudly. I bent down and scratched behind his ears. "I'll be back later, sweetie."

"Who is that?"

I'd locked Jitters in Lainey's room last time Ryder was over because he tended to not like other men in the house. My possessive little alpha cat. "Oh, that's Jitters. He's my main man."

Ryder bent down to pet him, and Jitters hissed in response.

"He doesn't like strangers. Takes him a little bit to warm up."

"I used to have a cat when I was younger. His name was Milo. Was more like a dog with his fetch skills."

"Jitters can play dead." I stood, aimed my two pointer

fingers at him, and said, "Bang, bang."

The cat flopped down on the floor onto his back.

He laughed and the sound vibrated through my chest. "Your cat kicks ass."

I scratched Jitters on the tummy and then said, "Well, we should get going."

He opened the door wider and put his hand on the small of my back as we both exited my apartment. Professional Me should have slipped away from his touch. I should have declined this evening altogether. Instead, I leaned in closer to his touch. Resistance was futile at this point. I'd broken my rules—why was I trying to abide by them anymore?

We made our way to the parking garage and stopped at his truck where he helped me in the passenger side.

As he pulled open his own door, he climbed in and gave a quick, deliberate perusal of me, his gaze snaking down my chest to my crossed legs, then back up again. He'd barely said a word since we walked to the car, which was very un-Ryder-like.

"Want to plug the address into the GPS?" When I didn't say anything, he glanced over at me and frowned. "What? Why are you looking at me like that?"

"I—nothing." Don't mind me, just having epic flashbacks. Hands, lips, neck…name a body part and my mind was coming up with very creative ways to make use of it. I cleared my throat and entered the address of the winery into his dash navigator. If he could keep it together, I certainly could as well.

Thirty minutes later we pulled into the drive of the winery. Twinkle lights wrapped whimsically around the tree branches, and soft music played through the outdoor speakers. It was the perfect spot for a…date. Yup, this was a full-fledged, bona fide date that I'd just agreed to go on. No backing out now, not when sweet and savory spices mixed in the air with the promise of wine that cost more than ten bucks for a two-liter.

Like I said, Lainey and I were frugal, but it got the job done.

Ryder put his hand on the small of my back as we entered the lobby of the restaurant. It was a light touch that was anything but friendly, and I didn't bother to pull away.

A hostess came to the front desk, looking at the laminated layout of the restaurant sitting on the podium. "Would you like to sit at the bar or at one of our tables?"

"Table would be great," Ryder said. He returned his hands to his pockets and moved his neck from side to side.

She led us to a table overlooking the vineyard.

The sun had already set over the mountains, leaving blotches of pinks, oranges, and deep purples punctuating the skyline. A gorgeous early spring night.

She handed us two menus, and I stared at the selections of reds, whites, and sparkling dessert wines, my mouth watering. Lainey and I drank boxed wine because it'd been customary from our days in college and fit our broke young professionals budget, but it didn't mean I didn't enjoy the good stuff every once in a while.

Ryder's gaze scanned the menu and then focused on me. "I've actually never done this before."

"Really? Lainey and I went all the time in college."

He set the menu down, folding his arms on the table. "Is that where you two met?"

It was intoxicating, having his full attention focused on me. I'd been on dates where the guy spent more time with his phone than having an actual conversation with me. Ryder's was nowhere to be seen. Instead, his hands were clasped atop the table, and he looked at me like what I had to say really mattered. "We've been friends practically my entire life."

I sat back and stared at the sunset. To think, a few weeks ago, I could barely stand to be in the same room as him. And now my heart threatened to pound out of my chest with just one glance his way.

The wine came first, and I'd downed the first two samplers in record time. The delicious factor wasn't even taken into account. It was a survival tactic. More food in mouth equaled less stupid crap said.

"You tell Lainey you were going out with me tonight?"

"Actually, yes." I drummed my fingers along the tabletop. "She sent a message with me."

His brow raised at this. "Yeah?"

"She said to be nice, or else."

"I'm not buying she was that diplomatic about it."

"Okay, she threatened to throat-punch you."

He smiled. "I like her."

"She's the best."

"Seems like it. Friends like that are hard to come by. The only person I've been that close to is my brother."

Lainey was the sister of my heart. "They are." She'd been there for me when my mom died. She'd been there for everything, and I didn't know what I'd do once the time came for us to move out and go our separate ways. I kicked back the jigger of wine. Damn, this was good stuff. "You just missed her when you picked me up tonight. She's going to be away for the weekend at her mother's."

"Is that so?"

Why was I telling him this? This had to be the wine taking effect. That could totally happen within five seconds of taking a sip, right?

He thumbed the knife on the table and gently clinked it against the spoon sitting next to it on a crisp white linen napkin. "About last week…" He trailed off.

I set my glass down. "What about it?"

So, I'd done the coward thing and ignored the situation, throwing myself into my work. It was about 23 percent effective.

"Are you really going to make me say it?" He lifted his

brow. When I didn't answer, he straightened and blew out a breath. "What happened between us was intense. I figured we needed to talk this out."

"Yeah?" I swallowed hard. "What about your whole one-night rule?" As much as I wanted to blame my entire reluctance on my job, this was the real reason I hesitated when it came to him. Not that I thought Ryder was going to play me, but because he wasn't the type to stick around.

His lips pulled into a thin line. "I think we know that I've screwed that up. I tried the relationship thing once, and it failed miserably."

"I've screwed up many times. Did you know I almost brought flash cards on this date?"

His lips tipped into a smile. "What would they have said?"

"I like to have random facts prepared, just in case there's a lull in conversation."

"Okay, lay one on me."

"You really want to hear my Guinness record-worthy knowledge of random facts?"

He took a sip of wine, and I caught the slightest grimace ghosting his features. "Hell yes."

"A shrimp's heart is in its head. And a crocodile can't stick out its tongue."

"Interesting." He smiled and my chest squeezed.

"And, just like fingerprints, people have different tongue prints as well." I worried my lip between my teeth. "Sorry. I'm ruining this, aren't I?"

"No, I could listen to you share trivia facts all night if it meant spending time with you."

Boom. Duke Renau had nothing on Ryder Covington. A scary thought, especially since I'd been burned by this guy before.

"Ryder, what happens when you start your circuit again?"

He frowned. "I don't know. And I'm not able to make any

guarantees. But I know I'd sit here and choke down wine if it meant even one more minute with you."

Okay, back the truck up a moment. I wasn't supposed to want this. I always went for the sure bet. The riskiest thing I'd done not pertaining to Ryder was to try to match a yellow armoire in a beige room. "I don't know what to say to that."

"Say yes. Give this a shot. It's not perfect, but I feel like we should at least try."

My mind fuzzed over. It was the wine. It had to be. This was why I stuck to Tom Collins. Something that I could sip and savor, something that lasted. But I'd guzzled down the wine like it was on a BOGO sale. Maybe it was because I was with Ryder—without us constantly bickering, I didn't know what to do with my mouth, so I kept it busy. Drinking.

"You know how much this job means to me." Coward. I was using my job as a buffer. Sure, this went against office policy, but I'd already broken that, so I couldn't even really claim it as an excuse anymore.

"I do. And I'd never jeopardize that. But we're two consenting adults. I won't let this get in the way of business if you don't."

"Okay."

He cocked his head. "Okay what?"

"Let's do this." Why not? Might as well stop fighting it and enjoy myself for once.

Three glasses later and the room spun like a carnival ride. There was a teensy chance that I'd overdone it, but the dessert wine was good enough where I just couldn't pass it up. And wow, Ryder was really cute. Like, really, really cute. Did I mention how cute he was?

I hiccupped and set my glass down on the table, giggling. "I can't feel my teeth." Everything was pleasantly numb.

He chuckled and sipped at his glass of water. "I don't think you can normally feel your teeth."

"But I really can't now." I tapped my canines. "Completely numb."

"If that's the case, maybe we should get you something else to eat on the way home, Flash." He paid the bill as soon as the waitress handed him the check, and we both got up. I pulled my coat off the back of my chair and put it on, making my way around to his side of the table.

His arm wrapped around me, and I might have leaned in and nuzzled his shoulder. His chuckle vibrated through my chest. He said, "Let's get you home."

"Are you coming with me?"

He shifted his gaze down to me and his brows pulled together. "I'll make sure you get there safe."

I bopped the edge of his nose, leaning most of my weight on him. "You know, you're actually pretty sweet."

"I'm glad you're finally coming around and realizing this." He smirked.

"That! Stop doing that!" I pointed at him.

His lips twitched in the corner. "Stop doing what?"

Dammit, why was he so sexy? It would be much easier to have a client I *wasn't* attracted to. And as for those moments of complete sincerity that upped his swoon factor to thirteen, seriously, what was with this guy?

"That whole smirky thing. Girls eat that shit up."

He chuckled. "I only care if it works on one particular person, Flash."

It did.

We got into our ride, and I scooted toward the middle seat of the bench and rested my head on his shoulder. God, it was so comfy. All those muscles. All that warm skin radiating through his button-up. He really should wear less clothes. It'd be a gift to us all. My eyelids felt heavier by the second, and I spiraled into a darkness filled with visions of Ryder without a shirt and his lips on mine.

Chapter Twelve

Ryder

Zoey was toasted. We stopped at Taco Bell on the way back to her place, and she fell asleep with a bean burrito halfway to her mouth. I was doing my best to hold her up so I could get her into her apartment.

"I like your hands," she slurred.

"My hands?" I'd get her in the apartment, make sure she guzzled a sufficient amount of water, and then get out as soon as I felt confident that she'd be okay on her own.

"Yeah. They're strong. They feel so good on my body."

Shit. Focus. Do not look her direction. Which damn key went into this door? There had to be at least twenty on the key ring.

"Ever since the night we got together, I've fantasized about your hands on me." Her fingers walked down my chest, and I fought the shudder her touch elicited. She was off-limits tonight with a capital O.

"Zoey. As much as I'd love to hear what you fantasize

about in regard to me, I think maybe we should save this for a different time."

Find the damn key.

"That mouth of yours. You just talk, talk, talk so much. It's so much better at other things." She clasped her hands over her mouth, her eyes wide. "Did I just say that out loud?"

"Yes. But I'll take the compliment."

I finally found the correct key and turned the lock a few seconds later, breathing a sigh of relief. I just needed to put her down on the couch, make sure she was okay, and then I'd be out of here to take care of business in the safety of my shower.

"Oh, Jitters. Sweetie, did you miss momma?"

Her cat purred loudly while nuzzling against Zoey's leg. He eyed me suspiciously as I helped Zoey onto the couch, propping her legs on a pillow. Murderous eyes continued to stalk me as I moved into the kitchen in search of a glass for water. Scary to think even the animals in this apartment had glares perfected.

After opening at least five different cupboards filled with enough ramen noodles to feed a small village—and the damn disgusting La Croix—I found the stash of pint glasses. I turned around to go to the fridge and almost stumbled over the cat. What was his name? Jibber? No, Jitters.

"Move it along there, pal." I went to maneuver around him and his back arched, the hair on his neck standing in a stiff line. He bared his teeth and hissed at me.

Okay. It didn't take a genius to know he was two seconds away from making a meal out of my leg.

His tail twitched from side to side, and his eyes widened, his pupils dilating to demon-level.

I thought back to the trick Zoey had shown me. "Bang, bang." I pointed to the cat.

Hell, did he just arch a brow at me?

"Listen, I'm just trying to get water for your owner." I tried to move toward the fridge again, and Jitters let out a low, don't-screw-with-me growl.

"Okay, what do you want me to do?"

Was I really talking to a cat? Last time I checked, I was the alpha species here, the one with the opposable thumbs. A creature that couldn't even open his own can of food was not going to exert dominance over me.

"Move it, pipsqueak." I brushed past him, working my way to the fridge. Just as I put my hand on the door, a sharp pain radiated up my leg. "Shit!"

I glanced down to find the cat latched onto my leg. Claws bit into my skin, and I let out a grunt, shaking my leg to extract him. The little devil clung on harder, kicking his back legs into me, scratching the shit out of my jeans.

I braced myself against the counter, kicking my leg, trying to get him to unearth his claws from my pants and my shin. The damn thing let out another low growl.

"What? Fine. I won't go to the fridge. If I use the tap, will you let go of my leg?"

The cat narrowed his eyes at me, considering. This was ridiculous. Cats didn't understand humans. Tormented them and probably scarred their legs, yes, but there was absolutely no point in running my itinerary by him.

A few of his claws retracted as I scooted to the sink. Okay, maybe we were on to something here. I inched closer again, and another couple of claws released from my jeans. By the time I made it to the sink, he was back on the floor and my jeans and the blood blooming across the fabric were the only evidence that he'd attacked my leg. "Dude, what did fridge water ever do to you?"

He let out another hiss.

I turned on the faucet and filled the glass, keeping the cat in my peripheral vision the entire time. As I turned to leave the kitchen, he sat in front of me, tail twitching, his pupils still large with the thirst for my blood.

"We cool, man?"

I shook my head. What the hell was wrong with me?

I probably had at least a good two seconds before he pounced.

Deciding to play it safe, I walked a safe distance around him, giving him the space he needed. He let out a loud hiss before I exited the kitchen. I glanced back and his expression was clear: I own you. You're my bitch.

As I made my way out to the living room, Zoey lay there, softly snoring on the couch. Her arm was draped over the side, her fingers grazing the wood floor. Her eyelashes fanned across her face, and her blond waves draped over her cheek.

My chest tightened at the sight of her. She was stunning. And mouthy. And perfect in every sense—except for her taste in animals and beverages. I'd do just about anything to be hers, and for once that didn't scare the shit out of me.

• • •

ZOEY

My whole world tilted, and my eyes sprung open. I expected the interior of Ryder's truck, and instead gazed at my living room. Alcohol tended to put me to sleep, but rarely before I made it back home. Last time that happened was during my trip to Europe when we'd had one too many glasses of wine at a restaurant in Tuscany.

Stupid. Damn that delicious dessert wine.

Ryder sat on the chair across the room, watching over me.

"How did I get in here?"

"I carried you in."

Oh. Seriously, girl? Good thing Ryder was a nice guy, because if he'd been a slimeball… I didn't even want to finish that thought. "Thanks. That was nice of you."

He handed me a glass of water and I took a sip. "I couldn't find anything in there but ramen and Doritos. Do you want me to get you anything to eat? I think there's still a bit of the burrito in the car."

I glanced at my surroundings, making sure I didn't have anything embarrassing hanging around, like a bra or a box of tampons. Nothing as far as I could see, just Jitters sitting on his perch by the window, his tail twitching wildly. "Thanks. And no, I'm good."

Sitting there, legs spread as he slouched in the chair, he looked so inviting. He'd undone the top two buttons of his shirt and it was now haphazardly untucked from his jeans. The sleeves of his shirt were pushed up to his elbows, and I desperately wanted to see the muscles jump under his skin as his hands worked over me. His lips were tinged a deep red that made me think of apples, and dammit, now I was hungry.

"I think you should get some sleep. And maybe more water." He shot up from the chair. "I'll be right back. Let me get that for you."

"Is being nice a part of your master plan?"

"Plan for what?"

Toot toot. What was that? Oh, just the truth-bomb express heading straight out of my mouth. "To get me into bed." Damn wine and its ability to turn me into Honest Abe. Next I'd be admitting that time in ninth grade where I slipped the answers to a chemistry test to my friend.

His expression hardened, like he was upset that I even suggested the idea. "I'm not an asshole, Zoey. And any guy who would try to put moves on you while you're drunk doesn't deserve your time."

I pouted. "You're a fun-sucker, you know that?"

"Zoey, I want you so bad it physically hurts. But I'd never take advantage of you. Also, I'm selfish, and want you to remember every damn minute I'm inside you."

"I see what you did there." I pointed at him. Or at least I thought I was pointing at him. Currently there were two of him, so I had a fifty-fifty chance. "Saying minutes instead of seconds. You're just trying to entice me."

He chuckled. "I didn't know the bar was set so low," he said, handing me a full glass of water. I downed it in a few gulps and set it on the end table.

"What's with all the packages?"

I glanced to the stack of stuffed mailers piled on the counter, which I hadn't had time to open before my date. "Leggings."

"Wow. That's an impressive collection."

"Ha. Not even breaking the surface, my friend."

"Friend?" He looked up, testing the word in his mouth like someone tasting a new wine. "I like the sound of that."

"Me, too. I can talk to you. Although that may be the alcohol speaking."

"Probably," he said. He chuckled and sat back down in the chair across the room, opening a book. I glanced at the cover and realized it was mine, the one I'd left sitting on the coffee table before I'd left for tonight.

He pointed down to the page he'd opened to. "This lord does have major game."

"Are you really reading my book?"

"Sure. Wanted to see what all the fuss was about."

"And?"

"Not something I'd seek out and read on my own, but he has swagger for someone in the eighteen-hundreds. Although if I ever read the words 'stiff rod' again, it better be about a fishing pole or else it's game over."

I giggled. "Ryder?"

"What?"

"Will you cuddle with me?"

"Cuddle." He cocked his head like I'd just spoken another language.

"Yeah, you know, big spoon, little spoon. You have cuddled before, right?"

He regarded me, his eyes wary. "I don't know if that's a good idea."

"I promise I won't get handsy. Plus, don't you need to make sure I'm okay from all the alcohol?" I batted my eyes at him.

His brows scrunched together. "Are you okay? Is something in your eye?"

I sighed. "No." Well, shit. Drinking totally cramped my seduction skills. "Please, I would love some company."

After a few moments of contemplation, he sighed. "Fine."

"Just wait here a few minutes, okay?" I bounded toward my bedroom and grabbed a pair of leggings and a tank. After I brushed my teeth, I hopped in bed and pulled the covers over my chest.

"Okay, you can come in," I called.

Ryder stood in the doorway, looking uncertain.

"I'll stay for a little bit, but that's it," he announced.

"Fine."

He tugged his shirt over his head, revealing a notch of muscled stomach inch by inch.

"Holy mother of Christ." I didn't know if I said this out loud or not, but those abs never got old.

A smile pulled at his lips as he eyed me. "Should I put it back on?"

"Only if you want me to weep tears of sorrow."

He grinned. "I'd never want to make you cry, Zoey."

"Does that mean the pants are coming off, too?"

"Not a chance. Damn, Flash—drunk you has a one-track mind." He shook his head, but his face still held a smile.

"Are you at least going to join me on the bed? Or is that

off-limits as well?"

"I think I can manage that." He slid onto my bed, not getting under the covers, though. He was serious about not doing anything with me in my current state, which was both swoon-worthy and frustrating as hell at the same time because, oh, did I want him to do something.

Was it hot in here? Just laying a few inches from him turned my body into an inferno. I kicked the covers off one leg, cooling myself down.

"Are those cats on bicycles?"

I ran my hands along the pattern. I bought this pair two weeks ago, during a particularly frustrating email exchange with Ryder. "So what if they are?"

"They're cute." He chuckled. "I've never seen anything but black yoga pants."

"Would you rather me wear my pair with hula-skirt-wearing rhinos?"

"I'd rather you wear whatever makes you feel comfortable. I wouldn't change a damn thing about you."

Damn him and his stupid, swoony mouth.

I turned on my side and propped myself up, my head in my hand. "You know you have the most gorgeous eyes?"

"The better to stare into yours."

I snorted. "Where did you come up with that line?"

He grinned. "Just read it in that book of yours. Thought it was worth a try."

I smacked him in the chest. "You can't use a British lord's words against me."

"Never said I played fair." He stroked his fingers through my hair, and I leaned into his touch, savoring every time his fingers grazed my scalp.

My head nestled into the crook of his arm, his bicep making an incredible pillow. "Ryder?"

"Yeah?"

"I'm glad you're working on the project with me."

The skin around his eyes creased as he smiled. "Me, too."

"CEO is a good look on you." I turned and grabbed his other arm, draping it over my side. "But I think I might like this look even better."

"Hey, Flash?"

"Huh?" My lids were getting heavier by the moment. I had to struggle to stay awake while I snuggled into the warmth of Ryder's chest.

"Thanks for giving me another shot."

"Just don't hurt me, Ryder. I think I could fall for you." *Wait, did I say that out loud?* But before I could retract the statement, the world went black.

Chapter Thirteen

ZOEY

To Do List:

• Find different place to live once realization of last night's events hits.

I woke up with the sun beating down on my face, which lay plastered against something warm. A wall of muscle enveloped my entire field of vision when I cracked open my eyes.

Oh holy crap.

I blanched at the stale taste of wine and the whole cotton mouth thing I had going. This was exactly why I stuck to Tom Collins. My trusted friend Tommy never left me with a hangover, and I always remembered what happened the night before. How did I end up in Ryder's arms? Better yet, why was he in my bed? I peeked down at my fully clothed body. My bicycle-cat leggings? Jesus, just take away my license and never let me drink again. My only solace was the fact that drunk me opted out of the Bieber Believer shorts Lainey got me as a joke for my birthday one year.

Ryder was still asleep, his breaths coming out in long and slow huffs. He looked so peaceful laying there. His feet dangled off the end of the bed. I took my time perusing his muscles, his glorious muscles on full display. Today was officially deemed Man Candy Saturday. Or would that be Sexy Stud Saturday?

A smile spread across his lips, and his low, gravelly voice hit me square in the stomach when he said, "You checking me out?"

I quickly averted my gaze. "Am not."

He cleared his throat. "I think you are. Or you were."

"You don't even have your eyes open."

"Don't need to. Everything you do has so much focus, Zoey. If you stare at me any harder, I might burst into flames. You do have a fire extinguisher, just in case, right?"

I smacked him on the chest. Always so in tune to my movements. I'd never met anyone quite like him.

I laid my head back down on his bicep and inhaled his scent, trying to pinpoint why I liked it so much, besides the fact it smelled delicious. It was more than that—it made me feel warm, safe. "Thank you for making sure I got home okay last night."

"No problem."

"I…" I swallowed hard. "I didn't say anything too embarrassing last night, did I?"

"Nope." He grinned.

"Now I know you're lying."

"A gentleman never tells."

A very unladylike snort came out. "You, my friend, are not a gentleman."

"True. So, I guess I shouldn't say that you told me that my design game is on point. And you were impressed with my mad CEO skills."

"That was the alcohol talking." Okay, I could deal with random compliments. But I couldn't shake the nagging suspicion I'd told him I could fall for him. Although if I had, he'd be long gone by now. Ryder may have managed to stay until sunrise, but his track record proved it wasn't a habit.

"Was it the alcohol talking when you said you wanted your legs wrapped around my neck?"

I groaned. So it was officially settled—I would never be drinking a drop of wine again.

Our gazes connected, and heat unfurled deep in my belly. I was Zoey Reynolds. I once talked my way out of a debate on global warming at the Model UN. I could certainly tell a grown-ass man my feelings while sober. "That wasn't the alcohol."

"And are you still under the influence of alcohol?"

I swallowed hard. "No."

"Then if it's okay with you, I'd really like to try that out."

Everything slowed down to the point where all I could focus on was keeping my breath even as every inch of my skin lit on fire. "Yes."

• • •

RYDER

Zoey's hair framed her face like a halo. She was a goddamn angel, staring up at me with hooded eyes. I'd traveled to the most exotic places in the world, visited awe-inspiring locations. This, right in front of me, Zoey underneath me, wanting me, was the most beautiful sight I'd ever seen. Sappy as hell, but the truth.

My hands worked over her skin, spreading her knees apart, and she mewled. This woman would be my undoing. Every shred of restraint was frayed beyond recognition.

I brushed my chin against her cheek and took the fleshy

part of her earlobe into my mouth. She exposed the delicate curve of her neck, leaning into me, silently begging for more. I'd give her anything she wanted. Her happiness was my salvation.

I nipped at her skin again and was rewarded with a groan and her fingers digging into my back. She arched into me, her breasts brushing against my chest, and I pressed my forehead into hers, fighting to keep grounded.

Her body was so soft beneath mine, squirming, the bedsheets rustling beneath us.

For once, I didn't feel the need to make an excuse to leave. For once, I wanted to offer something more than one night of pleasure, because Zoey was worth it. She was the real deal, and I'd do my best to give her everything she deserved.

"Please, Ryder." Her hips bucked into me, grinding against my erection.

"Patience, Flash." I smiled down at her. "I want to take my time with you." I wanted to take her to the brink until she pleaded my name. I wanted every inch of her to be seared into my brain. I'd stripped her down to her underwear, and that alone was enough for me to come undone.

My tongue trailed down her neck, and I inhaled the sweet scent of lavender as I made my way toward her breast, taking a nipple in my mouth. I ran my tongue in a circle and she arched into me, letting out a tiny gasp. The noise went straight to my cock, and I throbbed for her. I'd physically ached for her for months. I pressed my lips into the flat of her palm. "You are mine."

She nodded. "I'm yours."

Her words obliterated my world. The trust in her eyes, the way she looked at me like I was worth a damn—I'd hit the jackpot. She writhed under my touch, pressed her body against mine, and the urge to connect with her, to be in her, almost broke my resolve.

Sex came second nature to me. But every move now was dedicated to earning Zoey's maximum pleasure. I listened to her breathing, watched every sudden dip in her stomach. Her expressive body was the roadmap I'd travel until she begged me to be inside her.

I kissed along the freckles dotting her chest, to the muscles in her arm, to her delicate pink fingertips. No surface on Zoey's body would go unexplored before we left this bed.

"Your mouth is so infuriating," she whined, shifting restlessly beneath me.

I chuckled. "Usually you only say that when I'm talking."

"Extenuating circumstances." She raked a hand through my hair, and I leaned into her touch. "I might die before we get to the good part."

"Such a whiner. I still have the left half of your body to explore."

My mouth was on her neck, kissing down the flat of her stomach, to the curve of her hip.

"I'm not above retaliation when the time comes," she ground out, her words strained.

I smiled against her skin. "Fine." I rolled to the side and reached down for my jeans, grabbing a condom out of my wallet.

I shrugged off my boxers and sheathed myself, watching her track my every movement. I couldn't deny that I enjoyed the way she looked at me, with a hunger that made every grueling day on the mountain and at the gym worth it. The bed dipped below my knees as I knelt in front of her. I slowly traced my way up her legs until I landed on the scrap of material at her hips and quickly removed it.

A sweep of my fingers was enough to find that she was ready. I took a deep breath. This was it. I'd imagined this so many times while I was alone, with only the use of my hand. Nothing would ever compare to Zoey. She wasn't something that I could replicate; I could only savor every second and pray I didn't screw up again. She lay there, spread before me, her hands clawing at the sheets.

"Please, Ryder."

I positioned myself between her legs and lost all sense of reality when I slid into her. Better than the first time. A moan ripped out of her throat as I sunk in again. So. Fucking. Good. I could say Zoey was like a drug. That I'd had one taste, and now I'd be jonesing for my next fix forever. But that'd be a lie. Junkies sought out the next high, but it was never as good as the first. What Zoey was giving me was precious and pure and something that only got better with time.

I grabbed her legs and positioned them to fold over my shoulders, knowing that angle made her tick last time. She squeezed her eyes shut and clawed at my biceps, the sexiest moans spilling from her mouth. This woman. This beautiful woman who drove me absolutely nuts. Who managed to make me laugh at one of my lowest points. She'd given herself to me, and I'd worship her every breath.

I climbed toward my release, holding back to ensure she drifted first.

I thrust into her, still wondering how I ever got so lucky that she gave me another chance. She squeezed at my arm, and when I looked into her eyes, at the softness in her gaze, I lost it.

We spiraled together, and I knew I'd never get enough of Zoey Reynolds.

I covered her scream with my kiss, wringing out every last bit of pleasure from her body. When my mouth left hers, she smiled up at me with hooded eyes.

"Good morning," I said, planting a kiss on her forehead before taking care of the condom.

She let out a low, shuddering breath. "I like waking up this way. I could wake up that way every day if I had to."

I chuckled. "Same."

I dipped back onto the bed and resumed committing her skin to memory, kissing touching, nipping along every surface. I wanted to remember this—her touch, the look in her eyes—because I didn't know how long I'd have her.

The blissful state faded as I pulled her into my arms. "How is this going to work?"

Shit. Good question. I planted a kiss on her palm. "I think we are doing a pretty good job so far."

She bristled, and her designer mode was taking over in full force. "I mean it. How are we supposed to act when we're at the resort together?"

"Besides you giving me death glares from across the room?"

She shot me a look.

"See, you have that down to a science."

She laughed and swatted at my chest. "I mean it. If my boss finds out about this, I'm toast."

I'd never do anything to jeopardize her job. It meant too much to her. "He won't. You and I are the only ones who know. And you don't have to have a plan for everything, Zoey. How about we take this one day at a time?"

This was uncharted territory. There were no answers. One step at a time.

"The painters are coming on Monday. Are you going to join me?" She looked up at me with those eyes I could never say no to.

"You know I'd do anything you asked."

And I meant it.

Chapter Fourteen

Zoey

Rule #17: Never break the five commandments of the office, especially in the workplace.

Working side by side with Ryder proved to be a larger distraction than I'd thought possible. Even though our paint job moved at a glacial pace due to random barrages of kisses and ass swats, the remainder of the resort was well under way. Ryder and I had driven up together in his truck this morning. We holed ourselves up in one of the guest bedrooms while my team worked on the main area of the lodge. I'd chosen a pale blue for this room that would lend itself well to the four-poster bed and white-and-blue bedspread we'd settled on. All of that was scheduled to arrive by the end of next week.

I had exactly three more weeks to get this place in order before the production company sent someone to film. Lance and I had finalized dates this morning. It'd be a stretch, but I'd pulled bigger miracles than this one out of my ass.

"Mind if I play music while we work?" Ryder asked, pulling out his phone.

"Sure." I hadn't really thought about it, but it would probably make the time go faster.

He smiled over at me. "Good. I made a playlist."

"Look at you. This place really does bring out your early two-thousands roots."

"Hey, I didn't burn you a CD."

I shrugged. "Semantics, really."

He didn't bother with a response, just shook his head and started up the playlist.

The Queen track that had seemed to haunt me for the past few weeks blasted from the speaker on his phone. "Oh, you did not seriously put *Flash* on there."

"I thought you might enjoy it," he said, and then started humming along.

I put my hands on my hips, trying to smother my smile. "You do know that the song is actually about Flash Gordon and not the super hero, right?"

"What was that you said before? Semantics." He dipped his roller into the paint pan and spread a thick coat of the blue onto the wall, this time belting out the lyrics.

"Don't you use my words against me."

"What was that? I can't hear you over this awesome song." He continued to paint, smirking.

And with that, I globbed paint onto my roller, and before Ryder could move away, I rolled it across his cheek. I managed to get his ear, lips, and nose before he backed away. "You're just asking for it today. First in the bedroom and now with the painting. I'm beginning to think we have a problem."

"You're my only problem." I managed to get him on his arm this time, the paint splattering over his tattoos. I laughed at how ridiculous he looked, like he'd had a bad run-in with a Smurf. I laughed until my stomach hurt and tears blurred my eyes.

Cold paint smooshed in my hair and down my back as Ryder used my moment of weakness to get retaliation. "That mouth of yours is going to get you into trouble."

A throat cleared behind us, and I swiveled around to find Jason sitting in the doorway, looking between the two of us, his forehead wrinkled.

I gasped. "Mr. Covington." I set the roller down in the pan and made my way to Ryder's brother. "I didn't know you were coming to the site today."

"I wanted to see how the renovations were going, so I had my driver take me up for the day."

Shit. "So happy you could stop by." This looked bad. So, so bad. We were covered in paint, and he'd just witnessed us flirting. My stomach bottomed out thinking about the consequences. What if he told Lance? Unlike Ryder, Jason was a stickler for rules, and I didn't know how he would react to the scene in front of him.

He looked from me to Ryder again. "I like the color you picked," he said hesitantly.

"Thank you. Ryder helped pick it out." Silence spanned between us, the only noise being the stupid Queen song in the background. Awkward. So damn awkward.

"Yes, it looks like he's been very helpful." He gave his brother a knowing look. He wasn't dumb—it had to be plain as day what was going on here. The evidence was literally on our bodies.

"J," Ryder's voice was a warning.

Jason nodded and started to back out of the room. "Next time, try to keep all of it on the walls. This is my money, you know." But there was a hint of a smile.

I cleared my throat. "Right. Of course." I didn't know whether I should be relieved or terrified. Maybe both. This was my job, and the second time I'd put myself in a compromising position.

As soon as he left the room, the tightness in my chest eased up. How could I have been so careless? The crew wouldn't care if they spotted a little flirting, but anyone could come on the site, including my boss. If he saw? Cue the sad trombone and the walk of shame as I carried my possessions out of my office in a cardboard box. Sex really had turned my brain to mush if I let all my personal rules fade away when Ryder was around.

He strode over to me, his expression serious. "I can tell what you're thinking right now, and I know Jason won't say anything."

"That could have been Lance. If it was—" I shook my head, not able finish the sentence. This meant too much to me to botch it. "I think maybe we should work in separate rooms today. Or maybe you could take the day off and go enjoy the sun while I kill brain cells by inhaling paint fumes." I tried to keep my voice light, but I was too shaken up to put on an act.

"You're kicking me out of my own resort?"

"Yes." I shoved him toward the door. "Because I won't be able to concentrate if you're here."

We needed to be more careful. At least until this project was over. Forget being fired, I didn't want to give him any reason to question my work, not when this job was going to propel my career.

I'd barely spoken to Ryder the rest of the day. Instead, I'd tasked him with helping a few of the crew members apply coats of white paint to the baseboards while I continued to work in the bedrooms. I still couldn't shake his brother walking in on us, what it'd mean for my career if my boss found out. By the time Ryder dropped me off that evening, I could barely kiss him good-bye.

By nine, I'd bought another three pairs of leggings with two tops to match. Right as I was going in for a fourth, my phone buzzed.

Ryder: *Would you rather lose your sense of smell for a year or only be able to smell pickles for a month?*

I smiled. Leave it to him to come up with something completely random.

Zoey: *You're getting better at this game. And lose my sense of smell for a year. I hate pickles.*

Ryder: *Then ignore the pickle of the month club subscription I had sent to your house.*

I sank back into my bed and inhaled. The smell of Ryder still clung to my pillow. I'd take a month of pickles if it meant he'd sleep in my bed again.

Zoey: *Ha. Ha. Would you rather have round two of last night or have a flawless snowboarding career?*

Ryder: *Projecting on me? Round two for sure.*

Ryder: *You surviving over there?*

Zoey: *Barely*

Ryder: *How many pairs of leggings did you buy?*

Zoey: *One*

Ryder: *What's that saying? Liar, liar….*

I rolled my eyes. Dammit, why did he have to know me

so well?

Zoey: *Okay, fine you stopped me from purchase #4*

Ryder: *Would this cheer you up?*

A picture popped up of Ryder's smiling face, flecks of blue in his beard. My heart stuttered just looking at those ice-blue eyes. A color that should be chilly was so warm and inviting on him.

Zoey: *Maybe a little.*

Ryder: *What about this?*

Another pic came in, this time of his abs. Splattered paint managed to find its way onto his skin, even though he'd had a shirt on the entire time. Okay, now we were talking. No more need to impulse buy.

Zoey: *My one-click finger has been safely stowed away.*

Ryder: *Oh good. Do I get to see my dirty work, too?*

Psh. If I took a pic where some of the paint had embedded, I'd for sure be breaking state laws. Instead, I took a pic of the dirty dishes piled in my sink and captioned it: *This dirty enough for you?*

Ryder: *It's so dirty it needs a NC-17 rating.*

Zoey: *I thought you might like that.*

Ryder: *We good?*

Zoey: *Yeah, we're good.*

Ryder: *Good night, Flash.*

Zoey: *Night.*

Chapter Fifteen

Ryder

"Princess or round cut?"

Brogan held two rings in front of me, sweat dotting his forehead. They all looked the same to me—shiny and expensive.

I'd support my buddy in his quest to find the perfect engagement ring, but he had to know this was way above my paygrade in terms of knowledge. "I don't know, man. Which one do you think Lainey would pick for herself?"

There. A somewhat helpful answer. Always bring it back to the woman because she'll be the one wearing it for the rest of her life.

His frown deepened, and he appeared to be a few short breaths away from needing a paper bag. "I don't know. She likes simple, elegant stuff. She never wears any big jewelry."

If I had to guess what Zoey liked, she'd be into unique, antique rings. Something that fit her personality. She liked to be different from everyone, had her own style, and I liked that about her. Then again, knowing her, she already had printouts and an itemized list of rings in her planner.

I looked back at Brogan's selections. "Then I'd scrap the one in your right hand." I jutted my chin to the three-carat rock set in a cluster of smaller diamonds.

His brows knit together. "Yeah, you're probably right." He put the ring back on the black velvet cushion and reached for the next one in line, eyeing it so hard he was bound to burst a vessel before he made his pick. "Dammit, why does this have to be so hard?"

"I don't know, man. You'll find something."

I did find it annoying that it was up to the guy to pick something so monumental. If it were me, I'd at least take the woman to scope out jewelry before I proposed. Not that I was anywhere near that stage.

"Have you thought about how you're going to ask her?" I said, trying to keep him reasonably calm.

His shoulders relaxed a bit, and he studied the simple solitaire ring between his fingers. "I have something planned. We're working on an employee manual together. I'm thinking about slipping in a few specific rules in her copy."

"Nice."

"You think so?"

"Man, I'm the last person you should be asking for advice when it comes to that stuff. Look at my track record."

It was true. My dating history was shorter than a haiku. And then there was Brogan. An owner of a Fortune 500 business, about to pop the question to someone he loved enough to sweat it out in a jewelry store for over two hours. I didn't even know what I was having for dinner tonight.

What did Zoey see in me? A twenty-five-year-old snowboarding washout, if my last three runs down the mountain were any indication. She was on her way up the ladder at her design firm. If I didn't go back to sports, I didn't know what else I had to offer her.

"Doesn't mean you can't get back on track. It only takes one girl to change your mind." His face beamed. In fact, I'd never seen him so happy. "Before I met her, I was resigned to the fact I was going to be single until I retired. She lit up my life."

Damn. My friend had fallen hard for this woman if he resorted to clichés. But I got what he meant. Zoey didn't quite light up my life—more like incinerated it with a blow torch. I'd happily walk through the flames with her.

"Sounds like you found a keeper," I said. Even if I didn't trust her if any knives were within reach.

His smile broadened. "I did."

"Hope one day I'm lucky enough to have what you do with Lainey."

Just a few weeks ago, I couldn't even think past a night with a woman. Now, all I could think about was when I'd get to see Zoey again. My past self would have found this pathetic. But my past self didn't know what it had been missing the first time around with her.

I stared at the rings in the case. Maybe Brogan was right. It only took one woman to change everything.

• • •

ZOEY

To-do list:
1. Nothing.

T-minus fifteen days until this design job was finished. Four days and sixteen hours since I'd seen Ryder. But who was counting, right? With everything ordered for the project, the team was waiting on the final design elements to be delivered, which weren't supposed to arrive until later this week.

I'd managed a lazy Sunday so far. Forgoing my morning yoga, I slept in until seven. I hadn't even changed out of my sweats yet as I sat in front of the TV, watching Ina create another masterful dish. As far as days off went, this constituted as a win. Maybe not Ferris Bueller level in terms of excitement, but I'd take it.

"Just take a pinch of salt and add it to the pan. Make sure to keep stirring, because you don't want the butter to burn."

I knocked my head back against the couch and took a sip of my spinach smoothie. If only I could cook like the people on TV. But I'd proven myself unworthy of wielding a spatula in any capacity. And a stove? I glanced over at the hulking metal object in the kitchen that yielded nothing but charred crust and heartbreak. Yeah, I was staying far away from that.

I checked my phone again, looking to see if I had any new emails. Okay, so I sucked at this whole relaxing thing. I needed something to get my mind off the fact that the next few weeks would decide my fate at Bass and Goldstein. I just hated that I couldn't do anything about it. I was at a complete loss for something to control, and it made my mind spin.

I glanced back to the cooking show; Ina was making a batch of brownies and my mouth watered in a Pavlovian response. Lainey was the baker in the household, but she'd been so busy lately at work, she probably wouldn't have time to cook this week. And those brownies looked so damn delicious. My stomach growled in agreement.

Cooking looked like an excellent distraction. Plus, Ryder loved brownies. After he'd been so great about everything, especially making sure Jason wouldn't say anything to my boss, I thought it would be nice to make him a sweet treat. I squinted back over at the stove. It looked innocent enough at the moment. I mean, really, how hard could they be to make? I'd seen Lainey do it tons of times. We even had that bomb Costco Ghirardelli brownie mix in the cupboard that only required oil and an egg. A toddler could manage that.

I looked to the television for reassurance. If someone on the Food Network could do it, I definitely could.

Okay, it was decided. I'd make brownies. And okay, I'd eat half the pan before I packaged up a few squares for Ryder on a Dixie plate, but he didn't need to know that.

I grabbed Lainey's mixer from the cabinet and gathered all the ingredients on the counter.

Phew. I stretched my neck and cracked my knuckles. Deep breaths. It'd been a while since I mixed anything more than yogurt and granola, but there were literally four ingredients in this whole thing. If a child could manage an Easy Bake Oven, then there was hope for me.

I read the package, mixed the ingredients and poured them into a glass pan. I even remembered to grease it with Crisco. Zoey: 1 Stove: 0

By the time I plopped the brownie mix into the oven, I was on the verge of world domination. Or at the very least, would have tasty brownies in approximately fifty minutes. Just change my middle name to Rachel Ray, because my bad-luck baking streak was coming to an end. If only Lainey could be here to witness this. Of course, if she were here, she'd tell me to put down the spatula and back away from the kitchen, slowly. She didn't exactly have a lot of faith in my baking abilities. Not that I blamed her. There was that whole grease fire in college that nearly took out the apartment, so she had every right to not trust me. But really, this was a piece of cake—or brownies, I should say. I'd watch the oven closely, and these bad boys would be cooked to perfection. I could wrap them up nicely for Ryder and attempt the I-don't-know-where-we're-at-in-regard-to-a-relationship-but-here's-some-baked-goods dance around the topic.

I sat down on the couch and turned on an episode of Cake Boss. There was seriously nothing better than watching those beautiful cakes be decorated. Maybe after I made the brownies, I'd sign up for a cake class at the shop downtown. I could surprise the heck out of Lainey with my newfound kitchen ninja skills.

My phone buzzed and I grabbed it off the table. Ryder. Before I could catch myself, my lips had already pulled into one of those stupid, sappy grins, one that, if my face were put into emoji form, would have heart eyes and a kissy mouth. Is this what relationships did? Not that I was in one, of course. I mean, we were taking it one day at a time. But each day since we'd gotten together had been pretty darn awesome. Besides almost getting caught by Jason. Good thing we only have three more weeks and then Ryder was officially off my client list.

Ryder: *Want to meet up later?*

Zoey: *Sure. Give me a couple hours. I'm working on something.*

Ryder: *Does this something involve zero clothing?*

Zoey: *Nope, #teamfullyclothedinsweatpants all the way.*

I looked down at my clothes. I hadn't even bothered to change out of my sweats and tank top, because when I had the odd day off, I didn't really worry about things such as hygiene or being a potential biohazard. But crap, I had two hours to change my appearance from garbage fire to semi-presentable. I hadn't shaved since the whole wine tasting incident and things down there were getting a little scary.

Jitter plopped down beside me and rubbed his head against my elbow. "You think I should take a shower?"

He collapsed next to me, putting his paws straight into the air. "C'mon, that's just insulting. I didn't think I smelled *that* bad."

He thought better than to stick his tongue out. Instead, he meowed and nuzzled closer to me. "Seriously, we need to work on your tact. You're going to give a girl a complex." I scratched under his chin as I excavated myself from the couch, and when I turned around, Jitters had claimed my spot. I pulled up my music app on my phone and blasted my Taylor Swift station while pulling off my clothes.

After I ran the shower, I stood under there for a long time, letting the water stream over me. The Taylor Swift station was totally on point today, and I'd jammed out to at least half a dozen songs before managing the whole hair situation.

While I continued to un-yeti my legs, my mind slipped into designer mode. Showers always seemed to spark the best ideas. I needed one of those doodle pads that stuck to the wall so I could scribble designs. I was heavy into thinking about rich textiles to pair with these spectacular vases I saw at an antique store downtown, when a loud beep echoed through the apartment.

What the hell?

I peered around the shower curtain and my gaze locked on the smoke curling under the door.

Smoke?

What in the world…

And then it hit me.

The oven. My brownies that were supposed to be cooked to perfection.

No, no, no. The first time baking in months could not end in disaster.

How long had I been in here? Obviously long enough to set off the smoke alarm.

I shut off the water and grabbed my towel, booking it

out of the bathroom. The sprinklers hadn't turned on yet so it couldn't be too bad. I held a sliver of hope that maybe they were still salvageable. As I rounded the corner to the kitchen, black smoke snaked through the hallway. Double shit. Okay, the edible probability just dropped to 0 percent.

Flames poured out of the oven, and I coughed, holding the edge of my towel to my nose. All I needed was to get to the fire extinguisher before the whole kitchen went down in flames. Or before the sprinklers activated and turned our living room into a swimming pool. No big deal. Christ, Lainey was going to murder me. And then she would bring me back to life just to force-feed me the charred remains of my baking catastrophe.

Nope. Not happening. I'd get the extinguisher and put the fire out before that happened. I stared at the cabinet next to the sink, the one currently housing my little red life-saver. The cabinet next to the burning stove.

Okay, no need to panic. Towel. Yes, that would do. I unhooked the towel from my body and tried to tamp down the flames as I reached into the bottom cabinet. With ninja-like precision, I grabbed the canister in less than a second.

Fire extinguisher acquired. My pulse beat wildly in my temples as I realized I'd never used one before. Seriously, Past Zoey sucked big time for never bothering to study up on the instructions, because right now wasn't exactly an ideal time to spend precious seconds reading.

After a few times struggling with the release and handle, I finally got it to work and doused the flames. I knew enough to turn off the oven and let the flames inside die down. There was a glass half full aspect to this—at least I managed to get this all under control before the sprinklers—

Water shot from the ceiling as if by my just thinking it, the sprinklers decided it'd be a good time to turn on. "Yeah, you're a little late on that one," I yelled as I opened windows.

Jitters meowed and ran under the sofa, cleaning his drenched fur.

I looked out at the living room, the smoke detector blaring, a cloud of burnt brownies hanging heavy in the air. Disaster.

Um, yeah, totally screwed. Lainey was going to kill me.

"Flash? What happened?" Ryder yelled over the detector.

I swiveled around to find him standing in the doorway, his eyes wide.

"Help me turn it off," I yelled, pointing to the device on the ceiling that I wouldn't even be able to reach if I stood on a chair.

At this point, I realized I was still holding the fire extinguisher and I was bare-ass naked. He made quick work of unhooking the smoke detector and silence pulsed through the apartment. He rushed over to me and pulled me into his arms, taking in my disheveled state and frowned. "I feel like I'm overdressed for the occasion."

I banged my head against his chest, cringing at the mess I'd made. "Shut up. I had a situation."

His hand stroked down my cheek. "Are you okay? You're not hurt are you?"

"Yeah, I'm fine. I just tried to bake."

"Here, let me help you." He disappeared into the bathroom and came out seconds later with a fresh towel, wrapping it around me and pulling me into a hug. Jitters took a swipe at him as he walked by. "You do know that you're supposed to take stuff out of the oven *before* it burns, right?"

"Really? They don't mention that on the cooking shows," I deadpanned.

"Didn't Lainey ban you from the kitchen?"

"Yes." I groaned, looking at the apartment, the wood floors now a massive puddle.

Good news: the sprinklers managed to miss the electronics.

Bad news: the couch would be soggy for a week.

"Go get dressed. I'll find some more towels and start cleaning up the mess," he said, and kissed the top of my head.

"Thanks." I stood on my tip toes and gave him a quick hug before disappearing into my room.

After quickly changing into jeans and a T-shirt, I made my way out into the living room. Ryder was on his hands and knees sopping up the wet mess and fending off Jitters, who was charging him with each swipe of the towel.

"Jitters!" I picked him up and went to my room, giving him the stink-eye before shutting the door. "I'm sorry, I don't know what it is about him and new people. I promise, he is a nice cat."

"I'll believe it when I see it," he said. Ryder had moved over to the stove, extracting the badly charred glass pan from the oven. The contents were completely unidentifiable. It looked like an inkblot test, one where you were supposed to find shapes. Right now, I could spot Santa's coal and my twelfth grade calculus teacher.

"What was this supposed to be?" He bit back a smile, but I didn't fail to notice the edges of his lips curling as he tried to keep a straight face.

I crossed my arms and bit my lip. "Brownies."

"Well, you almost have the color right," he said, flicking a charred mound that disintegrated upon his touching it. "What possessed you to do this?"

"I wanted to make you something."

"Aw, Flash." His expression softened, and he set down the pan and pulled me into a hug, chuckling. "You almost burned down half your kitchen for me?"

I nodded. Seriously, why did I even think that was a good idea?

He smiled down at me and tucked a piece of my uncombed hair behind my ear. "That is the sweetest thing anyone has ever done for me."

"Really?" I didn't know if that spoke more to the fact he had *really* crappy relationships in the past or the epicness of my baking disaster.

"Zoey, the fact that you tried something that is way out of your element is sweet." He looked around the kitchen. "Although, I don't recommend ever touching anything that isn't pre-cooked in the future."

"Yes, I've come to realize I'm more of a hazard than anything else when it comes to kitchen activities."

His arms circled my waist. "You know what I like?"

I looked up at him. "What?"

"Store-bought brownies. They're even sexier than homemade ones." He guided me over to the towel-covered couch, and I swung my legs over his and leaned my head against his chest.

"Now, that I can do. I can even buy Little Debbies, the ones with the filling in the center," I said.

He groaned. "I like when you talk dirty to me."

He leaned down and swept my lips into a kiss. Everything about being with Ryder just felt right. Even with the rest of my life in utter chaos, he buoyed me, and I was thankful for that.

Chapter Sixteen

Ryder

I sat on the ski lift, letting my board dangle from one leg. Take number four down the mountain. After taking my doctor's advice and easing up on my leg, everything started to run a little smoother. I no longer worried that my teeth were going to crack every time I walked on it. Spending time with Zoey also helped bandage some of the pent-up anxiety about not getting out on the slopes right away.

With Zoey inundated with shipments arriving and final preparations at the lodge, I figured it was as good a time as any to hit one of my favorite passes and see if my career was in the shitter. The last three outings ended in more cussing and falling than actual boarding. I could only hope that the rehab and training I'd done on my leg these past few weeks helped speed up the process of getting back on the mountain, permanently. Because as fun as it was overseeing the construction of the resort, I had to get back to reality. Spring training resumed in a few weeks, and the deadline to give an answer on whether I'd be attending was fast approaching.

Andy had called twice a day this past week, and I'd hit the reject button each time. I didn't have it in me to tell him about the first bad run, and the fact that three times down the mountain had only added to my doubt about my career.

I sat at the top of the slope, watching others carve down the mountain. The back and forth of their boards cutting through the snow calmed me. Hard breathing, cold wind against my cheeks, muscles straining before performing a trick—this was my domain. My home. I'd make this work.

My attention turned to a little kid, maybe ten or so, a few yards from where I sat. A high-pitched shriek came from his mouth as an older guy, probably his dad, tried to comfort him. The boy's knees visibly shook under his gear, and if I had to guess, I'd say this was his first time going down a pass.

"Jeremy, it's okay. You've mastered the bunny hill, but if you're not ready for this, we can go back down on the lift," said the man.

"It's always scary the first time," I said, the words coming out of my mouth before I could stop them. It was none of my business if the kid decided to take the lift, but I'd had that same fear—one that my mom had calmed, patiently talking me into giving the trail a fair chance. Behind that kid's scared-shitless expression, there was a spark, a glimmer of excitement. I saw it, it was there. Hell, maybe I had the same look on my face at the moment.

The kid paused, his mouth gaping open. "Aren't you Ryder Covington?" When I nodded, a huge smile speared his face. "I begged my parents for a snowboard when I saw you on the X Games last year," he said.

"Jeremy, is it?"

"Yeah."

"There's always going to be something that scares you, but you just need to face it head-on. There's no such thing as failing." I unhooked my board and walked over to him. "But if you want a little advice, bend your knees, don't flail your arms—it'll put you more off-balance."

"What if I fall?"

"You will. A lot. But it's worth it if this is something you want to do."

"I do, more than anything."

"Good. Then you will. Just don't get discouraged if you don't get it the first time. Trails tend to be a little tougher than the beginner's slope." I smiled at him. Maybe I needed to take my own advice. I'd been putting so much pressure on myself to be perfect the first few times back, and all it had done was put me into a deeper spiral.

He was silent for a moment, seeming to mull over my words. "Thanks," he said, and then looked up at his dad. "I think I'm ready."

His father nodded to me, and then Jeremy started down the mountain. The urge to ride down there with him, to make sure he was keeping his knees bent, to make sure he got down the mountain okay overtook me. I had to dig my fingers into the snow to remain seated. When he made it to the end of the run, he looked back up at me and gave a thumbs-up. I smiled and gave him one in return. That kid would be shredding down this mountain in no time.

I walked back to my board and strapped myself in. Time to take my own advice and stop being scared shitless. It would do nothing except stall the inevitable.

Snowboarding had been my life for so long, I didn't know how I'd come to terms with it if I wasn't able to continue on the team. It would probably feel similar to what my brother was dealing with, and yet he was back in the office now, like nothing had happened.

Just do it.

Overthinking wouldn't get me anything but a frostbitten

ass.

I stood and positioned my board. And then I was off. Carving left, then right. The wind streaked across my cheeks, and I readjusted my beanie as it rode up on my forehead. It was a perfect day on the mountain—completely sunny, no wind. I'd left my jacket in the truck and enjoyed the warm sun on my skin. Damn this felt good. Much better than a couple of weeks ago. Before I knew it, I was down the trail and cutting my board to a stop.

Hell yes.

Another lift up the mountain and I sped down the course, executing the basics—Butters, followed by an Air to Fakie, and a simple 50/50 grind. The tricks were simple, but my leg held up. My pulse hammered and my muscles ached, but I kept going, pushing, testing my limits. I amped up my music, taking run after run, my snowboard carving its signature into the snow. By the fifth time down the pass, I ruled out today's success being a fluke.

I let out a loud *whoop* and people turned to watch. I didn't care. Because I was back in the game. It was a small run, but I could feel it. I was back.

I pulled out my cell and dialed Andy's number.

"Ryder, man. I wondered if I was ever going to hear from you again."

"Sorry, Andy. Been a little preoccupied with my brother's business." And the fact that I was too chickenshit to call him back until I had a definitive answer for him. "I'm on the mountain right now."

"And?" He trailed off, and the desperation rung clear in his voice.

"And I'll be at spring training." This was it—things were finally going to return to normal. My old life was on the horizon.

"That's what I was calling about. It starts in one week.

You'll be able to make it?"

One week. Right when the resort project finished. When the TV show was scheduled to interview Zoey. She'd asked me to be there, too.

"I have a few things to check on first, but for right now count me in."

This was it. My chance to get back out there. But this time around, leaving didn't sound as exciting as it used to.

• • •

ZOEY

Ryder: *I have news!*

Zoey: *Use of an exclamation point? Must be something good.*

Ryder: *I'll tell you tonight.*

Zoey: *You know I love cryptic messages.*

Ryder: *See you later, Flash. Hope you're up for celebrating afterward.*

Okay, I could deal with cryptic messages when it promised to include *other* things. I tossed my phone on the bed and went back to the task at hand—preparing for next weekend. I'd already picked out my makeup, and how I wanted to do my hair for the interview, so all I had left was my outfit.

"Green dress or black one?" I held both numbers up to Lainey.

"Dude. We're just going out for drinks at Dean's."

"No, I mean for the TV show. There's only one more week, and I want to make sure everything is perfect before they come." The design went smoothly—only a few snafus with the orders and a minimal amount of water damage near the fireplace. Wrong throw pillows and a missing armoire. Irritating, but not the end of the world, and fixed quickly with a phone call. One more final tweak before the interview next Saturday, and I'd be set. Lance had even made a trip to Divinity and said this was my best design yet. I guess I had Ryder to thank for that, because the first design I'd given him paled in comparison to the end result.

"The green one will bring out the hazel in your eyes. The black one will bring out the sinister part of your soul. Which one do you feel like broadcasting on national television?"

Somehow unlocking the gates of hell wasn't quite what I was going for. "Green it is." I draped the dress over the back of my desk chair and shoved the black one back in my closet.

I took a deep, contented breath and closed my eyes. I'd reached a Disney character level of happiness. The bird chirping, magic carpet ride, bust out into song kind. All I needed was woodland creatures to do my dishes and wash my clothes, and this whole scenario would reach the pinnacle of perfection.

Between my career about to take off and things with Ryder working out, nothing short of a meteor crashing into the resort could ruin my good mood.

Ryder and Jason had been very accommodating, especially in regard to the interview. I'd been fielding droves of emails from magazine journalists wanting to feature the resort in their next issue. Even a snowboarding mag contacted us.

"You excited for next week?" Lainey asked, sitting on my bed, thumbing through a magazine.

"Of course. But what if I mess up and say something really stupid?"

"You hear what half the people on those shows say, right? Sometimes I don't think they're even speaking English."

"I'm representing my firm, though. It's different."

"Zoey. If you can rap an entire Eminem song in front of a crowded bar without flubbing, I doubt you'll have any issues with mixing up your words. Plus, I hear they can do retakes. So even if you do mess up, you can get another chance to be your lovely shining self." She prodded me with the magazine.

Lainey was always right. And if anything, I could sneak in a few notecards in case I got tongue-tied. Ryder would be there, too.

I smiled again. Giving him a second chance to redeem himself was possibly the best decision I'd made all year.

I grabbed my jacket from under Lainey's legs and shrugged it on. "Ready to head out?" I asked.

"Always." She rolled off my bed, and we walked into the living room to grab our purses.

Twenty minutes later, we walked into Dean's. It was packed, and like any other Friday night, people squeezed into every nook and cranny of the place. Brogan and Ryder were sitting in a corner booth, both sipping from tumblers. I scooted in next to Ryder as Lainey sat next to her boyfriend.

Boyfriend. I hadn't really considered the word when it came to Ryder, but I guessed that was what he had become over the past few weeks. Maybe? I was never good at deciphering the label thing, but he was as close to a boyfriend as I'd had in over a year.

"So, tell me this news you were so cryptic about over the phone." I quickly glanced to Lainey, who was practically in Brogan's lap. Seriously, those two. I'd never seen two people more in love.

I turned back to Ryder, who had a smile splitting his face. "I went back on the mountain today," he said.

"That's great!" He had that glow about him, the same

one he had when he taught me how to snowboard when we started renovations on the place. "How did it go?" The last few times, he'd come back from the mountain in a piss-poor mood. This was an obvious improvement.

"My leg feels good. I think I'm ready to start back with the team. And my manager just called and said all of my sponsorships have been reinstated now that I'm back on the roster."

"Amazing." And it was. This was his dream, and he was making it happen, even after a devastating accident. I admired that perseverance. "When do you start?"

His teeth hooked over his bottom lip, and he took a deep breath. "That's the thing. I'd start next week."

Say what? I might have experienced a brain aneurism because I just heard him say "next week." *The* week. "But that's when the TV people are coming."

He frowned. "I know. I figured I could leave after the interview, if that's okay with you."

Oh. This was all happening so fast. I'd expected him to go back on tour—I wasn't delusional. But so soon? Was I a horrible person for wanting him to stay just a few more months, to live in this perfect bubble we'd created? I swallowed back the sudden lump in my throat. "Yeah, sounds good to me."

"Where are you going first?" Brogan asked.

"We'll start training on Mount Hood, so it'll only be a few hours away. And then I think my manager has us booked to go back to Chile at the start of the summer. Then if I'm back to 100 percent, we'll begin touring in the fall."

I plastered on a smile. "Great." My stomach bottomed out. This was all happening so fast. That was just…not enough time. The days we had left together were now on a ticking clock. I had so much I wanted to do with him—and what about the comedy show we'd just bought tickets to? My pulse throbbed in my temples, and I fought to keep my breathing level. "I'll be right back. Need to make a trip to the ladies' room."

His brows furrowed. "Okay."

I scooted out of the booth and booked it to the bathroom. Pushing through the door, I beelined for the sink, splashing water on my cheeks. I just needed to process this for a moment. It'd be stupid to assume he'd put his career on hold indefinitely. I'd never ask him to do that, or even expect that of him in a million years. But a week? The Disney chorus in my head came to a screeching halt. The Ghost of Christmas Future came barreling in, the one who promised lonely nights and an empty left side of the bed.

He had said he didn't do relationships because he traveled all the time…and now he was about to get back into the swing of things. I grabbed a paper towel and blotted my face, working on keeping my composure. This was important to him, and I'd be a complete monster if I wasn't 120 percent supportive. Even if the security of what we built was quickly crumbling like a lost game of Jenga.

A Tom Collins sat on a napkin in my spot when I returned to the table.

Lainey caught my eye as soon as I sat down. "Ryder was just telling us more about his good news." Her eyes widened ever so slightly.

I gave her a tight smile. "Yes, it's great." I took a sip of my drink, letting it burn all the way down to my stomach. "So great." Was I happy for him? Hell yes. But it didn't mean I wanted him gone full-time. He'd become a fixture of my everyday life, from texts, to calls, to more. So much more.

Ryder put his arm around me and pulled me closer. "I'm ready for things to go back to normal."

I took another sip of my drink.

I wasn't ready. Not even a little bit.

By the time we got back to my apartment, I was in a

particularly sour mood. I should have been happy for my boyfriend. He was getting his career back.

He stopped me in front of my door, stroking his hand down my arm. "Hey, you've been acting weird all night. What's up?"

I shook my head, trying to brush off this gloom that hung over me like a cartoon rain cloud. "It's nothing." I fished for my keys. If I looked at him, he'd see I was lying.

"If it's bothering you, it's not nothing. C'mon, don't shut down on me."

"It's just…when you go on tour, do you still want to give us a try?" I hated this, the in-between, the sharp sting of uncertainty. It reeked of weakness and vulnerability. Two things I prided myself on not having in my life.

He gripped my shoulders with both hands and looked at me with a sincerity that made my toes curl. "I'm not saying it'll be perfect, but I'm willing to try. The distance thing didn't work out before, but I think that's because I wasn't with you."

"You mean that?"

He held his fingers up. "Two-day-Boy-Scout's honor."

I laughed into his chest. "How do you always know the right thing to say?"

"I've been wrong enough times that I'm bound to get lucky once in a while." His thumb smoothed over my cheek, and I leaned into his touch, savoring his rough skin against mine. "And if it's all right, I'd like to take you inside. I've been thinking about you all night."

I nodded.

His lips were on mine. A blur of kisses, my hands in Ryder's hair, and a frantic search for the keys quickly ensued. He broke the kiss and growled, digging into my bag. "Seriously, how do you find anything in this Mary Poppins purse?"

"Magic."

He groaned, smiling against my mouth. "I'm going to miss

your cute jokes. Promise to text me at least one a day, so I don't miss out?"

"Promise."

After unearthing the keys, Ryder swung the door open and pulled me to him, my legs wrapping around his waist. My fingers tangled in his thick hair again, and he let out a shuddering breath.

"I'm sorry for getting weird tonight."

He pulled back, his blue eyes searching mine. It used to unsettle me, to know that he saw so much. Now it was a comfort, to know he understood, he got the real me, the one that was sometimes too chicken to say something. "You never need to apologize for how you feel. I just want to make sure we're on the same page now."

"We are."

I moved in to the curve of his neck, kissing, taking small nips at his skin. His taste, his smell, his touch—it all called to me on some deep level I never knew existed within me. How had this man, who'd driven me up a wall for months, managed to get under my skin this way?

"What did I do to deserve you? I was such an idiot the first time around."

I traced my thumb over his jaw, and he closed his eyes, practically putty in my hands. "Yes, you were. And you can't say stuff like that," I said.

"I thought we were being upfront and honest."

"We are, but you're supposed to make me angry, not sweep me off my damn feet."

"You mean like right now? Because I have to say, I really like your legs wrapped around me." He grinned.

I laughed and swatted at his back. "You know what I mean."

He looked at me, such intensity in his eyes. In fact, I'd never seen him so serious before. This man who could have his pick of women was now looking at me with laser focus. "I'm falling for you, Zoey."

"I'm falling for you, too," I admitted. Maybe I had been for a long time. I kissed him harder, pouring every emotion that had built up for the past several weeks into my lips, my tongue, trying to convey just how much he meant to me.

He carried me to the bedroom and lay me down on the bed.

"May I?" His fingers traced the buttons of my blouse and along my collarbone, sending goose bumps rippling across my skin.

I propped myself up on my elbows. "Yes."

He unbuttoned each one at an excruciatingly slow rate. But that was Ryder. He liked to take his time. He was methodical, driven, unrelenting.

"You know what would make this moment perfect?" he said.

"What?"

"If you were wearing your Flash underwear."

I smacked him on his chest.

"Hey, I'm only human. And had an extensive comic book collection as a kid."

His head dipped down, and his lips connected with my skin, lighting a fire in their path. "I want to savor every inch of your body. Every freckle. Every dip. Every swell. When I met you, I knew you'd be different. You make me different."

And that was how I felt about Ryder. I didn't want to have to rely on my planner to get me through life. He brought out a spontaneous side of me. One that took a big gamble on my designs…and almost burned down my kitchen. But it was worth it. He taught me that life shouldn't be lived by a script. It was okay to break my rules every once in a while.

My hands smoothed under his shirt and ran up the ridges of bunched muscles of his back. He sat up and pulled his shirt over his head, and I took a moment to really let it sink in—the veins cording up his arms, the expanse of his chest, the tapering of his waist. He may have been hard as friggin' granite on the outside, but he had an ooey-gooey center that melted me into a puddle of feels.

I sat up as he removed my shirt then sank back down against my pillow as he undid the button of my skirt. I lifted off the bed as he worked that down my legs. He continued kissing down my body, heat blooming between my legs. I let out a shaky breath as he grabbed a condom from his pants and then removed them, the belt clinking against my wooden floor.

He made his way back onto the bed and hovered over me. "Flash?" he said, his voice strained.

"Yeah?"

The muscle in his jaw clenched as he regarded me. "I'm more than falling for you. I hope you know that."

"Same."

And with that, he sunk into me. I let out a deep shuddering breath as he filled me. When it came to this, I'd never felt this level of connection.

My legs wrapped around his waist as he picked up the pace, his chest brushing against mine, our stomachs grazing. He stilled a moment and looked down at me.

"What?"

"I'll always be yours, no matter how far away I am."

I threaded my fingers through his hair and pulled him down to me. Did he feel that? I'd just given him a piece of my heart, something I'd never be able to get back. And I trusted him not to break me into a million pieces.

Chapter Seventeen

Ryder

There'd never been a time that I wasn't excited to get back to snowboarding. Ever. I stared at the gear packed in the middle of my living room, ready for the trip this weekend to Mount Hood.

Stupid. I'd been out of my goddamn mind last night when I practically proclaimed my love to Zoey, days before leaving to train. I'd never told a woman that. Though, I'd never felt this way about anyone else. The thought of leaving her, and my brother, it just didn't feel right. What was I supposed to do, though?

If I stayed behind, I was a college dropout with an untouched trust fund and no direction without sports. Andy asked me a few weeks ago to consider a second option in case my leg didn't hold, but that was the thing—I didn't have one. I had to make it work, because otherwise I'd be sitting on my couch eating Cheetos for the rest of my life. Zoey deserved a better man than that. One that followed through with things.

I drove over to Jason's early Sunday afternoon. If there was one thing I could count on, it was my older brother doing what he did best—giving his unsolicited opinion. This time, I'd gladly take the advice, because Zoey had been MIA today with last minute tweaks to the resort, and the caginess had hit me full force.

Jason was sitting on the bricked patio under an umbrella when his housekeeper let me in.

"How's it going?" he asked. His face and shoulders had filled out substantially over the past month, and I took this as a sign he was falling back into his routine. One less thing I'd have to worry about when I left for training.

"Good. We're all set for the soft open next weekend. All the licenses and permits are being mailed to your office." Heidi was a godsend and deserved a raise for all the crap she dealt with the past few weeks.

"Zoey sent me pictures. It looks great."

"Yeah, you guys were right. This resort really turned into something amazing." Better than I ever could have imagined. I thumbed at my bracelet. Mom would have loved it.

"Zoey has a good vision."

She had a lot of things, nothing I'd like to share with my brother, though. All I could do was nod.

He swilled his iced tea, took a sip, and then zeroed his gaze in on me. "How long have you been seeing her?"

"What?" I'd played it off casually the other week when he caught us flinging paint on each other. As much as I loved the dude, we didn't exactly have a ton of heart-to-hearts where I broadcasted my relationship status.

"Don't look at me like that. I'm not stupid—I saw you two at the resort. Plus, you're all dopey."

It took one hell of a woman to turn me into the worst of the Seven Dwarves. I sighed. No use playing dumb. He'd pester me until I coughed up the information. "A few weeks."

He dipped his head and scratched at something on the table surface with his thumb. "And somehow you don't seem happy about it."

"I told her I was going back on tour. And now I feel weird about it." She'd been so open, telling me how she felt, and now I was the one in crisis mode. The woman turned me into someone I barely recognized.

"Ah."

"What?"

His lips pursed together, like he was debating on what he'd say next. "Well," he said cautiously, "you haven't exactly been the poster child for healthy relationships while you're traveling."

"I know. It scares me." I'd never cheat, but there were a million different ways to screw up a relationship. It was the reason I instituted the one-night policy in the first place.

He stopped picking at the spot at the table and lobbed a heavy look my way. "Do you love her?"

"J. It's been a month. I don't think anyone can fall in love in that time." I couldn't say that I'd ever been in love with anyone before. I never really gave myself the chance, because I didn't want it messing with my career. But I'd turned into a sap around her. Hell, I'd kiss the damn ground that she walked on, because Zoey was just that awesome.

He gave me a look.

I shrugged. "I don't know." Did I? How was I supposed to tell if this was love? Everything was in flux, and my life was essentially snowballing down a mountain with faulty bindings. One wrong move and I'd be shattered.

I decided to turn the conversation elsewhere, to something that I hadn't been able to get off my mind. "Do you ever feel like your career is who you are?" Ever since I made the call to Andy yesterday, something didn't sit right. The proper reaction to starting to train again should be hopping in the car and setting up camp on the slopes, waiting for the rest of the team to arrive. My hands didn't itch to grab the keys to my truck. It sickened me to look at my bags in the living room.

He nodded. "Sometimes I feel like it consumed every part of my life."

"And that turned out well." I motioned to my surroundings. Jason was the most successful man I knew.

He huffed out a laugh. "Besides being miserable as fuck and lonely most of the time?"

From the outside, that seemed to be what he'd wanted. To be in his own little bubble of work, work parties, and anything to get ahead in his career. The guy had anything and everything at his fingertips, but maybe that wasn't enough.

I tapped my fingers on the glass table, swallowing hard. "If I don't take this opportunity, what am I going to do?"

"Ryder. Snowboarding is a thing you *do*. Not who you are. What would happen if you quit?"

"I—don't know."

"I'll tell you exactly what will happen. Nothing will change. The world will go on. If you quit, you'll still be the same annoying little brother you've always been." He smirked.

"You had me until the last bit."

"Seriously. If you're not wanting to go on tour, why not take the money you do have and invest it in something? If you tap into your trust, you can do pretty much anything you want."

I shifted in the chair. Just the thought of that money made my lips curl. "Not happening." Taking that money would admit defeat to my grandparents, taking pity funds. Ever since I was eighteen and eligible to use it, I'd made it clear I didn't want a damn thing to do with it. I didn't need that hanging over my head. Not that I didn't love them, but it'd be a cold day in hell before that happened.

"All I'm saying is that you have options. I know you don't

want to hear it, but you're good with people—maybe it's time you started putting your talents toward a greater cause."

"Like dealing with your mopey ass."

He smiled. "Exactly."

"I'll think about it." I didn't have much time to decide on my future. Six days and I'd be on my way to Portland. I'd be back to something that didn't seem that exciting anymore.

I stood and clapped my brother on the back. I'd officially filled my quota of heart-to-heart conversations for the next few months. "I need to head out and grab new bindings for my board."

"Ryder?" He grabbed my arm, and I turned back to him.

"Yeah?"

"Tell her how you feel before you blow your chance."

Chapter Eighteen

Ryder

The next few days flew by in a blur. Everything in the resort had been checked and rechecked by Zoey. I had to hand it to her—she was a miracle worker. She restored Divinity to something that everyone could enjoy.

Jason's words kept playing on repeat in my head. *Tell her how you feel.* Hell, maybe he was right. Maybe if I did, the tightness in my chest would disappear. I finished up the last of my reps, gritting through an intense workout at the gym. Anything to ensure my leg was ready to be back on the slopes. The last thing I needed was to get injured in training.

As I cut to my car in the parking lot, my phone buzzed in my pocket. My frown deepened when I saw my grandmother's number flash across the screen. I hadn't heard from her in over a week, which was both odd and a relief.

I slid into my truck and answered. "Hello?"

"Ryder. We're going to be in town tomorrow," she said.

My head knocked back into the seat. If she was looking

for another interrogation session, she was shit out of luck. The resort was finished, and rooms were being booked for the beginning of fall already. "What for?"

"There's a potential buyer for the resort. You did say it was completed, right?"

"Yes. Zoey put the finishing touches on just yesterday. And what do you mean potential buyer? Jason said he didn't want to sell."

She laughed, her condescending tone stiffening my spine. "Ryder, that is just silly. You could make more money from the land than that hokey resort. You said so yourself."

I had. But this resort was worth more than just a mountain. I was too stupid to see it before, but Zoey saw it. So did my brother. Sometimes I was a little slow on the uptake. "It's not hokey." Hell, it was amazing. She turned that place into something worthy of its moniker.

She scoffed, displeased I didn't agree with her. "Either way, Jason seemed very interested once he heard what the buyer was offering. He has a meeting with him tomorrow morning."

"What? Where?" And why the hell was I left out of something this monumental? I didn't actually have an official title in the company, but I'd been with this project since day one. And it directly affected Zoey.

"At the resort. He didn't tell you?" She practically purred the words. My grandmother always did take great pleasure in stirring up drama.

"No," I said, raking a hand through my sweat-slick hair. I was too damn tired to be having this conversation.

"Well, they'll be there at noon tomorrow if you want to stop by."

Stop by. If this was another one of my grandmother's schemes, she'd taken it too far this time. Now it was personal.

"Grandma…that's so close to the grand opening." What

was she playing at? Did she really expect Jason to sell after months of hard work? No way in hell he'd even think of doing that.

"This is the best thing to happen to Jason since his accident. Show a little respect for the man's decision, Ryder," she snipped. "He could use the money to invest in more profitable companies. The least you could do is make an appearance and support him."

I didn't trust her—she was up to something. "Fine. I'll be at the meeting." And I'd make sure this buyer didn't brainwash my brother into making a decision he'd regret.

"Very good." My grandmother huffed through the phone and then hung up.

As soon as I got home, my phone blew up again. Except this time, it was a text from Zoey. Specifically, it was a picture of cookies on a cooling rack.

Ryder: *Please tell me you are being supervised.*

Zoey: *Sadly, I can't take credit for these. Lainey baked. I'm just the taste tester.*

Ryder: *Best job. Want to come over tonight? Maybe share some of those cookies?*

Zoey: *Can't. Girls night. I'll save you one for tomorrow :-)*

Zoey: *You doing okay?*

I debated texting Zoey about the possible sale of the resort, but decided against it. Jason would never sell. And she was already stressed enough with the upcoming segment on the TV show. I shrugged it off and decided I'd let her know about it after the fact.

Ryder: *I'm good. Tell Lainey I say hi.*

Zoey: *She says she's still watching you, and is giving that creepy Robert De Niro look.*

I chuckled.

Ryder: *Night, Flash.*

God, I was going to miss her.

The next morning I drove to Divinity and parked next to a black town car, presumably my grandparents' ride.

Just as I got out of my truck, Zoey pulled into the parking lot. She was dressed casually today, in a pair of faded jeans, boots, and a jacket. She smiled at me as she walked over to where I stood. Shit, she knocked the air out of my lungs. I was such a sucker, totally consumed by her. I'd never understand how I got so lucky, besides the fact that persistence paid off.

"Hello, gorgeous." I pulled her into a hug and kissed the column of her throat.

She let out a soft sigh, clouds of crisp mountain air escaping from her lips.

"I missed you." I didn't even want to think about how weird it was rolling over to find no one there. Or the fact that Zoey had an official side of the bed. We'd come a long way since Valentine's Day when she threatened to decapitate me with her stiletto.

"Me, too." Her hands slipped under my shirt, smoothing over my skin.

I pulled back, bracketing her shoulders in my hands.

"I have to tell you something. My grandmother called, and Jason and I are meeting with someone about the resort this morning."

She stiffened. "Who?"

Stress rolled off her in waves, to the point where I worried she might actually bust a vessel with the hassle of yet another thing pertaining to this resort. There was no way I'd add to that if this meeting didn't pan out for the buyer. "Some guy that my grandparents want me to meet with. It shouldn't take too long. Nothing important." I hoped. Because if I had any say, the resort would be staying in the Covington name. It was too important of a place to just let go.

As if on cue, my grandparents wound their way down the brick path of the main portion of the lodge, wheeling my brother. They conversed amicably with each other. Again, odd, but nice to see. Maybe things would go back to normal, and Jason would return to Golden Boy status.

They stopped a few feet ahead of us, staying on the newly paved walking path. My grandmother's gaze moved from me to Zoey. She eyed her up and down and managed a stiff smile. Although I loved my grandmother dearly, if one unkind word about Zoey came out of her mouth, I wouldn't hesitate to put her in her place. Zoey didn't need to be subjected to my grandmother's shit.

"Grandma, Grandfather, this is Zoey. She was the genius behind this remodel."

They shook hands, and Zoey shot me a wink. Leave it to her to be unfazed by these two.

"Quite the renovation you did," my grandfather said.

Zoey smiled. "It wasn't too bad once we were on the same page."

She was polite enough to not mention I'd been a complete tool during the first half of the project. Just as I was about to say something, a green sedan pulled into the parking lot.

A man in his late forties stepped out of the car, shut the door, and headed our way. The construction and design work had finished days ago, so no one else would have a need to come up here. This had to be the buyer my grandmother mentioned yesterday.

The man's expression brightened when he noticed my grandparents. "Beatrice, George. Always a pleasure."

My molars ground together as I watched him kiss my grandparents' asses.

He turned to me and extended his hand "Jake Travers."

I shook it, a little harder than I needed to. He winced and, okay, yeah, maybe I was being a little bit of an asshole. Anyone who was trying to buy this resort out from under me deserved it. "Ryder. Nice to meet you."

He turned to my brother. "You must be Jason."

Jason nodded and stuck out his hand, shaking Jake's.

"And this is Zoey. She was the designer on the job."

"Nice to meet you." He smiled at her and shook hands. His gaze lingered a few seconds longer than necessary. I didn't like him. Or trust him.

I turned to Zoey. "Would you mind hanging out in the lodge while we meet with Mr. Travers?" I hated to bail the first time she met my grandparents, but Jason needed my support.

"How about I show you the grounds?" Zoey offered to my grandparents.

"That'd be lovely," my grandmother said.

I shot her a look that said she needed to be on her best behavior. My grandmother gave a snake's smile, which did little to settle the unease in my stomach. I'd never brought a woman home to meet my grandparents for this exact reason. I'd be subjecting a poor soul to their mind games. My grandmother had made people cry within ten minutes of knowing her.

"Are you sure?" I asked. Zoey really didn't know what

she was getting herself into. But if anyone could hold their own, it was her.

I kissed the top of her head, not even bothering to acknowledge my grandmother's gasp. Screw it, the job was finished. I wasn't her client anymore. It didn't matter if our relationship was public. "It shouldn't be too long. I'll come find you when I'm finished."

She beamed at me. "Sounds good."

Great. I'd get this meeting out of the way and then get back to Zoey and spend as much time as possible with her until I left for training. Everything was finally falling into place. I'd tell her just how I felt about her tonight. I bought that dessert wine she liked so much from the vineyard where we went on our date. And then I'd find *other* ways to show her just how much I adored her.

Jake took a seat across from me and Jason at the desk. My desk. Even if Jason had backed the money, I considered this place mine. It was something I was proud of. Something that I helped make. Maybe Jason was right—managing a business wasn't so bad after all.

"I came out here as a courtesy to your grandparents."

I looked to Jason and we eyed each other. It was clear neither one of us planned to sell the place. Who the hell did this guy think he was?

"Before you start, I just want to say there is no amount of money that you can offer for which I'd sell this place," Jason said.

"See, that's the thing. Your grandparents have already contacted their lawyers and checked the contract."

Jason scoffed. "Why would they do that? And why not tell me?"

"They used the phrase 'not fit to lead' a few times." A smile twisted that shithead's lips.

"Watch your fucking mouth," I said, slamming my fist

into the table.

He raised his hands in defense. "Apologies. Their words, not mine."

Yeah, he didn't look one bit sorry.

A fire lit in Jason's eyes, and I was legitimately worried for this Jake's safety. "Go ahead, tell me exactly what they plan to do behind my back," Jason said, his tone lethal.

"They've agreed that for the sake of the company, it is a better business decision to sell the property," he said.

Traitors. My grandparents didn't have a loyal bone in their bodies, not even when it came to blood. "They're selling it to you to make an extra buck?" I said. Un-fucking-believable. "I won't let this happen."

"Last time I checked, your name wasn't in the contract," Jake shot back.

True. But my ownership of the property was down to the marrow of the wood in this place. My sweat, my blood, it went into revamping this resort into something spectacular.

"What do you plan on doing with Divinity?" Jason asked, doing a better job at keeping composed.

I couldn't say I wasn't two seconds from connecting my fist with this guy's face. His arrogance unleashed every bit of pent-up anger I'd harbored for my grandparents. They couldn't keep their damn hands out of Jason's business for one minute. And now something that he loved was being taken away from him.

"Besides knocking it to the ground and adding four new lifts? Really, you guys missed the mark on capitalizing on the trails. Maybe I can get that hot designer to help me out with new plans. Did you see the tits on that woman?"

Within an instant, red blurred my vision, and I was ready to jump over the table. "You'd better shut the fuck up before I knock your teeth down your throat."

"Ryder." Jason gripped my arm. He turned back to Jake.

"What my brother is trying to say is that your misogynistic attitude will not be tolerated here. My designer is not a piece of ass." Jason leveled him with a gaze. "And I think there's been a mistake. We'll be opening for guests in a few weeks, and we have a design show taking a tour through the place this weekend."

Jake smiled. "No. It won't."

He pulled a few folded pieces of paper from the inside pocket of his jacket and placed them in front of us. "This place is mine, and I have a demo crew coming Saturday morning to start the process. We need to be ready in time for ski season."

Jason and I both leaned over to take a look at the piece of paper, which was the deed to the property. With Jake's name on there.

Fuck.

• • •

ZOEY

After Ryder and his brother disappeared into the lodge's main office, I turned to his grandparents and said, "Well, would you like to see the guest rooms?"

Ryder's grandfather seemed much more down to earth than the grandmother. I was used to dealing with those of the upper echelon since my start at Bass and Goldstein, so I wasn't too worried about handling Ryder's grandparents with tact.

"So you and my grandson are close?"

"Yes." I didn't really know how else to answer that. He hadn't introduced me as his girlfriend, and I didn't know if he wanted to keep that under wraps for now. Now that the job was done, we didn't have to hide our relationship anymore.

"Well, that's lovely," she said, disdain clear in her voice.

Brr, was it cold in here?

Yep. Not awkward whatsoever. Note to self: never offer to show people around the resort anymore.

"Here is one of the honeymoon suites," I said, walking into the room where I'd been stuck with Ryder a few months back. Gone was the hideous carpet, paintings, and faux wainscoting. In was a beautiful four-poster bed, rich blues, and creams that I wanted to bury myself in. A room that I'd want to be stuck in with Ryder. Heck, I'd take the horrid seventies version if it meant he was here right this second. Anything to make his grandmother ease up on giving me the stink eye.

"The designs seem a bit simplistic, but tolerable." Ryder's grandmother sniffed. Actually put her nose in the air and sniffed.

Wow. Now that was a new one, and I'd had some pretty difficult clientele.

What was I even supposed to say to that? My first instinct was to go for the good ol' throat-punch, though I doubted Ryder would appreciate that.

She didn't have a design degree. The people who mattered loved it, most importantly my boss. I decided to ignore her jab and moved on with the tour. "And here is the master bath. It even has heated tiles for those cold nights in the wintertime."

I looked around the room and sighed. Never thought I'd say this, but I'd miss this place.

I led them through the other guest rooms and toured the outside complex with the lifts, pointing out the area across the expanse.

"And those are the trails. Ryder is setting up new lift chairs to be installed in June."

His grandmother bristled. Seriously, I needed a sweater for all the shade this woman was throwing my way. Forget her blatant hate for my work—she should be proud that her grandsons had taken on such a big project and succeeded.

"I don't know why he spent so much time on this place,"

his grandmother started in.

Was this woman on crack? How could she not understand? "I'm not sure what you mean," I said. Ryder spent time on the place because he loved it. Sure, he wanted to burn it to the ground in the beginning, we all did. But he'd changed his mind once he gave it a fair shot.

"Beatrice, this isn't your place," his grandfather said.

"Really, George. Look around. All this time spent on this"—she looked around and grimaced—"redesign, just for it to be torn down. It's a shame, really." She casually studied her manicured nails, like she was talking about the weather.

Now I knew I must have suffered from a brain aneurism, because I sure as hell did not hear those words come out of her mouth. "Torn down?"

"He didn't tell you?" She shot me a pitying look, but I didn't fail to notice the gleam in her eyes. She was happy to dish out some gossip at my expense—a shark that smelled blood.

"The person Jason and Ryder are meeting with is buying the resort. He plans to demo the place within the week."

No. "Excuse me?" What the hell? I was in the loop for everything on this project, I think I'd know if the damn building was going to be torn down. No way would Ryder do that after the time we spent on this place. Months upon months.

"He's selling the resort to Jake. That's what the meeting is about this afternoon. Just finalizing everything. It was actually Ryder's idea to begin with. He knew this resort was a lost cause." She trailed her hand down one of the curtains. "Such a waste."

No way. I could not even begin to process this. There was no way this was happening. But those were Ryder's *exact* words. That it was a waste of time, that there was no point in even completing the project. Had he really been the reason the resort had sold? And if so, what did that mean for my meeting on Saturday?

Ryder returned to the main room where I stood with his grandparents, ready to throw down. His cheeks were devoid of color, his gaze hollow. I wasn't about to lay into him completely without getting the details first. I was giving him the benefit of the doubt that maybe his grandmother was mistaken. This Jake guy could have been anyone. A vendor, a patron, anything. He didn't have to be a person looking to tear down months of hard work. *My* work.

"Zoey, I have to tell you something." He paled even more, and the sadness in his eyes drop-kicked me straight in the stomach.

"It's true then? You're selling the lodge?"

He looked at me then back at his grandparents. "Yeah, how did you know that?"

"Your grandmother told me." My throat tightened, and the hot sting of tears pricked at my vision. What did this mean for all the hard work we'd done? "Told me that you're the reason it sold."

He shook his head and turned to his grandmother, his lips curling in disgust. "You told her what?"

"You're the one that told me it'd be better off sold for scraps. I just went ahead and followed through," his grandmother said. She looked particularly satisfied with herself. It made me want to do and say very unprofessional things.

"Are you insane? Like actually insane?" He practically spat the words. "You've just ruined months of work with your sick game."

She waved him off. "Your little girlfriend will get paid. Not to worry."

My eye twitched. Little girlfriend. The words rankled me.

I stared at her, with her crisp white pantsuit and that

blood red lipstick. A devil incarnate that just turned my world upside down.

My resort. My designs were null and void. Ryder instigated the entire thing. It was just too much.

"The cleanup crew will be here on Saturday to *dispose* of these little knickknacks," she said, her lip curling as she fingered an antique clock in the main room.

My designs. *Mine.* And she was looking at them like they were trash to be discarded. I didn't care who she was, she was walking into my job site and not bothering with a modicum of respect. A hot flash of anger ripped through me. This was my job. She just screwed over my job because my boyfriend told her the place needed to be sold. "You're a real piece of work, you know that? Take your head out of your ass for one minute and notice how amazing this place looks. Because of your grandson." And me, but that was beside the point.

"Excuse me?" She put her hand to her chest, flabbergasted.

"And I'm not just his *little girlfriend.*" After that I may have thrown around the terms misogynistic and entitled. I didn't really know what I was saying because all I saw was red. Hell, I saw the whole light spectrum as I lit into her. Because the one thing that had solidified my job was being bulldozed. Literally.

"Zoey," Ryder warned. "I can handle this."

"Yeah, I can see you're handling it real well. Thanks for getting the place sold. Glad I just spent three months of my life on this. I'm sure HGTV will be thrilled to hear there's no resort to showcase." Screw this noise. I was done with the whole damn family.

He reached for my arm, but I shrugged him away. "Don't touch me." Hell, I couldn't even look at him. This was my job, my chance to move up in the firm, and he'd just ruined it.

"Your supervisor will be hearing from me," his grandmother called as I walked off.

"Good. You can tell him I said the whole Covington family can rot in hell for all I care."

That may have taken it a tad bit far. Like, about ten steps. But I was so beyond caring. The pesky part of my conscience said I should have gone back and apologized, kissed her ass, and begged for her forgiveness. But what was the point? When Lance found out about this, my job was as good as gone. I might as well pack up my office tonight.

As soon as I made it to the parking lot, Ryder raced out behind me, gravel crunching under his feet.

"Zoey, please listen. I really had no clue."

"You wanted to get rid of this place from the beginning. I should have known." I laughed. How could I not see it before? I was so stupid. "I should have known that this was all too good to be true." My arms flailed out to the sides as my temper raged.

"You have to believe me. I would never ask her to sell the place."

"Well, it's done. God." My breaths came out in jagged huffs. "I can't even look at you. It just makes me sick. Please, just go. Do your snowboarding thing. That's all you ever wanted. We never need to speak again."

"Zoey." His voice was desperate this time. "Please."

I didn't listen, though. This was my fault. If only I'd passed him off to another designer to begin with. Jesus, men made me so damn stupid.

I got in my car and didn't bother to look back, just tore out of the parking lot and made my way down the mountain. I ignored the seven calls from my office and the fourteen calls from Ryder.

The tears didn't start until I made it to my apartment and parked the car. This was it—I'd really screwed up everything.

My fingers trembled as I clutched my phone. In my inbox was an email from my boss labeled: *We need to talk.* Had Mrs.

Covington already yelled at my boss? I knew my fate before I opened the message. Because really, when it rained…

I blew out a breath and banged my head against the headrest. Might as well rip off the Band-Aid that was my crumbling career.

Zoey

I just got a very disturbing call from Mrs. Covington. I would like to talk to you about your relationship in regard to Mr. Covington and your treatment of that whole family. For the sake of the company, I'd like you to take some time off, and we will meet next Wednesday to discuss the ramifications of this incident.

Best,
Lance Bass

This was it. Everything that I'd worked so hard for slipped through my fingers like water.

• • •

Lainey was waiting for me as soon as I walked in the door. God bless her, she had a bowl of ice cream in one hand and a spoon in the other, ready for my taking.

"What the hell happened?" She pushed the bowl into my hands and wrapped me in a hug. How had I gone so wrong? I knew better than to trust men like that. I thought he was one of the good ones. Guess the joke was on me.

I shoved a chunk of Chocolate Mudslide in my mouth. "He sold the resort." I still couldn't believe it. The Hulk-smash haze had faded from my vision, and I was left weary to my bones.

She led me over to the couch, and I numbly followed, sitting down next to her. "What do you mean? I thought you had your interview this weekend. The new owner seriously didn't want to keep anything you did?"

"Nope." How was I supposed to explain this one to the TV producers?

Um, hi. Yes, I'm calling about my design on Divinity Resort. Oh, yeah, the one you wanted to film for your resort special. Yeah, I'm sorry, it's actually going to be flattened to the ground before you get here. I'll just go eat my feelings now.

Good thing my leggings were one-size fits all. I'd be needing the extra fabric for the coming weeks.

Screw Ryder's family. I couldn't believe I ever put my trust in him.

I laid my head in Lainey's lap, and she took a piece of my hair, braiding it as tears rolled down my face. "Oh, Zoey. I'm so sorry. I wish there was something I could do."

"There's nothing. Except for maybe come with me to stand in front of the wrecking ball and throw a protest."

She laughed softly, my head moving with the flex of her stomach. "I don't think that works anymore. Plus, you don't need a criminal record on top of all this."

"True." I snuggled deeper into her lap. At least I could always trust her. I'd hoped I could say the same about Ryder, but he'd proved me wrong time and time again.

My phone lit up on the table. I grabbed for it, and as soon as Ryder's name scrolled across the screen, I chucked it to the other side of the room. I was done with him.

Chapter Nineteen

Ryder

"Come on, Flash. Answer your phone," I pleaded.

I hung up and dialed again. Two hours of complete shut out from Zoey was driving me past the brink of insanity.

A call came through my Bluetooth and I answered it immediately. "Flash?" The desperation in my voice bordered on pathetic.

"Uh, hey, man," said Andy.

Not my girlfriend. Of course.

"What do you want?" The words came out harsh, but I wasn't in the mood to talk to anyone that wasn't Zoey. I needed her to hear me out, to know I had nothing to do with this.

"I'm going to need you a couple days early," he said.

"Why? Training doesn't start until Saturday." I fisted my hand through my hair. Horrible timing. I couldn't imagine a worse time to leave than right now. Zoey wouldn't return my calls as I continued to field ones from my grandparents. As far as I was concerned, they were no longer my family. Not with the way they manipulated Jason and Zoey.

"I could use your help with setting up. You're usually available for these things."

Yeah, back in the day when I'd jump at the chance to avoid conflict when it came to women. Now, I'd throw myself into the pit of hell if it meant Zoey would hear me out for one damn second. I laughed, bitter that I was in the same place where I'd started in terms of my career, my relationships—or lack thereof. Everything gone.

"Can you give me a few minutes to think about it? I am kind of going through some shit right now."

"Take your time, man." And with that, the line went dead. I clicked off my Bluetooth and continued to drive around. Somehow I ended up parked in front of Zoey's apartment. Her car was sandwiched between two cars on the other side of the street.

I tried her phone one more time, but when it went straight to voicemail, I got out of my car and made my way to her apartment door.

After I knocked, Lainey opened the door. Her ice-cold glare cut straight through me. "What are you doing here?"

"I want to talk to Zoey. I want to straighten everything out."

"That's not happening."

"Just five minutes. That's all I ask." I wasn't above begging. I'd grovel at Lainey's feet if it meant I could see Zoey.

"There is no way you're coming through this door. You've already done enough damage. Aren't you supposed to be going back to your snowboarding training? Now would be a great time to leave." She crossed her arms, not budging from her post at the door.

"But—"

"Now. Leave now before I find something to stab in your

stupid meat-head neck." Her voice was a vicious whisper.

"Fine. Will you just tell her I'm sorry?"

She laughed. "You're delusional if you think a simple apology will fix things, Ryder."

And with that, she shut the door in my face.

Shit.

I walked down the hall and hit the button to the elevator. She was less than thirty feet away. So close, but she'd shut me out. I glanced at her apartment door one more time before entering the elevator. Lainey was right—I was delusional to think she'd ever believe me.

After an hour of wandering downtown and blowing off steam, I entered my apartment. I stared at the space, the complete silence deafening. It could be classified as barren compared to Zoey's place. Hers was warm and inviting and had the most important element of all…her.

I pulled out my phone and tried her number one last time. "C'mon Flash," I pleaded as the phone continued to ring. As with the last however many, this one went to her message box.

"Fuck!" I fisted my hand through my hair.

I couldn't go to Portland. Not like this. Damn it all to hell, she would expect that from me—to just up and disappear. But I wasn't that man she met months ago. How could I leave her when I was the root of all her problems? The resort demolition was my fault, and I had to make this right.

Then again, what did I have left if I didn't return to train with my team?

Jason's conversation played in my head. He believed I had more to offer than just my boarding skills. Hell, I'd had reservations about leaving even before this shit storm.

Whatever I did have to offer, it meant shit if I didn't have my girl. I was not going to prove her right again, not when I knew I'd changed.

I pulled up Andy's contact and dialed.

"Hey, man, you coming down tonight?" he said.

I paced around my living room. This was insane. The biggest gamble I'd ever taken. "No. Andy, I'm sorry to put this on you last minute, but I'm not going to be at training."

"For how long?" He could have been irritated, but I had a hard time giving a shit at the moment.

"I don't know yet, but as soon as I do, I'll let you know." At the moment, I didn't know anything.

"What do you want me to tell your sponsors?"

"Hell, I don't know. Tell them to give the money to charity." And then I hung up. The only person I wanted to talk to was ignoring me, so there was nothing to do but wait.

Hours later, Zoey still wouldn't answer my calls. I'd ended up on the couch, eating vanilla ice cream, but I had to stop halfway through the bowl because it reminded me of her shampoo. Fuck, I was pathetic.

I turned on the TV and the first channel featured a property renovation. Click. I flipped through a few channels and stopped when I landed on *Arrow*. I tore off my shirt and slid under the sheets and continued to watch. That was, until the Flash came onto the screen. My chest tightened, and I swallowed hard. Shit, I needed to get a grip. But I couldn't stand one more second of anything that reminded me of her, so I shut the show off, still just as clueless as to what the hell to do.

Being here was the wrong choice. Same with going to Portland. There was only one place I should be right now—Zoey's. Comforting her.

I looked around me, at the emptiness of my room. This would never live up to Zoey's apartment, or the feeling of her in my arms. Hell, the thought of spending a night without playing our stupid Would You Rather game gave me a headache.

What did I want? I wanted my resort back. And I wanted

my damn girl.

Again, I thought back to my conversation with Jason. I tried to picture what he'd do if he were in the same situation, what ruthless measures he'd take to get his life back.

Dread settled in my gut. There was a price I had to pay to make it happen. I knew exactly where I had to go in order to get one of those things back. Something I promised myself I'd never do.

I'm selling my soul for you Zoey.

I picked up my cell phone.

Chapter Twenty

Zoey

Rule #41: Never wake up Lainey Taylor if you value your life

A loud knock sounded at the door on Saturday morning. Way too early. The sun hadn't even peeked through my windows yet, which meant this was either an emergency or someone was really drunk.

I groaned and waited a few more seconds, praying that this person would go away. And then I heard it. A voice. A very familiar one. "Zoey! Open up."

I threw my pillow over my head. Nope. Not in a million years. He could rot out there for all I cared. I flipped him the bird for good measure, even though he couldn't see it.

"Zoey, I know you're in there, please, just hear me out."

Lainey yelled from the other room, "For the love of all that's holy, get the door, Z."

"You know who it is," I yelled back. "No way."

I loved Lainey, but she was the grumpiest of morning people, and there was no getting her out of bed unless I set the kitchen on fire.

Ryder continued to knock. I'd admire the persistence, but I was too busy hating him at the moment.

"I swear to you, Ryder Covington, I will find very creative ways to torture you and dispose of the evidence if you don't stop knocking," Lainey yelled again.

She told me he'd shown up at our door the other day while I was in the shower and she'd promptly sent him away. I'd do the same for her if Brogan was ever an ass to the *n*th degree again. But it looked like I was on my own at the moment.

"It's important. I promise I wouldn't bother you guys if it weren't," he said. Something in his voice held a desperation that I couldn't ignore. Plus, I didn't want Lainey to have murder charges on her record. If anything, I was answering the door just for her benefit. I rolled out of bed, pulled my robe tight around me, and yanked open the door.

Ryder stood there, his hair drenched, his clothes a sopping mess. Water beaded off his hair onto the floor, and he looked like he hadn't slept in two days, probably the mirror image of me in that respect. Still, the sight stole my breath. Even though he'd tossed my heart off a cliff.

I crossed my arms. "What are you doing here? You should be at training."

"I'm an asshole."

"Agreed. You can go now."

"You know that I hated the resort—"

I cocked my head at him. The nerve of this guy. "Seriously, save your speeches for someone who cares." I went to shut the door in his face, but he stuck his arm out, pushing it back open.

"Will you please listen to me? Just hear me out for one minute."

I crossed my arms. "Sixty seconds. Tick tock."

"Take this outside, assholes," Lainey groaned from the bedroom.

I glared at him, but for the sake of my roommate, I walked out into the hall and slid down the wall to sit.

"I'm listening," I said.

His eyes softened as his gaze roamed over mine. "What I meant to say was, I hated it at first, but that all changed when I got to know you. Your passion, your great ideas…you made something incredible out of nothing. Zoey, I admire the hell out of you." He dragged his hands over his face and groaned.

"That's nice. I know you can use pretty words. You've done so before. But it doesn't change the fact that in a few hours someone is going to mow down everything that I worked so hard to create. It also doesn't change the fact that your grandmother—who, by the way, is a jerk—called my boss and I'm probably fired." I could barely catch my breath as red swarmed my vision once again.

Ryder shoved his hands in his pockets and shifted from side to side. "I'm sorry for that. All of that. You have to believe me that I would never purposefully hurt you in any way. That was never my intention."

"I've had a change of heart with my career," he said. "As soon as I got a call from my manager to come to training early, I knew I didn't want to do that anymore. And it dawned on me what I really want to do."

"Why are you telling me this?" He should save this for someone who actually gave a shit.

"I'm getting to my point, and I have at least twenty more seconds before you slam the door in my face, so please let me continue."

I gestured to him. "Carry on."

"I want to run the resort. I want to create a ski school and work there."

I snorted. "You're a little late. Last I heard, it was sold. But maybe that Jake dude takes job applications. Listen, I'm glad you figured out your life. Thanks so much for ruining mine. I'm going back to bed."

I went to stand and Ryder grabbed my wrist, whirling me around. "Zoey, I bought the resort back."

"You what? How?"

"I did something I told myself I'd never do—I tapped into my trust fund. I always thought I'd be selling my soul to the devil if I used that money, but it is being put to a good use. My mother's memory. More families making memories. Future memories with"—he looked at me, his expression hopeful—"us."

"You are obviously delusional if you think I'm going to get back with you because you bought a resort. If you somehow forgot, I am probably jobless and have embarrassed myself with HGTV."

"That's actually what I came here to tell you." He smoothed a hand through his wet hair, giving that stupid smile that usually made me melt. "I made a few calls. The show is still filming today—if you're up for it, of course."

"I—what?"

He shrugged. "The producer was a little confused, but I made sure everything was straightened out. She's expecting you there for hair and makeup at two."

My voice wobbled as I said, "You didn't have to do that." But holy hell, he had. No one had ever done something like this for me. For us. "I don't even know what to say. I'm just… Wow."

"Is that a good wow or a bad wow?"

"I haven't decided." Tears blurred my vision. This was all just so much to process. First losing the resort, then possibly my job, which was still on the table, and now I had my interview. "Why?"

He shook his head, his brows furrowing, and that cute line between his brows appeared. "Why what?"

"Why did you do this?"

He looked at me, bewildered. "Isn't it obvious?"

"No, Ryder, it isn't. Because last I knew, you were going to training and weren't coming back."

He hesitated for a moment, mashing his lips together. "I love you, Zoey." He looked at me, those blue eyes so intense, searing a hole straight to my soul. "I'm not good at this whole relationship thing, and I managed to screw it up without even trying. But I've never felt this way about anyone before. And when my family hurt you?" He swallowed hard. "I saw the light go out in your eyes. You are the type of person that can do good in this world, someone I can only hope to deserve one day. I can't promise everything will be perfect, but I'm moving to Seattle permanently. I want to be a part of your life. God, Zoey, I love you so much I'd move a mountain for you if I could. Please don't shut me out," he pleaded.

"You bought one instead," I managed to say, laughing at how ridiculous that sounded. A mountain. He bought the resort back so he could stay here. With me. And he fixed the television shoot while he was at it. He wouldn't have gone through all that unless he truly did care.

Tears streamed down my face, and Ryder wiped them away with his thumbs.

"I'm not sure what's going on here." He frowned, his eyes tracking my face. "You're laughing. Does that mean you forgive me?"

I nodded. "You really did all this for me?"

"For us, Zoey. You're worth it," he said, pulling me into his arms.

"Say it again," I murmured into his chest, ignoring the raindrops soaking into my clothes.

"Say what?"

"That you love me."

He pulled me tighter, his hand stroking my hair. "I love you, Zoey. So much I haven't slept in two days."

God, I loved being in his arms. I loved his smell, the way he made me feel. "I love you, too," I said.

He pulled back and smiled. "Are you ready to do that interview?"

"Only if you'll be there with me."

He pressed his lips to my forehead. "Always."

Chapter Twenty-One

Ryder

Three Weeks Later

I made the best decision of my life by not returning to train. Zoey's clothes, specifically, more leggings than I could count, had taken up residence in one of my drawers at my apartment, and we spent most of our time over there, since it was closer to her work. She'd managed to keep her job at the firm. Funny how a well-known TV show seemed to smooth things over with her boss. That, and the fact my brother promised many more projects for Bass and Goldstein with Zoey as the lead designer. The grand opening went off without a hitch, but there was a recent addition to the resort I was excited to show Zoey.

Her fingers intertwined with my own as I drove her up to the resort. "Aren't you even going to give me a little hint as to why you're bringing me up here?"

"Nope. Would you rather enjoy the surprise or stare

daggers in my direction the rest of the car ride?"

She pouted. "You're no fun."

"I remember you singing a different tune last night," I said.

"You drive me insane." She smacked me in the chest, and I smiled back at her.

I grinned at her. She was so easy to rile up. "You love it," I said.

She nodded. "I do."

That would never get old. I didn't know what I did to deserve a woman like her, but I sure as heck wasn't going to screw it up again.

I put the truck in park, ran around to the other side, and opened the door for her.

We walked up the main path to the resort, and then I veered to the left, giving her a clear view of the side of the building, the area where people could purchase lift tickets and equipment rentals.

I motioned to the sign carved out of wood, hanging at the apex of the roof.

COVINGTON SKI SCHOOL

"The perfect final touch to the resort," she said, beaming.

It was all because of her. I would have never had the courage otherwise to take such a big risk.

"It is. And I'm going to offer free lessons to children and adults with disabilities." I'd been thinking a lot lately, and decided I could combine two things that I loved—working with kids and snow sports.

I hadn't talked to my grandparents since they tried to sell the resort to Jake. Honestly, I didn't know if I'd ever talk to them again after what they did to Zoey and Jason. I'd cashed out my trust fund and wouldn't feel a damn ounce of guilt. It went toward something great.

Zoey squeezed my hand. "This is perfect, Ryder. The best

part of the place by far."

"I have a few people who are interested in investing and starting up other resorts and ski schools around the nation if this works out."

"That's amazing, Ryder." She beamed at me, and it melted my fucking heart. "I'm so proud of you."

"I told them they could use the company name under one condition."

"What's that?"

"They use your design firm."

"Oh, Ryder. You didn't have to do that, but thank you." She leaned into me, and I wrapped my arm around her. Nothing ever felt so right as when I was doing something with her.

"You're my partner in crime, Flash. We stick together."

Acknowledgments

As always, I am forever indebted to my fabulous and insightful editor, Candace Havens. Thank you for guiding me and helping me through this book.

Thank you to my rock star agent, Courtney Miller-Callihan who is always in my corner.

A shout-out to my author friends and my reader group, whose love and support always brightens my day. Love you guys.

To those who sent me lovely emails and messages about *The Rule Book*, thank you times one billion. Your kind words and excitement for Zoey's book got me through a very tough time.

And, as always, thank you to my family. My books wouldn't be possible without you.

About the Author

Jennifer Blackwood is an English teacher and contemporary romance author. She lives in Oregon with her husband, son, and poorly behaved black lab puppy. When she isn't writing or teaching, she's binging on *Veronica Mars* episodes and white cheddar popcorn.

Want to know when Jennifer Blackwood's next book releases? Sign up for her newsletter.

www.jenniferblackwood.com

Discover more New Adult titles from Entangled Embrace...

Falling for the Player

a novel by Jessica Lee

Bad boy and former NFL running back Patrick Guinness is tired of meaningless sex. Ever since his scorching hot one-night stand three years ago, no one has interested him. So when Max Segreti wanders into his mechanic shop—and his life again—Patrick can't stop thinking about the totally-out-of-his-league law student and the possibility of getting him out of his system once and for all...

Branded

a novel by Candace Havens

The last thing I need is a Texas princess like Cassie messing with my head. But there's something more to this spoilt little rich girl than the perfect image she works so hard to keep. There's only one rule to keeping my job and a roof over my sister's head: stay away from the boss's granddaughter. But I'm not always great at following the rules.

No Kissing Allowed

a novel by Melissa West

Cameron Lawson is partying it up before she starts her dream job at New York's biggest ad agency. Her task? To hook up with a random guy, and, the super-sexy guy sitting next to Cameron is definitely game. No names. No details. Just one hot night...until the first day of work when Cameron discovers that her hook-up is none other than Aidan Truitt—her boss. But sometimes the only way to get what you want is by breaking a few rules. Even if it means putting *everything* on the line.

Crazy Pucking Love

a *Taking Shots* novel by Cindi Madsen

I just met the girl of my dreams. Megan Davenport is funny and smart, and she's as much of an insomniac as I am. She's also my team captain's little sister, which I only found out *after* our passionate kiss. Megan is completely off-limits—her brother makes that very clear—and I know better than to think I can keep a relationship going during hockey season anyway. But that doesn't mean we can't be late-night friends, right?

Discover the Rule Breakers series

THE RULE BOOK

More New Adult books by Jennifer Blackwood...

UNETHICAL

FOOLPROOF

Adult books by Jennifer Blackwood

LANDING THE AIR MARSHAL

CPSIA information can be obtained
at www.ICGtesting.com
Printed in the USA
LVOW08s1428240117
522002LV00001B/61/P